A STONE'S THROW

BY DEBBIE DE LOUISE

10/16

Debbie DeLouise

A STONE'S THROW

Limitless Publishing, LLC
Kailua, HI 96734
www.limitlesspublishing.com

Formatting: Limitless Publishing

ISBN-13: 978-1-68058-365-6
ISBN-10: 1-68058-365-4

DEDICATION

In loving memory of:
Carolyn De Louise–Huebsch

CHAPTER 1

Standing barefoot in her bedroom with an empty suitcase by her side, Alicia Fairmont contemplated her plans to travel to the small upstate New York town where her husband, Peter, had been born. Six months earlier, Peter had been killed in a hit and run accident. They'd never visited Cobble Cove together, and he'd never spoken much about it except to say it was a backwards town he and his parents moved away from when he was ten and his sister seventeen. To her, it sounded charming. It would be lovely this time of year with the autumn leaves scattered along its paths, but more importantly, it might be a place she could find the answers to questions Peter avoided about his family during their fifteen-year marriage.

Alicia walked to her desk in the corner of the room where piles of mail sat unopened and a silent phone contained as many unreturned messages as her cell phone. There was only one gold-framed photo beside the mess, a shot of her and Peter on a beach in Bermuda, taken on their honeymoon by a fellow tourist. The absence of baby photos or school portraits ghosted the rest of the space.

An out-of-date Baker and Taylor calendar hung on the beige wall next to the desk. Alicia flipped the May 2015 page forward to November. Noting the date—November 13—she realized she had been on leave from her library for six months since the day a police officer came to her door and related the news about Peter's death. Although the main reason for her taking the time off was to help her recover from her terrible loss, a deeper reason was she was no longer happy at her job. Having worked there full-time as a reference librarian for seventeen years, it was time for a change. But at forty-two, she was too young for retirement, her attempts at selling some novels she'd penned had failed, and Peter had never felt a need to take out an insurance policy to support her if anything happened to him.

Sitting on her bed in the dark room, she wondered if anyone in Cobble Cove knew Peter or his family. Even though Peter and his relatives hadn't been close, had, in fact, stopped talking to one another years before she married him, it still seemed odd Peter hadn't kept their addresses. There was no one from Peter's family Alicia could contact. Only their co-workers and her friend Gilly attended the funeral. Peter had requested cremation, so there was no casket. Her last memory of him was when he left for work early that misty May morning, taking his usual one-mile jog to his office.

Even though she had no children or pets, Alicia still needed to make arrangements for her trip. She got up, went to the phone, and called Gilly, who she hadn't spoken to in over a week. Gilly was the only person she'd kept in contact with these past months. She lived nearby and worked part-time as a clerk at Alicia's library. The two had become close friends over the years.

She was relieved when her friend answered the phone. "Alicia, are you okay? I've been worried about you."

"Sorry I haven't called. I haven't wanted to bother you. I know you're busy with the kids." Gilly had three young boys who kept her running from baseball to soccer to martial arts events.

"Nonsense. I always have time for you. What's up? Have you made an appointment with Dr. Phillips?" Dr. Phillips was the psychiatrist Gilly saw regularly to deal with the issues from her divorce five years ago. She had recommended him to Alicia to help her overcome her depression.

"No, but..." Alicia paused. "I'm going to Cobble Cove for a few days, and I was hoping you could look after my house."

"You're going to Peter's old hometown? Is that wise?" Gilly was always skeptical and even more so since she discovered Frank had been cheating on her while she was pregnant with their youngest son. Alicia had been the shoulder Gilly cried on when she'd found erotic text messages between Frank and his secretary on his cell phone. Gilly had taken it upon herself to return the favor many times over since then. After Peter's death, they'd shared many late-night visits where Gilly acted as a sounding board as well as providing Alicia with much-needed hugs, comforting tea, and cookies. Alicia respected

3

Gilly's advice, but this time she knew she'd made the right decision.

"It isn't exactly Peter's home town. He lived most of his life on Long Island. He only spent a part of his childhood in Cobble Cove."

"Even so, running away isn't the answer, honey." Alicia could hear Gilly's washer in the background tossing a batch of the boys' clothing.

"I'm not running away, Gilly. You might say I'm taking a breather from things. I've made up my mind. I need to see if I can locate any of Peter's relatives."

Gilly knew Alicia well enough not to argue. Alicia could imagine her friend standing in her kitchen in fuzzy slippers and a robe shaking her dark curly head and trying to control an impulse to convince her that she was crazy to go chasing people from Peter's past. After a pause, Gilly said, "If that's what you want, I'll be glad to keep an eye on your house."

Alicia glanced at the November calendar page. "I should be ready to leave by next Friday and spend the weekend in Cobble Cove. I'll drop a copy of my key at your house. I really appreciate this, Gilly."

"No problem." Gilly didn't sound happy but seemed resigned to Alicia's decision.

"One other thing. When you go to work today, say hello to everyone at the library for me, but please don't mention anything about my coming back. I haven't made up my mind about that yet."

"Okay, Alicia. Keep in touch. I'll see you before you go if not sooner. Take care of yourself, honey."

***

During the next week, Alicia kept busy for the first time since Peter's death. In preparation for her trip, she managed to tidy up the house and even went to the library to return some unread books that were overdue. Her fines were waived, but many of her colleagues at the library asked her when she would be back. She didn't know how to answer, so she just told them she would try to be back soon.

On the morning of November 20, after breakfast, Alicia took a walk. Gilly lived just a few blocks away, and Alicia stopped at her house to drop off her duplicate key. Gilly's beagle greeted her at the door, the smell of baking rich on the air.

"Hi, Alicia. I'm making chocolate chip cookies for Danny's and Joey's Boy Scout troops," Gilly explained when she answered Alicia's knock. "Come on in. You can have some." She was nibbling a cookie as she opened the door wearing a sweat shirt and pants covered by an apron with a large Santa Claus face, even though Christmas wasn't for another month. A tray of fresh-baked cookies lay cooling on her kitchen counter. "I can put on some coffee for you too."

"No, please don't bother. I just wanted to drop off my key. I've already had breakfast."

Her friend furrowed her dark eyebrows. "You can use a few more calories, unlike me." She chuckled. Gilly wasn't fat, but she could afford to lose a couple of pounds. Her whole body was round including her face, which gave the impression of a cherub. She was shorter than Alicia, which was part of the problem. Both women were in their early forties.

"Go on. Have a seat," Gilly insisted as she pulled out a chair from the kitchen table. She placed a few cookies on a paper plate with a holiday design. Ruby, her five-year old dog, sat begging below the table.

"Stop, Ruby," Gilly commanded in a firm voice. Alicia suspected Gilly secretly fed the dog some cookies even though chocolate wasn't good for dogs. Ruby had arrived in the Nostran home as a puppy from the North Shore Animal League a few months after Gilly left Frank. The boys adored her, and she was Gilly's fourth child.

Once Alicia relented and took the offered seat, Gilly sat next to her and grabbed another cookie. She looked Alicia in the eyes. "Tell me what's going on. What's this trip all about? Is it safe?"

Alicia sighed. She couldn't return her friend's gaze. "I'm only visiting Peter's childhood home. I'm thinking I may find some people who knew him or his family. Maybe I can locate his mother and sister."

"Oh, sweetie." Gilly placed her hand over Alicia's. "I know you're still hurting, and it takes time to get over a loss like you've had, but leaving town isn't going to help. Why don't you come back to the library? Everyone misses you."

"Not now." Alicia felt the warmth of her friend's hand. Hers felt cold in comparison. "I think I just need to get away for a bit."

Now Gilly was the one to sigh. "I understand, but be careful. I'm here if you need me, like always.

How far is the drive to Cobble Cove?"

"It's a few hours. I MapQuested it. It's in the Catskills."

"Make sure your cell phone is charged and you have your AAA card."

"Yes, Mother." Alicia smiled. Gilly was a year younger than she, but Alicia appreciated the maternal concern. "I better be going." She stood up, reached in her sweater pocket, and handed Gilly her duplicate house key.

Gilly took it and got up too. "Have you booked a hotel? Do you have a number besides your cell where I can reach you if I need to?"

"I'll be at the Cobble Inn. It seems to be the only place to stay in town." Alicia remembered trying to find information on TripAdvisor and even Googling "Cobble Cove, New York, hotels" without any luck. She finally located a number for the Cobble Cove Library and called to ask where she could stay if she wanted to spend a few days in town. A man answered who identified himself as Mr. McKinney, the head librarian. He told her there were rooms at the Cobble Inn only a block from the library. She called the number he gave and booked a room for three nights. The price was reasonable, but the woman said they didn't accept credit cards. She found this strange but realized they probably didn't get many tourists.

"I'll call you on my cell with my room number when I get there and am all settled," Alicia promised.

Gilly nodded. She let Alicia pass by to get to the door. "Have a safe trip."

Alicia smiled. "Thank you." She paused a moment and then hugged her friend. Gilly gave her a kiss on the cheek, leaving a sweet smear of chocolate.

***

How can a woman be married to a man for fifteen years and know nothing about his family? Alicia mused over this as she sat in traffic on the Grand Central Parkway headed for the George Washington Bridge. After Pete's death, she had tried to search for relatives with his last name on Facebook in the hope someone would turn up, but Fairmont was a common name, and she didn't even know his sister's first name or if she was married with a different surname. Although Alicia's parents were dead and her mother had also been an only child, Alicia still kept in touch with relatives from her father's family who lived in other states. She received a Christmas card from her Aunt Phyllis each year, and her cousins called occasionally or sent Facebook messages. It wasn't the same as seeing one another, but she couldn't imagine why Peter had been so cut off from his family.

As she got closer to her destination, she almost missed the turn onto Cobble Road that would take her to the inn. The sign was covered with bright red leaves, although most of the trees in the area were already bare. It was a sharp turn, but Alicia took it slow. For a quarter of a mile, she was still driving along the twisted road, upset she had such a late start because, after visiting Gilly and dropping off her key, she had gone home, realized she forgot to pack a few things, and decided to postpone her drive until after lunch.

Her GPS said she had another two miles to go. No homes were in evidence unless they were set back from the road. She checked her gas meter, afraid she might run out of gas without a gas station nearby. The needle was steady at three-quarters full, another thing Gilly had reminded her about before she left her house. She had screamed it from the door as Alicia was getting in her car. "Make sure your tank is full!"

***

When she finally arrived at the inn, it was growing dark with the early fall sundown. She climbed three wide rickety steps to a porch with hanging wicker flower baskets bursting with natural-looking purple geraniums. Maybe real ones had filled the pots earlier in the season. She noticed the paint was chipping on the railing and white front door. She rang the bell, and after a few minutes, was about to try again when a slim lady who appeared to be in her mid to late sixties answered.

"You must be Alicia Fairmont," she exclaimed. "Welcome to the Cobble Inn." Her voice and expression, however, didn't seem welcoming.

"Thank you," Alicia said, entering the vestibule as the woman held open the door.

"I'm sorry, but we don't have a bellhop, so you'll have to carry your bag upstairs."

Alicia hadn't packed much, so she only had one

light overnight bag with her. After signing the inn's register, a tattered book containing few signatures, she followed the woman upstairs to the second floor. The place was eerily quiet, as if she was the only guest.

"I think I explained on the phone I need payment in cash up front," the woman said as she led Alicia down the hall, their footsteps echoing on the hardwood floor.

"Yes. I have that for you." She thought, *Will you at least let me get settled in my room?*

The woman, who hadn't introduced herself, opened a door on the left. Alicia noted the peeling, blue-flowered wallpaper and a double bed with a lace canopy. A patchwork comforter covered the bed. There was one dark wood nightstand with a lamp on it. There was no evidence of a TV or dresser, but she glimpsed two more doors inside and thought they might be a closet and bath.

"You can put your clothes in the closet to your left. The bathroom is on the right, but the water in the shower doesn't get too hot."

Alicia shrugged. "That's fine." She lay her bag and coat down on a chair next to the bed. The eagle-eyed innkeeper seemed to be staring at her purse, so she opened it and took out the envelope with the money she set aside for the room.

The woman nearly snatched the envelope out of her hand. "Your check out will be promptly at ten Monday morning," she informed her. Alicia found this odd, as she'd already paid, and there didn't seem to be a list of people waiting to claim her room.

"We also have a complimentary breakfast downstairs from six to seven, but if you want dinner, you should go to Casey's on Gravel Way." With that advice, the innkeeper turned and left the room.

It was twilight, but the room seemed even darker. She assumed this side of the inn received sparse sunlight. She glanced out the window and saw a pond below. It appeared quiet and peaceful, yet she didn't feel comfortable. She wondered if she'd done the right thing or if she should have left the past behind and moved forward as Gilly advised. But she'd come this far. It was only for a weekend. She decided to leave her bags and get a bite to eat at Casey's and then come back to unpack. Tomorrow morning after breakfast, she would explore the town, maybe visit the library and see if she could find anyone who'd known Peter or any of his relatives.

Casey's was easy to find, although Alicia had to ask for directions. She'd gone downstairs and found the woman who checked her in seated on a sofa reading a book in the inn's guest parlor. When Alicia walked in, the woman didn't put down her book. Alicia cleared her throat. The woman kept reading.

"Excuse me. How do I find Casey's Restaurant?"

The woman answered from behind the book. "It's not Casey's Restaurant. It's just Casey's. You might say it's a diner. Right up the hill from here. You can't miss it."

The rude innkeeper was right. When Alicia drove up the road, the only building after the inn had a red lit sign that read *'Casey's'*, even though the bulb in the last letter had probably gone out long ago. She parked her car in the small lot in the back and walked in the front door. It was more of a bar than a diner with green leather stools around a counter behind which stood a variety of liquor bottles and a wall-mounted TV broadcasting the news. A few empty round tables were scattered in the back. Casey, or who she supposed was Casey, a stout man in his late forties or early fifties, stood behind the bar reading a newspaper. He hadn't put it down when she entered. What was it with these Cobble Cove people?

Alicia approached the bar. "Hello," she said. "I'm staying at the Cobble Inn and the…" *uh, she should've asked the woman's name…* "proprietress—" *did that sound too upscale for these country folk?* "—suggested I come here for dinner."

Casey peered over the paper at her. He wore thick glasses and had a salt and pepper moustache. "The menu's on the chalkboard." He indicated the blackboard behind the bar where most of the items listed were either burgers, cheeseburgers, or hotdogs with French fries. The prices next to them were on par with McDonalds, if there was one in the area. "I also have a paper one on the tables."

"Do you have any salads?" She wasn't particularly fond of fast food.

"Sorry. What's on the list is all I've got." He went back to his paper. She felt like turning around and leaving, but she had no idea how far away the next restaurant was located.

"I'll have a cheeseburger with fries, medium well, and a Coke, please." She sounded unfriendly to herself, but she was simply matching his tone.

"You can have a seat back there." He finally put the paper down and gestured to the empty tables. "It'll be a couple of minutes."

Alicia took one of the tables. While she waited, she looked around. The walls were decorated with posters from the sixties and seventies. She saw one of the Beatles with Ed Sullivan. Another featured the Vietnam War protest with hippies holding up a *'Make Love, Not War'*, sign. There was even a mock yellow submarine model hanging from the ceiling along with an Apollo 11 moon module.

The couple of minutes Casey promised turned out to be almost half an hour. She didn't expect much when the food finally arrived, but it was actually tasty. Casey, who had yet to introduce himself, seemed to have no wait staff. He dropped the bill on the table with the food, but after she had taken a few bites, he came back and unexpectedly started to chat with her.

"Sorry if I was a little preoccupied before. I don't get many visitors out here. I've owned this place for twenty years, and I have a few regulars at lunch hour—but not many show for dinner. If I wasn't the only choice in town, I would've had to close long ago. My name is Casey, Jim Casey." He extended his hand.

"Nice to meet you. I'm Alicia Fairmont."

His face changed. "Ah, Dora said you were coming this weekend."

Alicia wondered why the innkeeper, whose first

name she now knew was Dora, mentioned her coming, but she assumed talk traveled fast in a small town like this. She was starving, but she thought it would be bad manners to continue eating during their conversation, and she was interested in what else he had to tell her, especially if he might know anything about Peter's family.

She had the opportunity when Casey asked, "So, what brings you to these parts, Ms. Fairmont, or can I call you Alicia? Most people in Cobble Cove go by first names, but I prefer Casey to Jim."

"Well, my husband lived here as a child, and I thought I might find someone here who may have known his family. And sure, you can call me Alicia."

Casey considered her question. "Hmmm. Fairmont. Name's not familiar to me. What year did they live here?"

Alicia did the calculation in her head. Peter had just turned fifty-five, so he must have lived in Cobble Cove during the sixties. "My husband left Cobble Cove with his family around 1970."

"Is your husband visiting with you now, Alicia?"

Alicia forgot she hadn't told the restaurant owner she was a widow. "No." She shook her head. "He passed away six months ago."

"Oh, my. Sorry to hear. I've never been married, but I lost an older brother to a heart attack last year. It makes you realize how short life is." Casey took a seat across from her. "I guess your best bet for finding anyone who lived in Cobble Cove would be to visit the library."

"Mr. McKinney is the head librarian, right?" she

asked, remembering the man who answered her call about a place to stay.

Casey smiled, showing a few uneven teeth. "That old geezer? I guess he fancies himself in charge, but he gave that job away when he started losing his marbles. He probably can't even remember the Dewey decimal system now, although he still keeps a nice local history collection. Sheila Whitehead would probably be a better bet to help you. She's the director and is pretty sharp. Too bad Tina isn't around anymore. She was a young thing right out of library school. She was even trying to automate the library. I think we're the only library in the tri-state area still using a card catalog."

"I happen to be a librarian, myself. I was planning to visit the library tomorrow."

"What a coincidence," Casey exclaimed. "If you do, don't be surprised if Sheila offers you a job. She's desperate since Tina left because she wants to retire out West to be near her grandkids." He looked back at the screen now showing an old Clark Gable movie. "I'd best leave you to your dinner. If you need anything else, just holler."

He got up and walked away, and Alicia went back to eating. The burger had cooled but was still flavorful. She left most of the fries and a nice tip for Casey, who had given her more information than she'd expected.

CHAPTER 2

Alicia woke to a ray of sunlight peeking through the inn curtains. She'd slept surprisingly well in the inn's bed considering it wasn't her own and she had so many things on her mind. She probably had been exhausted.

She got up, undressed, and stepped into the shower. She noticed some homemade soaps in the tub. There was also a bottle of pink liquid with a handwritten label that read:

Shampoo

When she opened it, she smelled the sweet scent of strawberry. She wondered if Dora, the innkeeper, had made the toiletries.

After she'd bathed and dressed, Alicia headed downstairs, sniffing the aroma of cinnamon drifting up to her. She had chosen a casual yet chic outfit for touring around town—a navy pantsuit offset by a deep pink eternity scarf. She'd brushed out her long chestnut hair and, although she'd forgotten her curling iron, she managed to scrunch some waves through it.

"Good morning." The innkeeper greeted her at the foot of the stairs. Alicia was almost taken aback by the woman's smile. It seemed to her this lady was a morning person or somehow her personality had become friendlier overnight.

"Come, I've made fresh cinnamon rolls and muffins." She led Alicia to a room that served as a small kitchen/dinette. "This is the breakfast nook," she explained, pulling out a chair for Alicia. There were three tables in the room with two chairs at each. "I'm afraid our other guest is not coming to breakfast this morning. He usually sleeps late." She waved her hand. "Ah, well, you can eat his share."

Other guest? Alicia hadn't heard anyone come in yesterday and didn't notice any signature above hers for this date in the guest register, but maybe someone arrived while she was at dinner. "This looks delicious," she said, reaching into the breakfast basket and placing a piping hot cinnamon bun on the delicate china plate in front of her. "I also enjoyed my bath. Did you make the soaps and shampoo?"

The lady's smile grew into a beam. "Yes, I did. I use all natural ingredients. I have an herb garden in the back by the pond. I include many of them in my concoctions." The innkeeper took a seat across from her. "Since it looks like John isn't going to make it today, I'll join you."

Alicia was reminded of Jim Casey and how he changed from distant to chatty in a matter of minutes. Maybe these townspeople just had to warm up to you. "That would be nice."

"My name is Dora, by the way, Dora Kantor, but please use my first name." She didn't extend her hand but widened her smile.

"Nice to meet you, Dora. You already know I'm Alicia Fairmont."

"It's a small town. We know who all our visitors are and, of course, you signed the inn's register."

"Who is the other visitor?" Alicia was curious about the sleeping guest.

"Oh, John." Dora chuckled. "He's not a visitor. He lives up the road, but he stays here occasionally. I think it's just to keep me company, but he says the atmosphere inspires his writing. He also does some chores for me."

"He's an author?"

Dora chose a cinnamon bun and spread butter on it. "He's actually our town's newspaper publisher. He also keeps the town's records, but he's working on a book too. He stays busy. I guess it helps him recover."

This was interesting. If this guy John kept the town records, maybe he could track down Pete's mother and sister. But what was he recovering from? Alicia was hesitant to ask. Maybe the man was in rehab for alcohol or drug addiction, or perhaps he had cancer or been in an accident.

"Talking about me again, Dora?" They hadn't even heard him in the doorway. The man who stood there didn't look drunk, sick, or injured. He was tall, even taller than Pete, which would probably make him about six feet. He was thin but muscular, and he didn't look like he spent a lot of time working at a computer. His hair was dark and thick with only a few strands of gray. He was clean shaven, but what drew her attention first were his deep blue eyes.

"Ah, good morning, John. You've woken before the rooster crows." Dora got up. "I have some cleaning to do upstairs. Why don't you come and meet your fellow guest, Alicia Fairmont? She's traveled here from Long Island." Alicia recalled she had filled in her home address in the inn's guest book.

John bent forward as if to bow. "Pleased to meet you, ma'am." He extended his hand. "John McKinney at your service."

McKinney? "Are you related to Mr. McKinney at the library?"

John smiled as Dora made her exit, muffin in hand. He sat in the chair she left. "He's my dad."

"Interesting. I had dinner at Casey's restaurant last night. He mentioned your father and also told me Mrs. Whitehead is the library director. I'm a librarian too. I'd like to speak to them when I visit there." She left out the part about Jim Casey alleging that John's father had 'lost his marbles.'

"That should be easy to arrange. Dad is only too happy to show folks around, and I'm sure he'd be thrilled to talk to a fellow librarian. Sheila will also like to meet you. She enjoys sharing Cobble Cove information, or gossip, you might call it. " He grabbed a muffin. "That's how small towns are. Some people find them boring. Not enough news and too much gossip."

Alicia had her opening. "I hear you're the local

newspaper publisher."

He smiled and she noted a dimple in his left cheek. "Guilty—if you consider the *Cobble Cove Courier* a newspaper. It's one sheet back to front and only comes out monthly."

"But you also maintain the town records?"

"That doesn't take much of my time." He bit into the muffin and swallowed a piece. "Dora may have told you I'm writing a novel. It's halfway done. I may self-publish it because I don't expect to land an agent. There's too much competition today, but maybe I can sell some ebook copies."

"I write too."

"You do?" His smile widened, along with his dimple.

"Well, it's a hobby for me. I've never published anything."

He took another bite of his muffin, and then wiped his mouth with the matching napkin next to his plate. "If it gives you pleasure, it's worth it." He paused. "So what brings you to Cobble Cove besides our wealth of sightseeing attractions and your interest in the library?"

Alicia knew he was kidding about the tourist sites. She replied to his question the way she had to the same one posed by Casey. "I lost my husband this past spring and thought some people here in the town where he grew up might know how to contact some of his relatives. That's why I wanted to talk to your father and Mrs. Whitehead."

John finished his muffin and wiped his mouth again. "Sheila might be able to help, but Dad has some trouble remembering stuff lately. Would you like me to walk you over to the library after you've finished breakfast?"

"Is it within walking distance?" Although she knew the inn was close to the library, she hadn't noticed it on her drive there or up to Casey's.

"Everything around here is within walking distance. I have no plans for today, so I could take you. It gives me a chance to visit Dad."

He got up and tossed his crumb-filled plate and crumpled napkin into the waste basket to the right of the door. "Actually, if you'd like a tour of the town before you visit the library, I can give you one and also show you the town hall and my newspaper office."

Alicia thought that was a great idea. Maybe he could help her check for Pete's relatives during their visit to where the town records were housed. "Thank you. That would be very nice."

***

After breakfast, Alicia accompanied John outside. "The tour should start here," he told her. "Cobble Inn has an interesting history. My dad is also the local historian, and he's passed a lot of information down to me."

"It reminds me of a bed and breakfast. Don't tell me it's haunted." They were standing outside the inn facing the road that curved toward it.

"No, sorry." His dimple creased and his eyes twinkled. "Nothing that exciting. It's old, though, at least a hundred years. The original innkeepers, Kurt McKinney and his wife Lydia, also opened the first school here. Nowadays, the kids are bussed to New Paltz. That's why our demographic has changed. You'll notice most residents are over fifty. I'm actually one of the youngest, although I'm getting there." He touched a strand of gray hair.

"It sounds like Kurt was a relative of yours."

"Indeed. He was my renowned grandpa. There have been McKinneys here forever. Come have a look at Dora's herb garden. She's very proud of it."

As he led her toward the back of the inn, Alicia absorbed what he told her. He seemed to be about a decade younger than Pete but possibly a few years older than she. If he grew up here, he might've been too young to know Peter, but maybe his dad had.

The herb garden was a square plot surrounded by white fencing. Small gardening sticks served as labels for parsley, rosemary, and other herbs that grew in neat borders. They looked as if they were tended lovingly.

John walked toward the bench across from the pond. "We can have a little rest before we continue." He sat on the bench and patted the area next to him. He leaned back and sighed. "I love the fall. Just enough coolness to the air. It can be relaxing but also invigorating."

Alicia accepted his invitation. She noticed two swans gliding on the pond. From her room in the inn, she hadn't seen them. She was reminded of a pond in Roslyn outside a restaurant where she and Peter went for their first anniversary, although this one was smaller. She also recalled how Pete insisted on not discussing his family.

After their meal, they had walked in the warm summer night to the town's duck pond. They sat on a large rock, and Peter tossed some stones into the water.

"Be careful not to hit the Canadian geese," she warned.

"I'll aim for the swans." He laughed as he put his arm around her. "I love you, Alicia." His kiss was warm, and she felt so happy, even though his insistence on not discussing his past still nagged at her.

"Can't you tell me about your family?" she asked tentatively, hesitant to break the magic.

"Not much to tell. Typical dysfunctional relatives. My dad worked hard to support my mom and sister. He had a heart attack at sixty-five. They took off with his money, and sis..." He paused.

Alicia squeezed his hand, prompting him to continue.

He shook his head. "I don't care where she is now. I haven't heard from her in years, and that's just fine with me." He gave an irritated laugh, throwing the stones into the water harder. Large ripples appeared, forcing the swans and geese to swim quickly away to avoid the waves. After a moment, Peter's temper dissipated. "You're my family now, Alicia, and that's all that counts," he said, pulling her close.

Shaking herself back to the present, Alicia said, "Since your family's been around so long, you must know everyone around here."

John shrugged. "Not really. I left to go to college

and was gone a bunch of years. Before that, I was your usual self-absorbed teenager, although I was more absorbed in TV and books than the kids are today with iPads, cell phones, and computers."

"Is Dora a widow? Does she have any children?"

"Dora's a spinster. She never married, although, between you and me, I think she once had a crush on my dad. He's older than she is, though. He just turned eighty. I think Dora's around seventy."

"I would take her for younger." The innkeeper was another person who might know some of Pete's relatives, but if she recognized the name, why hadn't she said anything?

John got up. "I don't mean to rush you, but I have a lot to show you before we stop at the library, and I don't want to miss Dad. He only works half days now. There'll be a lot of walking, so I hope you're wearing comfortable shoes." He glanced down at her flats. "Oh, they look fine. Are you ready to go?"

Alicia nodded. "I think so. Thanks again for being my tour guide."

He smiled as she joined him at the gate.

***

The first stop was the post office. They had walked up the hill toward Casey's and made a right turn. Alicia noticed John had no trouble dealing with the steep climb, which further reinforced her initial impression of his athletic prowess. Alicia, on the other hand, was a bit winded when they reached the top.

"Sorry, I'll slow down if you want," he said, noticing her breathlessness. "I usually walk four or five miles a day. It's great exercise, and it doesn't pay for me to afford the expenses of a car in this town, but I do have a pickup for travel."

Alicia was still catching her breath. "Don't tell me your dad does that much walking."

He smiled, and she saw his dimple again. "Well, the cane slows him down, but he does walk to and from the library each day."

"Do you live with him when you're not at Dora's?"

"Yes. Our house is part of the tour, but first...here is the town square. It's a good spot to get an initial view, but there's a better one I'd like to show you another day." Alicia looked down the hill at the picturesque view below. A dozen or so brick buildings and a white-spired church gathered in a circle around a green. Cobblestone paths led to offices and shops bordered by a variety of flowers and shrubbery. A bunch of nearly bare trees and weathered wooden benches were scattered around the area's perimeter with a gazebo at its center. A spraying fountain stood next to a sign reading **'Cobble Cove Square'**, its low gurgling a gentle contrast to the sounds of bird calls and insect buzzing. The quaint town, golden-hued in the sunlight, reminded her of a Thomas Kinkade painting. Autumn leaves made a colorful, crunchy path as Alicia followed John to the farthest building on the left atop which perched a steel eagle with large wings. A few mailboxes stood outside. "This is the Cobble Cove Post Office," he announced.

"That eagle is supposed to flap its wings on the hour." He glanced at his watch. "It's almost ten. We may be in luck. The kids who visit here love this."

They waited a moment in silence and, sure enough, the mechanical bird's wings spread and began moving. Alicia laughed. "That's wonderful. It reminds me of the one on Long Island in Stony Brook. I guess it's not a unique tourist attraction."

"Ours was probably first. This is an old town. Oh, and by the way, we no longer use Pony Express. Come on in and meet Ed, our Postmaster."

He held the heavy wood door open for her. The interior of the post office was more modern than its exterior. It was like walking from the nineteenth century to the twenty-first. A gray-haired balding man stood stamping some manila envelopes behind a long pine-colored counter. Several commemorative stamps and other postal products were displayed through the glass-fronted cabinet that also contained a postal scale and telephone.

"Good day, Ed," John said. "This is Alicia, a visiting librarian." Alicia assumed everyone called each other by their first names, but she wasn't sure how she felt about being addressed as a visiting librarian. She was here on purely a personal, not business basis.

"Hi, there," Ed said. His smile was slightly crooked. "Got any letters to mail?"

Alicia laughed. "Not today. How is business?"

"Slow, but it'll pick up soon when people start shipping for the holidays."

"I'm giving Alicia a tour of Cobble Cove," John said.

"Great idea. Be sure to bring her over to Wilma's. She might want a makeover." His ruddy cheeks suddenly darkened. "Sorry. You look fine. Very pretty in fact, but Wilma has a nice place. The only beauty parlor in Cobble Cove."

Alicia laughed. "I'm sure she does, but I'm not staying long. I only booked until Monday morning at the inn."

"I see. Well, if you change your mind and extend your stay, Wilma will probably give you a new customer discount."

"We'll see. Thanks for the information."

"Take it easy, Ed," John said as he beckoned Alicia to continue their tour to the next stop.

***

They spent the next hour and a half visiting the rest of the buildings on the green. Names and faces whizzed by Alicia as she met Duncan, the grocer; Camille, the bank teller; Irene the Cobble Cove gift shop owner; Claire the baker; and of course, Wilma the hairdresser, who wanted to make her an appointment for that afternoon, but John suggested he take Alicia to lunch first and the appointment could wait until later if she was interested.

"Are we going to Casey's?" she asked, because she knew it was the only restaurant in town.

"No. I want to make you one of my special PB&J sandwiches even Dad enjoys. You can see the McKinney homestead at the same time. It isn't far from the library."

Alicia was wondering what type of issue John

might be recovering from. She was also confused as to why he stayed at Dora's inn. While they walked, she asked him about it. "I hope I'm not being too nosy, but do you pay Dora when you stay at the inn?"

John smiled. "She won't take my money. We have a barter system. I help her with some stuff at the inn, plumbing, wood cutting for the fireplace, those types of things, and she gives me a nice quiet place to write."

Alicia recalled the inn was in need of a good paint job, but she didn't want to mention it. As if John could tell what she was thinking, he added, "I meant to do some painting of the exterior a month ago, but I never got to it. It's still on my list."

"How is the book coming?" They climbed uphill again. She glimpsed a few houses they were passing. Most had large plots with plenty of room between them.

"Slowly, but I think I'll finish before the end of the year, at least that's my goal."

"Have you ever published a book?"

"No. Just articles here and at Columbia."

"Columbia?" She remembered he mentioned going away to school.

"I attended Columbia Journalism School. That was twenty years ago. The newspaper field has changed significantly. Here…it's right up this path."

They turned onto a road with the sign **'Stone Throw Road'**. Again, as if reading her mind, John said, "I think my parents chose our house because of its cute street name and also because everything is only a stone's throw away from it."

They were facing a small ranch house with wildflower borders. A shady willow tree flanked its door. Unlike the rest of the houses they'd passed and the town green buildings, John's house was made of stone instead of brick. He took a key out of his khaki jeans and opened the door, holding it for her so she could pass. "Watch out for Fido," he warned. "He's our watchdog." Fido turned out to be an old, overweight golden retriever who greeted John with a slobbery kiss. He didn't even bark at Alicia.

After John said hello to his dog, he followed Alicia into the foyer. "Oh, gosh," he exclaimed. Papers were strewn over a table that looked like it was meant for dining and, in the first room they entered after going down three short steps, a couch was covered with coats and other clothing. "I guess I've been gone too long. Dad is such a slob sometimes. It's his memory. He has so much stored in there from the town history and library archives he forgets to put his stuff away."

Alicia stood in the beige living room while John did some tidying up, hanging the coats in a hall closet and neatening up the piles of paper so there was room to set the table. She was interested in pursuing the topic of John's college years but also wondered if his father might have some information for her about Pete's family.

"Have a seat while I prepare the sandwiches. I make the peanut butter with fresh nuts and my special recipe. The jelly is preserved by us. Dad has canned varieties of other fruits and jams in the garage. It's one of his hobbies."

Alicia sat on the now clear couch. A glass-fronted mahogany grandfather clock stood in the corner. Its hands indicated the time was a quarter to twelve. There was a fireplace in the living room in front of which Fido had gone back to sleep despite the fact the logs inside it were unlit. The stone theme continued on the mantel. Even the walls were bordered in stone. French doors opened onto what looked like a small patio with a few chairs and a table. She got up to take a better look.

"Would you rather eat outside?" John called to her from the kitchen. "It's a nice day, and the kitchen is messy. Dad also left some dishes in the sink, and I don't want to take the time to wash them now."

Alicia was reminded of her house at home and how neglected she'd left things before she'd decided to visit Cobble Cove. "That would be nice. Thank you."

"You're welcome. Go have a seat on the patio. I'll bring the sandwiches out in a minute."

Alicia wanted to offer to help, but it seemed like he had things in hand. She opened the unlocked side doors—she was surprised at that, but figured there wasn't much crime in Cobble Cove—and stepped out, shutting them after her in case Fido decided to follow. A basket of the same silk geraniums as the inn's served as a centerpiece for the wicker table. The backyard was large with an above-ground swimming pool, covered now the season was over. There was a flower bed and what also looked like an herb garden similar to the one Dora tended. The two chairs at the table were rockers with comfortable tapestry cushions. She'd just sat down when John came out balancing a tray with two plates containing sandwiches and two tall glasses.

"I hope you like iced tea. If you want something warm, I can put on coffee."

"No, that's fine. The coffee at Dora's was sufficient. I only drink a cup a day."

John took a seat across from her. "I hope you like the sandwiches. I use sourdough bread spread with a small amount of jellied preserves over the peanut butter. There are a few secret ingredients in the preserves, but my dad doesn't allow me to reveal them. Our family members are peanut butter connoisseurs." He smiled. "I also make mean deli sandwiches. Duncan has a good deli department."

Alicia bit into a triangular sandwich wedge. It was quite tasty, with a slightly sweet flavor. "Very good," she told him. "I don't eat much peanut butter, but this is better than any Skippy I've tried."

John took a bite of his own sandwich and washed it down with some tea. "I'm glad. I like to impress Cobble Cove visitors."

Alicia wondered what other visitors he had impressed, but she was more interested in what he had started to tell her about his college years. "How long were you at Columbia?" she asked. "If you don't mind my asking."

He laughed. "As I said, this town is built on gossip. I left for New York at eighteen and was there until I was twenty-five. It's hard to believe it's been twenty years since I've been back. When I was a kid, I thought everyone over forty was old, but I

31

still feel like a kid."

Alicia figured that was because John kept in such good shape. She'd turned forty-two last month and was starting to feel it. Pete's death had also aged her. "So you studied journalism at Columbia. I hear it's a good program."

The sun was bright, but a sudden cloud passed over the backyard. Alicia felt chilly. She was glad for the long sleeves of her suit jacket. She took a sip of iced tea while waiting for his reply. John was busy finishing the first wedge of his sandwich. He swallowed and said, "Yes, a fine program, but newspapers are not what they were back then. Today, a lot of the print ones are gone because of the Internet. I left Cobble Cove because I was bored with country life and needed to explore. I wanted to see what life was like in the big city."

"What did you discover, and why did you return?"

The clouds were in John's eyes now, turning them a lighter shade of blue. He answered her second question first. "My mom became ill with cancer. I came back to help my dad care for her. I'm an only child, you see. My parents had a hard time conceiving me. Mom was thirty-five when I was born and had lost five babies before me. My dad was still working at the library full-time back then."

"That must've been hard. I'm also an only child, and I lost both my parents to cancer too, shortly after I married."

"Sorry to hear that. Life can be tough, but my mom wasn't the only reason I came back." He pushed his plate away, leaving the other half of his sandwich uneaten. Alicia wondered if he had lost his appetite or if the topic had taken it away.

She was afraid to probe and ask what happened. Maybe it was the clue to whatever recovery Dora said he required.

John finished his drink and glanced at his watch. "Maybe we should get going. I want to catch Dad at the library, and Sheila is probably back from lunch by now." Clearly, he had closed the page on his story.

CHAPTER 3

The library was near John's house, and Alicia saw his dad could easily manage the walk with his cane. Unlike the walk from the town green, it was on flatter pavement. They only needed to turn down Stone Throw Road and make a right on Bookshelf Lane. Alicia was becoming fond of the street names and also the town's quirky characters. As for John, she found him friendly, but there was something not entirely open about him. Reflecting on this, she acknowledged the same could be said of her. People who have suffered a great deal usually close part of themselves up. She wondered what had caused his pain besides his mother's death.

Cobble Cove Library was small. It may have once been a house. Brick, like many of the town's buildings, it had a porch similar to Dora's inn with flower baskets hanging from its eaves. Out front, there was a statue of a boy and a girl holding a book. The sign next to the statue read, *'Cobble Cove Library'*. along with a graphic of an open book lying on a bed of cobblestones and, etched underneath, *'Est. 1915'*. The sliding glass front doors seemed out of place. It looked as if they were recently added. Alicia walked through the turnstile in front of John, who urged her inside first. She guessed the man at the circulation desk was John's father. The older man's eyes, the same color as his son's, lit up when he saw them. "Hey, there, young man," he said, "I see you've brought us a pretty visitor."

Alicia had never been one to blush, but she felt heat rise to her face and imagined it might be reddening.

"I sure did," John said, walking over to the desk. "Dad, this is Alicia Fairmont. She's a librarian from Long Island. Alicia, this is my father, John Senior. You can call him Mac. Everyone does."

Alicia stepped forward as the old man came from behind the desk, leaning on his cane as he approached. He extended his wrinkled hand for her to shake. "Nice to meet you, young lady. I'm always happy to meet a fellow librarian." She accepted his handshake, which was quite strong considering his age.

"Alicia is doing some research on her husband's family. Unfortunately, he passed away last spring. Alicia thinks you or Sheila might be able to help her."

"Sorry to hear about your husband. Ms. Sheila will be back from lunch soon, but I'd be glad to show you around the library before she gets here."

Alicia noted the half eaten peanut butter and jelly sandwich on the counter next to Mac and the scarcity of patrons. In her library at home, there were always people around, if only using the computers. She saw just one person reading at a table in the far corner next to the card catalog John had mentioned and one other at a lone PC. "I hope I'm not interrupting your lunch?"

"Nah. I'm about finished," Mac said, taking a few more bites and placing the remainder of his sandwich back into its tinfoil wrapper. Rolling it into a ball, he tossed it into a nearby trash bin and smiled when it made its mark. "Two points!" he exclaimed. "I shouldn't be eating at the desk, anyway. Sheila would have a fit."

John laughed. "Dad, you know how to handle Sheila by now. Incidentally, I treated Alicia to our homemade PB&J recipe. She will never go back to Skippy."

Mac's grin widened, showing a few missing teeth. "Good boy, John."

"I guess I can go then. Good luck, Alicia, and don't tire Dad out." He winked. "I know we didn't get to the newspaper office or the town hall, even though I pointed them out when we passed them. I promise I'll give you a tour of both of them before you leave town. I'll see you back at the inn later. You remember how to get there, right?"

"I can take her," Mac offered. "I'm only working until two today."

"Perfect." John turned. "Bye, Alicia. Bye, Dad." He waved as he exited the library.

Alicia faced Mac. "Do you have more books upstairs?" she asked, eyeing the stairway behind the desk.

"No. That's a living quarters. Tina used to stay

up there. She was our homebound librarian. Sheila uses it sometimes in bad weather. We get some wicked snowstorms. Oh, and Sneaky is a guest up there, too."

"Sneaky?" She wondered who would have such a strange a nickname.

"I'll introduce you two when I show you around. He usually spends a lot of time in our local history section."

Local history. Maybe the material at the library as well as in the town hall could help her locate Pete's relatives. She followed Mac around as he pointed out the fiction area with a small display of bestselling authors including James Patterson, Jodi Picoult, Debbie Macomber, and Stuart Woods.

Mac walked through an archway that led to the non-fiction collection. He said that part of the library was the reading room. Biographies were in front, followed by travel, and then history books. There was a long table with several chairs around it and a magazine rack filled with a few popular issues. Although it seemed the Cobble Cove Library used the Dewey decimal classification for its books, they didn't seem to offer many books in each section. At the very back was the local history collection. One book stack bore the sign *'Cobble Cove History'*. A basket containing a plaid blanket lay at the foot of the stack and, curled up in a beige ball in the blanket was a Siamese cat.

"There's Sneaky," Mac said. He touched a wrinkled finger to his mouth. "Shhh! He's napping."

Alicia laughed. She should have known. "Is he

your library cat?"

"Yes, ma'am. Sneaky the Siamese guards our collection, but he often sleeps on the job."

Alicia liked Mac's sense of humor. "Where did you get him?"

"Get him? You don't get a cat. They get you. He came to the library door one morning and Miss Tina begged us to take him. She said it would be advantageous to us if he was a mouser and would keep the mice away. Luckily, none of us are allergic, and Ms. Sheila doesn't mind too much. She's not too keen on cats, but he's grown on her."

"How long has he been here?"

"Over a year. We don't know if he was a stray, but no one has claimed him. We think he's about five years old. His litter box and food are upstairs."

Alicia nodded. "Why did you name him Sneaky?"

"Sheila named him. She says all cats are sneaky, but especially Siamese. I think she was thinking of Sneaky Pie in the Rita Mae Brown series, although Sneaky Pie is a female tiger cat. Sheila had a Siamese when she was young. They can be talkative but quiet when they want to be. I think she was heartbroken when her cat died, so that's why she doesn't like getting close to them anymore."

Alicia thought Mac could tell her something about his son's secret injuries, but that would have to wait for another time. Just as she was eyeing the DVD and audio offerings on a few shelves in the corner, a bell rang at the back door. She assumed it might be a staff entrance. A woman wearing a fur jacket entered. Her red hair was tied back with a white headband, and she was wearing a long black woolen skirt. Alicia's guess at her age was early fifties. She was holding a few books against her chest. "Mac, can you please take these? They're for the fiction to film rack. People keep asking for *Gone Girl* and the *Fifty Shades* books, although I don't know why they want to read or view such trash. Our classics section is dwindling, and they aren't even requiring that reading in school anymore." She glanced at Alicia with hazel cat eyes. "I'm sorry. I just came from delivering and picking up homebound books." She walked towards her. "I'm Mrs. Whitehead, the library director. Is Mac helping you?"

Alicia figured the woman took her for a patron but, before she could clarify, Mac introduced her and explained that she and John were staying at the inn together. "I've shown Alicia around a bit, but I think she would be better off checking out the yearbooks at the town hall once John has some time to take her there," Mac said.

Sheila raised a red eyebrow, and Alicia felt as if the woman was assessing her. "Hmmm, Alicia Fairmont. A librarian. I see." She handed Mac the three books she was holding as she came to shake Alicia's hand. She had long fingers with bright red polish, and there were rings on several fingers except the one reserved for a wedding ring. From what John told her, Sheila was a young grandmother, and Alicia surmised she was a widow or possibly a divorcee´.

"Nice to meet you, Alicia. Please call me Sheila. Let's go upstairs to be private, and perhaps we can chat about your husband's family." She nodded toward Mac as she turned toward the stairs, and Alicia couldn't help but notice the look that passed between them. She had no idea what it meant, but it made her feel uneasy.

As Alicia followed Sheila's high heeled boots up the stairway, the cat, who had risen, glided past them. "I assume Mac introduced you to our library cat. See why we call him Sneaky? He's always so stealthy on those padded paws."

The upstairs featured a small kitchen off of which was a sitting room with a couch scattered with a few rose-colored pillows. "Have a seat. I'll put on some water for tea if you'd like."

"No, thank you. I'm fine unless you want some."

"No, I'm too jittery today even for herbal tea." She waited while Alicia sat and then joined her on the couch, moving a pillow behind her back. "Make yourself comfortable, Alicia." She paused. "What do you think of our library from what Mac showed you so far?"

Alicia noticed Sheila's teeth were white and straight. "It seems well stocked, considering its size, but I saw there weren't many patrons here today."

Sheila folded her hands in her lap, clinking some of her rings together. "This is an older community. We get more people in the morning and some after work on weekdays, and we have a sizeable list of people who need homebound deliveries. That was Tina's job. She left to care for her ill mother. I've been doing her work, but I can use some help. I've considered advertising a position, so it's a coincidence you've shown up on our doorstep like our library cat." She gave a short laugh. "Do you think you might be interested?"

Casey had been right about warning Alicia she'd be recruited once Sheila knew she was a librarian. It seemed ages since Alicia had worked at a library, although it had only been six months. Her goal in traveling to Cobble Cove was to find Pete's mother or sister or anyone who knew them. She hadn't expected a job offer the day after she arrived. "I'm just visiting here, Mrs. Whitehead—I mean Sheila. If I even considered the position you mention, I would have to give my own library notice and put my house on the market. It would take some time, and I'm not even—"

"I understand." The library director cut her off. "There's no need to rush. Maybe John can help you find an agent for your house or you could travel between here and home for a while before you get settled. You could even live here." She waved her hand to indicate the upstairs. "There's a guest room down the hall and a bathroom. The library closes at six p.m. each night and opens at nine a.m., so you could have the place to yourself before and after those hours. It's also open Saturdays and closed Sundays."

"It's not that," Alicia paused, "I have to be honest. I'm still getting over my husband's death, and I can't commit to anything right now. You said you were considering advertising the position. Weren't you planning on interviewing candidates?"

A shadow passed over Sheila's face. Was she expecting Alicia to jump at her offer? "This isn't a civil service position. I'm not restricted to a hiring list. I can hire anyone I want. It seems like fate you would come here at this time. As I mentioned before, we don't have a large population, and I prefer not to advertise the opening to strangers. Since your husband once lived here, that makes you almost a resident."

"Did you know my husband or his family? He had a sister. They lived here until 1970."

Sheila's face remained shadowed. "I grew up here, so it's possible I knew him as a child, but that was long ago. I also read some of the nearby papers besides our local one John publishes, and I do vaguely recall an obituary for a Fairmont killed in a hit and run accident in May."

Alicia suddenly felt stuffy, as if she couldn't breathe. "I'm sorry, Sheila, but I think I need some air."

The director stood up. "Of course. Come downstairs with me. I'm sorry to have even mentioned the obituary and the library job to you so soon."

Alicia felt better once she was back in the public part of the building. Sneaky, the cat, who had been nowhere to be seen while they were talking upstairs, had followed them down and headed back to his bed by the local history section.

"Do you think Tina will return?" Alicia asked, curious about the woman Sheila was trying to replace and wondering if the job offer was only temporary.

"I'm afraid not. She's in Florida with her mother. I doubt she'll be back."

"Why would anyone return here?" Mac stood in

the reading room alcove. "I put those books where you asked, Sheila, but I'm headed home soon. I need my afternoon nap. Are you all done with Alicia? I offered to walk her back to the inn."

"Yes, I'm done with her for now, Mac. I've offered her Tina's position, but I can understand her hesitancy." She looked at Alicia. "How long are you staying at the inn?"

"Until Monday."

"Can you stay a little longer? Ask Dora to extend your stay a few days. Just get back to me with your decision before you leave. I can't offer you as much money as you make back home, but the cost of living here is much lower, and in my opinion, the people are nicer."

"Maybe I'll stay a few more days," Alicia agreed. She had no reason to go home.

On their walk back, Alicia remembered she had tentatively scheduled an appointment with Wilma the hairdresser, but she was too tired, so she asked Mac to take her directly to the inn. He surprised her by his spryness. Even with his cane, he could keep pace with her.

"I know some things may seem strange to you," he said as they turned onto Cobble Road. "But everything happens for a reason. As you grow older, you'll learn that saying is true."

Was he referring to Pete's death or her coming to Cobble Cove? Or, like Sheila, did he believe her visiting here was prophetic?

***

Dora and John were sitting in rocking chairs on the porch when they arrived. "Come join us," Dora said. "I was just about to bring out some tea and cookies."

"I would rather head home, thanks," Mac said. "It's time for my nap."

"Are you sure? I made my special peanut butter cookies you love." She winked.

"If you insist," Mac said, pulling up a wicker chair next to his son. Alicia sat across from them.

After Dora had gone in to get the cookies and tea, John asked, "How did your tour of the library go?"

"I'm not sure."

"Sheila hired her on the spot," his father explained, "but she has to tie up stuff at home. You know what that's like."

Alicia noticed the clouds pass through John's eyes again, but they cleared quickly. "Sheila is an impulsive woman. If Alicia needs more time to make that decision, she'd be wise to do so. I know her primary reason for visiting here is to locate her husband's family."

Alicia didn't feel so wise at that moment. Dora returned with a tray full of peanut butter cookies and a few muffins left over from breakfast, along with four tea cups and a steaming teapot.

Mac quickly grabbed a cookie and she laughed. "I knew you couldn't resist these because you're such a peanut butter fanatic."

Once they were all eating and drinking, Alicia asked Dora about staying a few more days. Unlike her initial request for Alicia to check out promptly by ten on Monday, Dora smiled and said, "Of course. It's not like I have an inn full of guests right now, and I think John is staying until the end of the week, so you'll have company and maybe he can finally get to that painting."

"Keep him as long as you need," Mac said. "I'm enjoying my privacy."

John laughed. "You're right up the road, Dad, a stone's throw, right? I'm in the thick of my book right now and am being inspired by this place. And," he glanced toward Dora, "I'm planning to do some painting this week if the weather holds."

She smiled. "Great. Would you three like to stay for dinner? I'm making meat loaf and there'll be plenty of it." She looked at Alicia. "You won't catch me dead in Casey's joint with all that fast food."

"I'm leaving after I finish these cookies," Mac said. "Don't worry about me. I'll have some of the crockpot stew John left in the refrigerator."

"John is actually a better cook than I am."

"Thanks, Dora. Maybe one day this week, if you let me in the kitchen, I'll treat you and Alicia to a chicken recipe my mom used to make."

"Only if you clean up afterwards."

Alicia began to feel better. The fresh air and comfortable porch was erasing the feeling of suffocation she'd felt upstairs in the library.

"Okay then, folks," Mac said, getting to his feet and leaning on his cane. "I'm off." He turned to his son. "Take care of our visitor and possible new librarian."

***

Dinner was delicious as promised and, afterward while Alicia helped Dora with the dishes despite her protests, Dora invited her to the regular Saturday night bingo game at church.

"No, thanks. I think I'll make it an early night and snuggle up with a book. I'm a little tired." She was planning to call Gilly to tell her she was staying longer than anticipated. She had forgotten to let her friend know she'd gotten there okay and was a bit guilty about waiting so long to contact her.

Dora nodded. "All right. If you need anything, just ask John."

John was clearing the table. "Yes, I'm not going anywhere tonight. I think Dad will be fine with Fido."

When Dora left, Alicia went to her room and dialed Gilly on her cell phone, which was on the nightstand, fully charged. She didn't want to add long distance fees to the inn's phone.

The phone rang three times and then was answered by one of the boys. Alicia had a hard time telling them apart. "Who is this?" she asked.

"Danny. Are you selling anything?"

She laughed. "No, it's Mrs. Fairmont. Can I speak with your mom, please?"

"Mom, it's for you," he yelled. She heard the phone drop and then it was picked up. Gilly came on the line, sounding out of breath as usual.

"Sorry to interrupt. Were you eating dinner?"

"Alicia. Oh, thank goodness you called. No, I was just cleaning up. I've been worried. Are you okay?"

"I'm fine, Gilly. I forgot to call when I got here. Sorry about that. Listen, I won't be coming home Monday. I'm staying in Cobble Cove a few more days."

Alicia heard a crash in the background and then, "Danny, what did you do? I'm on the phone. You'd better clean up, young man." Gilly came back on the line. "What about finding Peter's family? Any luck?"

"No, but the library director wants to hire me."

Gilly was quiet, and Alicia wasn't sure if she was dealing with Danny and whatever he dropped or if she was shocked by what Alicia said. It seemed to be the latter when Gilly spoke again. "Hire you? But you already have a job. I thought you were only taking a short trip. You don't even know anyone there."

Alicia sighed. Gilly was right, and yet Sheila's job offer had given her something to think about. She still wanted to find Peter's family, and staying in Cobble Cove longer would give her more of an opportunity to do so. "That's true, Gilly, but I need more time."

"I know what's gotten into you." Her friend's tone had changed from disbelief to acknowledgement. "You think staying there you'll eventually find someone who knew Peter, but you need to let that go, honey. I know it isn't easy, but you have to. Believe me, it's for the best."

Alicia realized Gilly was talking from her own experience after the divorce of having to let Frank go. "Thanks, Gilly. Just give me a few more days."

"Of course, sweetie. By the way, I checked your house today and picked up the mail for you. Mostly ads, of course. No mail tomorrow, but I'll check again on Monday. You take care now. I better go see what Danny and the other boys are getting themselves into while I'm occupied."

"You take care too." She disconnected the cell phone, missing her friend a little but not feeling homesick at all. Just as she was planning to pick up the book she was reading, there was a knock at the door.

"Alicia, can you answer?"

She was glad she hadn't undressed. She got up and turned the knob to face John.

"Sorry to bother you, but I thought you might want to sit out on the porch with me for a few minutes. It's not too cold, although you might want to bring a sweater."

Alicia was no longer tired, and thought this might be a good opportunity to ask John some questions about the town's local history and the Fairmont family, but she felt guilty to consider this when he was probably just offering a friendly chat. She wondered, not for the first time, if he had ever married. He wore no wedding band, but maybe a broken relationship was the cause of the secret pain he didn't want to share. She grabbed a sweater and accompanied him down the stairs and out to the porch. The stars were just coming out, and the stillness of the night had a magic to it. She and Pete often took walks at night at home up until it got too cold. She switched off those memories as she sat next to John on the same chairs they'd occupied when they'd all had tea after her library visit.

For a while they didn't talk. John seemed lost in thought, and she assumed she appeared the same. There were only the sounds of crickets and a light wind blowing through the trees.

She broke the silence by asking John about Tina. "Sheila said the girl she wants me to replace left the library when her mother became ill. Can you tell me more about her?"

He shrugged. "Not much. She wasn't from Cobble Cove. She turned up for an interview for the ad Sheila sent to the papers. She recently graduated from library school, and Sheila hired her right away. She worked at the library for about a year and a half before she left for Florida." It seemed Sheila was impulsive when it came to hiring new librarians.

John changed the subject. "What do you think of Cobble Cove so far, Alicia?"

What could she say? The small town was lovely, and the people were friendly once they got to know you. "It's very nice."

"A nice place to visit, but would you want to live here?"

She had to be honest. After all, John had lived both here and in the city. "I'm not sure. I don't have many ties at home." Now was the time for her to tell her story, but should she trust him? He already knew most of it.

"I read about your husband, you know," he went on as if reading her mind again. "I still subscribe to the New York papers, so I can use some of their news when our grapevine runs out." He must've noticed her expression because he quickly added,

"Of course, I didn't repost your husband's obituary. I wouldn't do something like that."

"I guess you're an ethical journalist."

He smiled. "One of a rare breed."

Alicia decided to be upfront with her curiosity. "John, do you think you could do me a favor and look through the town records for information on my husband's family? I haven't been able to locate any of his relatives, and I know he has a sister and mother."

"Strange he wouldn't have given you that information himself. I know some families become estranged, but you were his wife."

Alicia recalled asking Peter about his family early in their courtship.

"So when am I going to meet your family?" she'd asked while they were having coffee at a Starbucks in Westbury.

Peter stirred his mocha latte, a quizzical look on his face. "You lucky girl, there's no one to meet. You have me all to yourself, and no in-laws to worry about."

She wasn't appeased with this reply. "Seriously, Pete. Are your parents alive?" She had a weak spot in this, as her own parents had both been diagnosed with cancer a year earlier, and she knew it would not be long before she lost them.

Pete shrugged. "I have an older sister and a mother. They're around somewhere. We're not a close family."

Alicia brought herself back to the present and

decided to counter John's comment with a question. She hadn't meant to ask so fast, but the timing was right. "What about you? Were you ever married?"

She regretted the question when he stood up and walked to the porch rail. She felt the impulse to follow him, but she stayed where she was. He turned back to her, his face sad in the moonlight. He glanced down at his left ring finger. "I stopped wearing my wedding band a few months ago. Dad was on me about that for ages. He said I had to let go of the past because I wasn't attracting many women that way." He laughed, but it was a hollow sound. "I met Jenny at Columbia. She was a journalism major in some of my classes. I wanted to bring her back here with me, but she preferred the small apartment we managed to rent in the city."

"What happened?" Alicia tried to keep her voice gentle.

"She died." He nearly choked on the last word. "We were planning a big family. Since I was an only child, I had hoped to have a few kids. We were married a few months when she told me she was expecting." He turned back and looked out toward the sky as if he could see his wife in heaven. "She died in childbirth. So did the baby. It was a boy. I don't know what went wrong. I thought she was in good hands. The doctors said they'd tried everything. Her blood pressure was high at the end. They'd induced labor because she was running late, but our son was stillborn."

Alicia walked to him. She lightly touched his back. "I'm so sorry, John." When he turned to her, his eyes wet, she fought the urge to kiss him, to heal his pain so like her own.

"Life stinks sometimes."

He laughed, although the sound came out almost a sob. "You bet. Hey, you want to take a walk around the pond?"

"I'd love that," she agreed.

As they circled the pond, John continued his story. "I came home after I lost Jenny. Mom had just been diagnosed with stage 4 cancer. When it rains, it pours. I helped Dad get through it, and he helped me as well. I started a new life here."

"Don't you ever get bored? Lonely?"

He composed himself. "You can be bored and lonely in the big city too. It's what you make of your life. I'm happy." He paused. "You might be happy here too." What had his father said? Everything happens for a reason.

"I know you need time. It took a while for me too. I had to put the past behind me. I'm not even sure I've done that successfully yet." His grin was serious. "I wallowed in self-pity for a bit. Fido helped. Animals can be quite therapeutic. Dad was there too, but he was getting over his own loss."

"I think I would get over mine faster if I knew my husband's family," Alicia said, and it felt like a revelation.

He nodded. "I'll help you. I need to start painting for Dora, but I'll fetch some town records for you tomorrow afternoon. I can open the hall on a Sunday even though it's usually closed. Do you go to church?"

"I haven't been to church in years."

"Church is a social activity here. If you don't go,

there's talk. I'd like to take you. The church here is non-denominational Christian. They usually serve coffee and cake afterwards. Services start at nine. Will you accompany me?"

"I guess so. Do women wear hats to church?"

He grinned. "Only the older ladies."

"Good, because I don't wear hats."

"Sheila has a closet full of them." Alicia wondered how he knew. For a second, she thought she felt a tinge of what might be jealousy. Sheila was about five years older than John, but she looked good for her age. Alicia shooed away those thoughts. Both of them had too much baggage right now, but maybe one day something could develop if she decided to stay. In the meantime, they could be friends.

"It's a date then," he said.

"I guess it is," she agreed.

They spent another half hour talking on the bench by the pond, but it started growing cold, so John brought her back to her room. They said goodnight at her door. She was no longer in the mood to read, but she was inspired to do some writing. When she took out her old writer's notebook she'd brought along on a whim, she found what she was writing would fit a romance more than the mystery she was working on. She wondered what John's novel was about. She wondered if he was feeling the same attraction to her as she was to him. Most importantly, she wondered if she dare feel this way so soon after Peter with someone she'd just met. She turned off the light and lay in bed pondering all these thoughts until she fell into a deep sleep.

CHAPTER 4

Alicia woke early to the smell of cinnamon and figured Dora was making breakfast. She showered and chose an outfit for the day, glad she'd brought along a few extra clothes. Besides a second pantsuit, she had packed a dress, two pairs of jeans, two tops, and a sweater. She still had to ask Dora about laundry service. She assumed Dora had a washing machine at the inn, and she wouldn't mind doing her own clothes if she were allowed to use it.

She slipped on her navy dress that she felt would be suitable for church and went light on makeup. She never used much, anyway.

After heading downstairs and entering the dining nook, she was surprised to see John at the oven. "Good morning," he said as she entered the room. "Did you sleep well?"

Why did she feel heat rise in her face as if she was blushing again? "Yes, thank you. Where's Dora?"

John smiled, and the dimple in his cheek widened. "She called me last night after we came in

55

and said she wouldn't be back until after church. It seems she stayed with one of her friends after bingo." He paused on the word 'friends' and winked. Alicia guessed one of the bingo players was a boyfriend of Dora's. "She does that occasionally when I'm here. I don't mind. I like having the place to myself, but I like it better when I have some company as nice as you." He placed a plate of steaming cinnamon rolls on the table. "Have a seat and see how my breakfast compares to Dora's."

She sat and he joined her. There was a pot of coffee between them, and John poured them each a cup. Sugar cubes on a tray and a small pitcher of milk stood next to the coffee pot. Alicia added some of both, but John kept his coffee black.

"You look like you're ready for church. That dress looks attractive on you."

She nearly choked on her piece of cinnamon roll. "Thanks, John." He was already dressed in a dark blue shirt and slacks that complemented her dress and his eyes.

They chatted a bit, but conversation was kept to impersonal observations such as the day's weather that was predicated to be cool but sunny and his ideas for the exterior painting. "If you want to lend a hand later," he said, "I'd like to start after church. We would need to change, of course. But I haven't forgotten about taking you to the town hall. We could stop there right after the service and get to the painting when we come back."

"Sounds like a plan." Alicia thought her jeans would be okay to wear while painting and made a note to be sure to ask Dora about the laundry, so she would have something to wear the next day.

***

John was right about church being a social activity for the citizens, especially the ladies, of Cobble Cove. As soon as they entered the white-spired building that she'd glimpsed the day before on their tour of the town green, all eyes were focused on Alicia. She recognized many of them— Irene from the gift shop in her fur wrap; Camille, the bank teller in a long sweater dress; Wilma, the hairdresser in a simple black top and skirt; the postmaster, Ed, in a pinstripe suit; Duncan, the grocer, in navy slacks like John; and Jim Casey in green corduroys and matching jacket. There were a few other unfamiliar faces, but the bells were already ringing and John didn't stop to introduce them. She felt most of them knew who she was already through the infamous town grapevine. Everyone nodded or smiled at her, and those she had already met said hello. Wilma took her arm briefly and had her promise to come by the beauty shop the next day for a complimentary visitor makeover.

John led her to a pew a few seats from the altar where Dora was already seated next to a man about her age with a gray moustache who was likely Dora's bingo 'friend.' The church was packed, and Alicia wondered if this was the only service and if the churchgoers were the entire population of Cobble Cove. While everyone was getting settled with their bibles and missals, Mac ambled down the aisle and sat next to John on the end of the pew. He smiled at Alicia.

Sheila, who she hadn't noticed in the back of the church, walked up to the pulpit and read the first of the readings. Alicia was surprised when John got up to read the second. Singing of hymns followed and then the minister, a stocky balding man of middle age, read the gospel and gave a long sermon about being kind to one's neighbor and helping those less fortunate. When the collection basket was passed around, Alicia added a few dollars to it. John had an envelope he tossed in, and his father dropped in a few singles.

When the service concluded, they gathered in the foyer of the church where, as John promised, coffee and baked goods were provided for the parishioners. A banner strung across a table at which Sheila stood, read: **'Cobble Cove Ladies' Parish Group'**. A few other women Alicia didn't recognize manned the table with Sheila.

"Come have some muffins, Alicia," Sheila called to her. "We have fresh brewed coffee too. It's nice to see you in church today."

Alicia and John walked to the table. "Thanks, but I had breakfast already."

"I'll just have a cup of coffee," John said. "I think I'll take it to go. I have some things to show Alicia at the town hall."

Sheila raised a red eyebrow. "Working today? It's the Lord's day." She turned to the two ladies next to her. "You both know John, but this is Alicia Fairmont, our new librarian-to-be if she accepts my offer, which I dearly hope she does." The two women, one tall and the other short, both smiled at the introduction. The tall one was older. They shared similar features. Both had short red hair with freckles. The elder had some gray streaks in her hair; the younger wore glasses.

"These ladies are my cousins, Edith and Rose," Sheila said, explaining their likeness to her.

"Nice to meet you both," Alicia said. They nodded, as if neither of them had voices, but they both seemed friendly.

"Rose baked all these delicious muffins," Sheila continued. "Edith brewed the coffee. A few of us take turns each Sunday. If you decide to stay, you are welcome to join our social committee."

Why did Alicia feel pressured by her words? The invite sounded friendly enough, but for some reason she felt the offer was more obligatory than voluntary.

"Thank you, Sheila and ladies," John said, indicating the cousins. "But we really must be going now. I still have to start the inn painting today." Placing his arm on Alicia's back, he ushered her toward the door.

***

John had shown Alicia the town hall on their previous visit, although they hadn't gone inside. She recognized the building with the white door and bare rose bushes under its windows. John climbed three short steps to the office and unlocked the door. Both high and low file cabinets lined the room.

There was an oak desk with a large bookcase behind it filled with binders and school yearbooks. Alicia's home library housed the local high school yearbooks, but it seemed they did things a little differently in Cobble Cove.

"Have a seat," John gestured toward the desk and the only chair in the room. "I think we should start with the yearbooks, but I have to ask you a few questions first."

Alicia hesitated. "I think I'd rather stand. What would you like to know?"

John went to the bookcase. Turning toward her, he said, "I'm just curious, Alicia. I know you're trying to locate your husband's family, but they only lived here until he was ten. Why didn't you start your search on Long Island where you two met?"

Alicia sighed. "I've already done that without any luck. I had very little information. I met Pete when he came to my library when I first began working there. He was a salesman who traveled to various libraries in the area, endorsing his company's products." She paused, thinking back.

There was Pete, tall, blond, and handsome with that great smile and charm walking through the library door with catalogs under his arm. "Good morning, Miss. I have an appointment with Miss Arnold in Reference this morning."

"I'm Miss Arnold. You must be Mr. Fairmont."

"That's me, but please call me Peter." He put out his hand. "Excuse me, but I thought you were one of the young clerks for a moment. You must've

just gotten out of college."

It was true she'd graduated the previous year, but she didn't consider herself young. She was getting close to the big 3-0 that women her age feared because it meant their chances of catching a single, straight man were slim to none. "Yes, I just started here after Mrs. Crimmons retired last month."

"Then it must be my lucky day." He moved closer to the desk. "I visit quite a few libraries, but this is my first time here. I must say it's a beautiful library."

"Thank you. I heard they remodeled last year." Although Alicia was naturally shy and had been a bit reserved meeting her new co-workers, she'd been befriended by one of the part-time clerks. Mrs. Nostran, who insisted Alicia call her by the nickname, Gilly, had filled her in on all the who, what, where, how, and whys of the library and its staff. She could see Gilly now standing at the OPAC helping a patron search with one eye on the computer and the other on the stranger by Alicia's side at the reference desk.

"Is there somewhere private we can talk? I have some materials to show you. I won't take much of your time."

It was quiet in the library that day, but Alicia was alone at the desk while Mrs. Blake, a reference librarian who had worked there for twenty years, was taking her morning break. She looked around, wondering what to do.

Suddenly, Gilly was there. "Need some help, Alicia? I can watch the desk until Barbara gets *back."*

"Thanks. That would be great." She walked around the desk, exchanging places with Gilly.

Peter Fairmont smiled at Gilly. "That's very kind of you, ma'am. I promise I won't keep her long."

As Alicia walked away with him, Gilly winked at her.

"Are you allowed to leave the library?" Peter asked as they rounded a book stack. "It's a beautiful day, and I can show you what I have just as easily outside. That's one of the things I love about my job—traveling and being away from a desk most of the time."

"I think I can manage that." They walked through the doors and out into the sunny day.

Alicia brought herself back to the present and continued her story for John. Changing her mind about sitting, she took a seat behind the desk. "Peter had an apartment where he lived alone. He never mentioned any relatives and pretty much shut me down when I asked about them."

"What did you think of that?"

"I was concerned at first. As an only child, I couldn't understand why he wasn't close to his sister, but the few men I'd dated before weren't particularly open about their families. One of them was actually too close to his mother and that broke up our relationship. You probably would've considered me a late bloomer. I was also painfully shy. I still am to a degree, but I think you grow out of that as you get older. Too many other things to worry about than yourself." John smiled.

"My parents were still alive then, and we spent a lot of time with them. My mother really liked him, and neither she nor my dad asked him about his family. I think they knew he was sensitive on that topic, and they didn't want to pry. He was good to them, even at the end when..." She paused, choking up. "Mom went first and Dad a year later. Both of them were in hospice. Peter relieved me when I couldn't be with them. He had me continue to work while he, with his flexible hours, visited them. He said work would be the best medicine for me, and he was right. I have no idea how I could've made it through those dark days and after without him." She looked up at John, and she knew he saw the tears ready to drop from her eyes. "I know you must've gone through the same with your mom, and you had no one there to share the burden."

She didn't expect him to lean down and gently kiss her cheek. For a crazy moment she wanted to move her head so his lips were on hers, but she hesitated too long and he pulled away.

"Sorry, I..."

He turned back to the bookcase. "I think we would start with the yearbooks. Peter and his sister didn't graduate from my grandfather's school, but maybe their parents did. What year do you think that would be?" He slid his fingers over the volumes of the leather yearbooks ranging from 1920 to 1950 and rested them between the last five volumes. 1945 to 1950.

Alicia recalled Pete once told her his parents were the same age. Since he was born in 1960, it was possible they graduated high school in the late 1940's or possibly 1950.

"Maybe we should work backwards," John suggested, taking down the five yearbooks he was touching and arranging them with the oldest first. "You have no other names to go by except Fairmont, right?"

Alicia was thinking of his light kiss where her cheek still felt warm, but John seemed to have forgotten it ever happened, or maybe he was trying to.

"Yes," she finally replied, placing her hand on top of the pile he had laid on the desk. "I have no idea of his mom's maiden or first name. His father may have been a Peter as well, but I don't know for sure."

As she was about to open the 1945 yearbook, there was a light rap at the door.

"Who could that be?" John asked. "Everyone knows this office is closed on Sundays."

He opened the door, and Alicia watched as Sheila walked in carrying a Styrofoam cup. "Sorry to bother you two," she said, entering the room, "but John forgot his coffee. I thought he might want it while he works."

John took the offered cup. "Thank you, Sheila. I kind of rushed out, and I could use it, although I'm not really working today except to help Alicia find some information."

Sheila's hazel eyes lit up. "Information? Well, you know I'm the library director. Maybe I can help." She stood before Alicia in front of the desk.

"What is it you're looking for?" Her eyes

scanned the yearbooks. "I've lived in Cobble Cove more than fifty years. After my husband died suddenly, I raised my daughter alone. She has two young girls now, and they live in California. I'm still planning to move out there one day to be close to them. But if your questions have anything to do with town residents who graduated from Kurt McKinney's School, I think I may be able answer them."

Alicia hesitated. For some reason, she felt her search was safer with John than with her possible employer.

Before she could reply, Sheila tossed back her red hair that, unlike her cousin Edith's, contained no hint of gray. Today, it wasn't constrained by a headband. "If you're seeking information about your husband's parents, they both graduated in 1950, the last year the school was open." She picked the bottom yearbook from the pile and paged through it with her long, red nails. "Here you go. There's Paul Peter Fairmont." She handed the book back to an astonished Alicia. Staring at her from the page Sheila was tapping, was a face that looked like a younger Peter.

"You knew Peter's father? When we met, you said you didn't."

Sheila smiled her Cheshire cat smile. "I didn't know him personally. I was born in 1963, so I was only seven when the family left Cobble Cove. But Mac knew them well. I'm surprised you asked his son and not him for help." She raised her eyebrows again, at John this time.

"Mac is having some memory issues lately,"

John explained.

"Strange, but he seems to remember the old days better than I do." She laughed. "They say that happens as you age. And of course, some teachers remember their favorite students. Carol Parsons was the apple of Mac's eyes back then." She took back the 1950 yearbook and turned a few more pages to the students with last names beginning with P. "There she is. Miss Most Likely to Succeed before she became Mrs. Fairmont." She handed Alicia the book.

Alicia accepted it with trembling hands. The young woman on the page was fair like Peter, and while Peter had more of his father's features, she could also see something of him in the black and white photo staring back at her.

John cleared his throat. "Dad never told me about the Fairmonts. I grew up in this town with you too, Sheila, even though I was younger and left after high school."

"Mac liked to talk about his students to Tina. I overheard them a few times when I was shelving books. I think he enjoyed teaching more than reference work, although, in many ways, they're similar occupations."

Alicia still had her eyes on Carol Parsons. She couldn't take them away.

"Okay, mystery solved." Sheila turned to John. "I guess you can go back to the inn and finish painting for Dora now."

"Wait a minute." John walked to the desk and gently claimed the book from Alicia. The thought occurred to her that he feared she would break

66

down again, and he couldn't wipe away her tears with a kiss this time while Sheila watched them. "Nothing's been solved, Sheila. These are just faces. Alicia knows nothing about these people."

"Then she needs to talk to your dad." She paused. "I'm leaving now. Oh, and Alicia, I hope you're still considering my offer. I think things will work out well for you at the library." She smiled again and left quickly on high heels that barely made a sound on the wooden floor.

John sighed. He shut the 1950 yearbook and placed it back on the pile. "I'm sorry, Alicia. Sheila can be a bit authoritative. I had no idea my father taught your husband's parents. If you want, I can ask Dad to come to the inn today while we're painting, and you two can have a chat."

"I can't understand why Mac didn't mention he knew Pete's parents when he met me, but I don't want to force the issue."

"You can't force anything with Dad." John smiled. "Let's go back, change our clothes, and start painting. Dora will probably be home by now making lunch. When she sees us working, she'll put some out for us. I'll ask her to invite Dad."

"And you're sure he won't feel cornered?"

John laughed again. "One thing you'll learn about my dad. He craves a rapt audience."

***

Dora was at the inn when they got there, and she'd brought her bingo friend. They were on the porch when Alicia and John arrived. "Hey, guys," she greeted. "I don't think either of you have met Charlie Sullivan. He's new in town like Alicia. He just bought the old Fenwick place."

Alicia followed John up the porch steps where he shook Charlie's hand. "Nice to meet you, sir. I'm John McKinney from the *Cobble Cove Courier* and this is Alicia Fairmont from Long Island. We're both staying at the inn this weekend."

"Dora's been filling me in," the man said, shaking John's hand and then Alicia's. "Glad to meet both of you."

"Charlie and I are going to a play in Carlsville this afternoon," Dora said, dousing John's plans for lunch. "I know you said you'd start some of the painting today, and I didn't want to be in your way." She glanced at Alicia, and there was something in her expression that hinted at her leaving them alone for another reason. Alicia wondered if her feelings for John were that transparent. She herself didn't understand them.

"We'll be fine," John said. "You two enjoy yourselves. Alicia's going to be my assistant. We'll start right after we change out of our Sunday clothes."

"Wonderful!" Dora turned to Charlie. "I told you John helps me at the inn with little repair jobs and maintenance. I'm lucky to have him." She smiled. "I guess we should get going if we want to be on time for the show."

"All right, kids," Charlie said. "See you both later. It's been a pleasure. Have fun painting." His wink had Alicia considering him an accomplice to Dora's plan to give her and John some privacy.

Dora and Charlie left them standing on the porch as they got into a black Ford Alicia figured belonged to Charlie. She never saw another car at the inn, so she didn't think Dora drove.

"Don't worry about lunch," John said. "I can whip something up. Meanwhile, I'd like to begin working. I'll meet you back here in about a half hour. I have the paints, brushes, and drop cloths for the porch in the garage. I'll bring those out." As he opened the door for Alicia to enter the inn, he added, "And when we take our lunch break, I'll call my dad over, so you two can talk."

***

The touch-up painting turned out to be more fun than work. John made it so. He opened a music app on his phone where he'd downloaded some songs and let the music play as they painted. He cracked some jokes about Sheila, such as how she always looked like she was balancing books on her head and Tom in the firehouse said he could start a fire with her hair.

"What's with the cousins—Edith and Rose?" Alicia asked as she dipped a paintbrush into the can of white paint to help touch up the inn's shingles.

"That's a joke too." John grinned, exposing his dimple. "She calls them cousins, but they aren't. They're actually my cousins."

"Your cousins?" Alicia was confused. "They look like Sheila."

"Lots of people in this town look alike. It's mixed blood. Small town people often marry those with whom they grow up."

"Like my husband's parents."

John nodded. "Right. A lot of Irish settled here when the town was first established—the Caseys, Duncans, and, yes, McKinneys. I inherited the dark Irish from my mom, and Edith and Rose got the light Irish from my dad."

"So Edith and Rose are Mac's sibling's daughters?"

"Nah." John was painting the left shingle while Alicia was doing the right. "They're distant cousins. Dad had a younger brother who died in the war and an older sister. I think she's in a nursing home in Florida now. She left a few kids. They're not living here, but I think Edith and Rose are from that branch of the family. It's hard to keep track."

"I would think, as the town archivist, you would've done a family tree."

John dipped his paint in the white can again for a second coat. "That would be an interesting project."

"I still don't get it. Why does Sheila refer to them as her cousins?"

John added the second coat to the shingle. "Some people around here refer to everyone as cousin, but people kept remarking how much Edith and Rose look like Sheila, so she decided to 'adopt' them as her cousins. Hey," he stood back and admired their work, "we've done a good job. Dora will be pleased. Let's clean up, and I'll get started on lunch while the paint dries. I know you're eager to speak with my dad."

Why did Alicia feel uneasy about that prospect?

CHAPTER 5

Mac arrived with Fido at his heels. The dog kept pace with his owner. Alicia calculated if they converted dog years into people years, the two would be about the same age.

"Hey there, son, Alicia," Mac greeted them. "I see you've done some painting. Dora will be happy."

"Alicia is a natural painter," John said. "To reward her, I've made my special peanut butter and jelly sandwiches again. I was glad to see Dora had all the ingredients in her kitchen."

"Wonderful. I hope you have an extra sandwich for Fido." The dog looked up eagerly, and Alicia imagined he was excited about the prospect of people food.

"Of course," John said. "Let me get everything. There's plenty. Have a seat with Alicia, Dad."

Alicia knew the extra time John spent inside allowed her time to talk with his father.

She wasn't sure how to begin as she sat next to Mac on the wicker patio chair. She decided plunging in was best. "John was helping me find information about my husband's family at the town hall after church today. We found something interesting."

"John is great at research. Instead of studying journalism, I wish he would've followed in my footsteps and gone to library school, but he seems happy with the path he chose."

"Yes, he does." Alicia had expected Mac to ask what they'd found. "Sheila showed up just as we were looking through some yearbooks, and it seems she knew Pete's parents or at least knew of them. She said they attended the last class at your father's school. She also said you taught there." Alicia waited for Mac's reaction before she mentioned Paul Fairmont or Carol Parsons. His expression remained the same.

"Sheila likes to exaggerate. I didn't exactly teach at the McKinney school. I was only fifteen that last year and attending classes myself, but I was a bit ahead of the crowd. Dad let me tutor some students in English."

"Was one of those students Carol Parsons?" Sheila said Carol had been the apple of Mac's eyes. Alicia tried to imagine him a pimply teenager infatuated with her lovely mother-in-law.

"Ah, Sheila told you about Carol." It wasn't a question.

Alicia didn't want to accuse the old man of dishonesty, but she had to ask him, "Why didn't you tell me you knew Peter's parents?"

He seemed to be telling the truth when he replied, "I didn't see the point. That was a long time ago. I have no idea where they are now."

Before they could talk further, John arrived with lunch. He set the plates down on the table. "Sorry to interrupt your conversation, but you can continue while eating. I know you probably have a lot to talk about."

Mac grinned. "You bet, son. Sheila's been at it again with her stories. She told Alicia about me and Carol. I might as well fill her in on the rest. Fill you both in on it."

John sat down and waited while his father and Alicia took their sandwiches. Fido, who had been sitting quietly by Mac's side, suddenly began whining and extended his paw.

"Here you go, Fido," Mac said, placing one of the extra sandwiches on the floor by the dog, who eagerly chewed it up.

"Boy, he's hungry, Dad. Haven't you been feeding him?"

Mac laughed. "He eats all the time. You know that, John."

"Looks like your dad spoils that dog," Alicia said, but she was hoping Mac would return to the topic.

After a few minutes, while everyone ate, Mac laid down his half-eaten sandwich and resumed his story. "Okay, I'll try to remember as best I can how it all went down." He turned to Alicia. "Your husband's mom was a beauty back then. All the guys in school, even those in my grade, had crushes on her, but she had this thing going with Paul. They went to all the dances together and also the prom. Paul was bright and so was Carol, but she wasn't much interested in studying. I guess she figured she would get married and raise a bunch of kids like the other girls. But my dad believed in equal education for men and women, and he felt Carol needed some additional help with her classes. He asked me to tutor her an hour after school once a week so she would be able to raise her grades enough to graduate."

He took a sip of lemonade. "I got to know her pretty well." Alicia suddenly noticed Mac had a dimple like his son and also a propensity to blush, which he was doing now. "She wasn't like the girls my age. Of course, she was more mature, but there was something about her." In Mac's eyes, she could see him traveling back to the past. She waited while he paused and then continued.

"She told me what she really wanted to do when she got out of school was dance. There was a dance school at Cobble Cove back then, and she had attended it since she was seven years old. She showed me some of her steps." His cheeks reddened. "Like so many of the other fellas, I think I developed a crush on her. Then there was that day toward the end of the semester..."

Mac was still reliving the past, his eyes staring ahead. "She came to the lesson crying. Paul told her he was leaving for Korea to fight in the war. She was afraid she'd never see him again. I tried to comfort her." He paused. "I was only fifteen but big for my age. She was a tiny thing at eighteen. I kissed her. It was my first real kiss. I thought she'd punch me like some of the other girls when I tried, but she smiled instead. She said I was such a nice boy. She showed me the friendship ring that Paul gave her. She said he promised he'd replace it with an engagement ring when he returned. I was hurt. I told her I was sorry, but I had to go home and couldn't finish our lesson. I didn't see her for a long time afterwards. Dad asked me why I wasn't tutoring her, and I couldn't tell him the truth. I just said I was too busy with my newspaper route and my own school work." He took another sip of lemonade and cleared his throat.

"After graduation, which I didn't attend, I knew Paul went off to war. I didn't see Carol and then I heard she'd gone to New York City to study ballet. I was surprised when I got a letter from her a few weeks later. I expected she'd be writing Paul. She invited me to come visit her and offered to send me some traveling money. It was summer, so I wasn't in school. I told Dad I wanted to go away on vacation. He didn't even ask where or with whom. He knew I was old enough to see the world if I wanted to and figured I'd saved some money from my paper route."

He cleared his throat again. "That was the beginning of my summer visits with Carol. She hadn't had a word from Paul. The summer I turned eighteen, I asked her to marry me."

John took a deep breath, "Dad, I…"

"Please, let me continue, son…she said no. She was still in love with Paul. I was hurt again. I knew she was three years older than I was, but I felt like no other girl I met could compare to her."

Mac was deep in thought as he spoke, not looking at either of them. "I told her I wouldn't be back the following summer. I wouldn't be treated as a second fiddle. She cried. She begged me to stay. She was lonely. She said she would let Paul go. So I stayed. I couldn't bear her sadness. We started an affair."

He spoke lower, almost in a whisper. "She was my first girl. I'm sorry, John. It was an infatuation. I realize that now, but I hadn't met your mom yet."

When Mac was quiet for several minutes, John asked gently, "What happened after that, Dad?"

"What I supposed would happen all along. Paul returned. He had been injured quite badly but had earned several medals. He claimed he hadn't had Carol's address in the city and had written letters to her in care of her parents in Cobble Cove. Carol never received those letters. It didn't matter. They picked up where they left off. She gave up dancing and married him shortly after he came back."

Mac sighed. "Seven months later they had a daughter. The Cobble Cove grapevine was ripe with rumors the baby's father wasn't Paul."

"Were you the father?" John asked. I was still trying to absorb it all. Could Pete's older sister be related to John?

"I never knew. Even though I was heartbroken, I wished Carol well. I didn't run into or look for her around town. I began dating some of the ladies. I eventually met your mom after I graduated library school. I was almost thirty. You know that story, John, and I doubt Alicia would be interested in it. Not that it wasn't as romantic, but first love is always more dramatic."

Mac got up. "If there's anything else you want to

ask me, Alicia, I'm not going anywhere. Don't listen to Sheila. She tends to get carried away. Thanks for lunch, John. I'm going to walk Fido home now."

"Wait," Alicia said, standing. "Do you know what happened to Paul and Carol when they left Cobble Cove? Did you know Pete?"

"Like I said," Mac reached for Fido's collar, "I didn't keep up with them. That may be hard to believe, and it isn't easy in a town this size, but we never crossed paths again."

Alicia watched Mac go, leaning on his cane while the dog ambled by his side.

"Did you have any idea about that?" she asked John when Mac was out of earshot.

"I didn't. It's an eye opener. I may actually have an older sister somewhere."

"I wonder why he doesn't care to find out."

"Oh, I'm sure he does, but sometimes the past is better off buried."

"Is it?" Alicia didn't believe that. She felt it was always wiser to know the truth despite how cruel it might be. "I wonder if Peter was really more like his dad than I imagined. I mean, Paul doesn't sound like the nicest guy from what Mac said about his leaving Carol hanging."

"But he came back for her. That's what counts."

"Poor Mac."

"Dad recovered, and he ended up with my mother. Things happen for a reason. Dad says that all the time, and it's usually true."

"Okay, enough of this philosophizing. Where does that leave me now in my search?"

"Now you have the names. We could Google them, maybe check Facebook. Our cell phones could handle it, but I think we might be more comfortable using a desktop. I could open up the newspaper office and we could use my computer there. I was planning to stop by later to start work on next month's issue. Would you like to come with me?"

Alicia was slightly afraid of what they might find, but she knew she couldn't turn back now. "Sure. Sounds like a plan."

***

The newspaper office was a few doors past the town hall, a similar brick building, but its door was brown with an evergreen bush outside instead of roses. Alicia couldn't help but feel they would run into Sheila again. The woman was shadow-like.

When John unlocked the door, she sniffed a musty odor. Alicia recognized the microfilm cabinets. There were copies of the *Cobble Cove Courier* scattered on a long table along with a few New York papers. A computer stood on a desk in the corner.

"Have a seat," John said, moving some dusty books and a jacket off one of the two chairs in the room. The other chair was behind the computer. "Ah, and have a look at my baby." He handed her the November 1st issue of the local paper. It was double-sided as he'd told her and printed on heavyweight parchment. "I publish it in-house, only three hundred copies." He sat at the computer and booted it up.

Alicia sniffed. "No wonder they call some newspaper offices morgues." She glanced at the copy he handed her. It appeared to be more of a newsletter than a newspaper. The front-page headline read:

Marge Simper Wins Big at Bingo.

She laughed. "I guess there aren't any major crimes to report here."

"All news is good news," he replied. "When I run out of material to feature, I consult the local grapevine or steal something from one of the nearby papers." The monitor was coming alive. "I subscribe to some of the national databases too, but let's hope Google does her magic with the names we have."

Alicia liked the way he said 'we.' "Thanks, John."

His fingers tapped the keys, and the day's Google logo came up—leaves falling on autumn-colored letters spelling the famous search engine's moniker.

"Let's try Paul first. I know you said he's dead, but Carol may have remarried, so we can't be sure which surname she's going under—Parsons, Fairmont, or another name."

Alicia nodded. "I think Paul passed away in 1997. Peter said he had a heart attack at sixty-five."

"There might be an obituary," John said, typing Paul Fairmont into the search box. "If I can't dig it up from Google, I'll search one of the microfiches from the New York papers from that time."

Alicia nodded. She held her breath.

The search was fast. John smiled. "The wonders of the twenty-first century. Got it on the first hit."

Alicia gazed over his shoulder at the search results. The first one wasn't from a newspaper but a publication called the *Gold Coast Gazette* published in Brookville, New York. Alicia had attended the C.W. Post campus of Long Island University where she'd earned her library degree from their Palmer School of Library and Information Science. She knew Brookville, the location of the college, was home to many wealthy residents, but she had no idea Peter's parents were rich.

Even though Alicia was looking on behind him, John read the article aloud.

"Paul Peter Fairmont, Industrialist, Lieutenant U.S. Army, Korean War, passed away at his Brookville home on March 3, 1997 from cardiac arrest. He is survived by his wife, Carol nee Parsons; daughter, Pamela Fairmont Morgan; son-in-law Mark Morgan; granddaughters Cynthia and Caroline Morgan."

"We got them," John said.

Alicia was surprised Peter not only had a mother and sister who were still alive but also two nieces. She supposed they must be in their twenties or older since the article was published eighteen years ago.

"Shall we keep looking?" John asked. "Maybe we can find something more recent by checking on the Morgans. It's amazing how the Internet has made privacy a thing of the past."

"That's not a good thing."

"It is when you're looking for people like you are."

Now she was getting close, Alicia wasn't sure she should continue. Already, her husband's relatives seemed as if they were from another world than the one she'd shared with Peter. "Do you know what an industrialist is, John?"

"Fancy word for businessman, but the question is what type of business? Looks like your hubby's folks had quite a bit of money. I hope he left you with a good nest egg."

"I don't know what he left me. He never made out a will. We had a joint account but not much savings. There were always expenses even without kids—upkeep on the house and so on. He never invested in anything, either, said it was too risky. After he passed, a friend of mine told me to consult a lawyer." She thought of Gilly and how she'd recommended hers, although he was a divorce attorney. Alicia ended up finding one in the yellow pages.

"What did the lawyer say?"

"Not much, but he charged me a fee for the consult, of course. Without a will and because I didn't know all of Pete's assets, I was out of luck."

"But he had to at least have life insurance?"

"Nope. He didn't believe in it. He said his work pension was enough because we didn't have kids."

"Wow!" John seemed startled. "Have you collected the work pension?"

"They're still processing that, but it doesn't matter to me." Alicia always assumed she'd go on working until she retired and never considered John would die and she would have such problems just getting out of bed after his death. Coming to Cobble Cove had changed that, and yet she'd never considered the questions John was asking and how her answers were showing her something maybe she didn't want to see. "Let's go on, "she said in an attempt to change the subject. "Can you Google John's mother and his sister to see where they are now?"

John's puzzled expression remained but another quality entered it. Alicia feared it was pity. "Sure. Sorry we got sidetracked."

"Wait, John." As he was about to enter a new search term, she had second thoughts. If these relatives they found had been 'dead' to Peter all these years, what good would it do to contact them now? And if they were as wealthy as they appeared and still lived on the Gold Coast of Long Island, why hadn't they attended the funeral or even called to offer their condolences? Alicia recalled the humiliation that added to her pain when Pete's boss took her aside at the funeral and, after a hug, whispered, "Where are Pete's relatives? Doesn't he have any family?" She could only shrug, dry eyed but crumbling inside. How could she tell him she had no idea?

"I've changed my mind," Alicia told John. "I'd rather you not continue."

John paused. "That's fine. We can come back another time. Just let me know."

82

Alicia got up. "Thanks for your help, but I think I'll work on this on my own."

"Whatever you want." John switched off the computer. "I have somewhere else I'd like to show you and then maybe you'd want to have an early dinner at Casey's? It's Dora's night off on Sundays, and I'm sure she'll be going to dinner with Charlie by the theater."

"I thought you never ate at Casey's, and what about Mac?"

"Dad is a good cook himself. He likes to share leftovers with Fido, as you've noticed. I occasionally eat at Casey's, but if you're in the mood for something more nutritious, we could drive somewhere else. I know I still owe you and Dora a chicken dinner, but let's save that for another time, okay?"

"Okay. Casey's is fine."

***

The day had grown cooler, but Alicia enjoyed the fresh air after the mustiness of the newspaper office. She followed John past his house on Stone Throw Road, keeping pace with his long strides.

"Let's take the secret path," he said, turning into a wooded area where a dirt road picked up into the hills.

"Secret path? Where are you taking me?"

John grinned, quickening his pace. "Sorry, but no Cobble Cove tour is complete without this stop, and I promised to show it to you before you left town. If I'm going too fast, let me know. It's a bit of a climb."

A bit of a climb turned out to be an understatement. After a few minutes of huffing alongside him, she felt like she was ascending a mountain.

"We're headed for the highest point of Cobble Cove. This was my favorite spot as a child. My dad showed it to me once, and I spent a lot of time here. I sometimes brought my buddies, but mostly I came alone."

Alicia could imagine the young John standing atop his secret spot looking down on the residents of Cobble Cove pretending to be king of the mountain or a pirate or whatever his mind conjured up as a little boy.

"You can see the whole town from this vantage point." They had reached the top, and Alicia followed John's outstretched arms to survey the sight below.

"It's breathtaking," she exclaimed.

"Literally." John laughed as she caught her breath.

The entire village lay before them, golden-hued in the setting sun. She could see the tiny houses, both brick and stone, smoke puffs shooting out of miniature chimneys, the twisting roadways and paths she'd followed in her car and on foot. Dotted throughout were trees and gardens, valleys, and other smaller hills. It was an enchanting Lilliputian sight.

John sat down among the wildflowers and asked her to join him. "This would make a nice picnic spot. Too bad we didn't bring along any food."

"It's so peaceful," she said as she watched a few birds fly overhead. Her voice seemed to carry a low echo.

"That's what I loved—love about it." John leaned back and looked up at the almost cloudless sky. "Tell me something, Alicia, would you mind if I called you Ali?"

"Of course not. My parents used to call me that all the time."

"What about your husband?"

"No, although I often called him Pete."

"I guess there's an advantage to having a one syllable name. I always thought John was rather plain, and then dad started using Mac." He grinned, and she saw his dimple again. "Okay, Ali, so what are your plans for the rest of the week now you've extended your stay?"

She thought a moment. "I don't know. I promised Wilma I'd come down to her shop tomorrow morning for a free makeover, and I need to ask Dora about the inn's washing machine because I didn't pack enough for the week."

"Sounds exciting." He smiled. "After you're done with Wilma and Dora, would you mind spending more time with me?"

Alicia felt a blush coming on again. "Well, you are the only other guest at the inn." She suddenly realized the insult in that remark. "I mean, so far you've been wonderful. I would've been lost here without you, but surely you have other ways to spend your time."

John looked down, grabbed a small pebble and threw it over the hill. "I think you must've guessed by now all my little jobs in this town—news editor, town hall manager, and inn assistant—are voluntary. I'm not independently wealthy or anything, but I had some savings when I came back here and—" he paused, "Jenny and I had both taken out life insurance policies when we married. I'm living off that right now, but it won't last too long. Dad's semi-retired. You don't get rich by working part time in a small town library, but his pension will take care of things. I should be moving on. I'm not young anymore." He tossed another pebble down the bank. "It won't be easy finding work if I go back to the city. The journalism field has changed with the Internet. That's why I'm hoping to finish the book…but that won't be enough."

"How do you know? Look at James Patterson, Stephen King…"

"It took those big names years to get established."

"But you're not old. Some writers still write in their seventies and eighties."

John looked at her. "Enough about me. Are you happy being a librarian? Are you considering Sheila's offer?"

She was glad he didn't mention what they had learned about Peter's family. "I guess I have to consider it, but there are some things I need to finish first. At least, I thought I had to finish them. Now I'm not sure. Like you said yesterday, some things are better left buried."

"You're talking about closure. I know all about that. I'm not giving you any advice because it's ultimately up to you, Ali, but in my opinion, if Peter was so set against you knowing anything about his family, you might be sorry to start digging in that soil."

"Maybe you're right."

"Okay, then. Now you've seen Cove Point. Let's go down to the water."

"Water?"

The grin on John's face was boy-like. "Close your eyes and turn around."

Alicia laughed as she obeyed, putting her hands over her face. "When can I open them?"

John moved closer to her and gently removed her fingers from her eyes. On the opposite side of the hill, she saw a river with sailboats.

"I wish I'd brought my binoculars. Now you know why they call this town Cobble Cove. It really does have a cove. Follow me."

John descended the hill faster than he'd ascended it, but it was easier going downhill, and Alicia had no problem keeping up. When they arrived at the bottom, they walked to the river. The scene was lovely.

"When I first came back, this is where I came. It relaxed me."

"Yes." Alicia had spent time at the beach with Peter and had always enjoyed watching the water. "I know what you mean."

"This is a charming town," John said. "I missed lots of things about it when I was away, but I never realized how much I'd missed them until I returned. Does that make sense?"

Alicia nodded. She wondered if she'd feel that way about Long Island if she decided to return.

After they stood a few minutes looking out over the cove, John glanced at his watch. "It's almost four. Would you mind an early dinner at Casey's? I'd like to do some writing tonight, maybe grab a scene from here."

Alicia suddenly wanted to take his hand on the climb back up, but she knew it wasn't a wise move. The kiss in the town hall had been a sympathy gesture, nothing more. "I am getting a little hungry," she admitted.

Then, unexpectedly, John seemed to read her mind once more. "Would you like a hand up? The rocks on this side are pretty steep."

The reason it took her a minute to reply wasn't from hesitancy but from surprise. She finally managed to say, "Thank you. That would be helpful."

He took her arm, and together they climbed up the hill. "Now I've really worked up an appetite," John said, smiling down at her and, for some crazy reason, she wasn't sure if the appetite he was referring to was for food.

***

Casey greeted them as they entered the restaurant. "Good afternoon, John, Alicia."

"Hey, Casey." John smiled. "I'm taking our visitor on a tour of the fine restaurants of Cobble Cove." He winked.

Casey laughed. "You mean the only restaurant in Cobble Cove? Would you two be up for drinks?"

John glanced at Alicia with a raised eyebrow.

"No, nothing now. Thanks."

"Me neither."

"Then have a seat. The menu's on the table and the blackboard as usual. I'll give you a few minutes to decide."

As they walked to a table by the window, Alicia noticed Edith and Rose seated further back. They still wore their church dresses. Their empty plates sat before them, and they seemed engrossed in conversation. When they saw John and Alicia, they seemed to stop mid-sentence, and both of them waved.

"Howdy cousins," John said. "Fancy meeting you ladies here."

"We always come here on Sunday," Edith said in a squeaky voice. Rose just smiled.

"Yep," Casey said, arriving with a tray of two water glasses he placed on their table. "Edith and Rose help me stay in business. Before you order, would you like a soda or something?" He seemed to be talking directly to Alicia.

"I wouldn't mind a cup of coffee, if it's not too much trouble."

"Not at all. And you, John?"

"I'll take coffee too, and I'll go with my regular well-done cheeseburger platter when you're ready."

Alicia added, "I'll also have that. It was very good the other night. Make mine medium, please."

"Good choices. Be back with your fine meals in a few minutes."

The early dinner was as tasty as Alicia's last one there, but John was a bit quiet as they ate. Even when Edith and Rose left, waving goodbye to them and leaving a tip on the table for Casey, he still wasn't saying much. Alicia thought she should break the silence. "What's wrong, John?"

He looked up from his plate, where only a quarter of his burger had been eaten and the fries sat in an untouched pile. "I guess I'm not as hungry as I thought."

"Is that all? You seem quieter than when we were on the mountain."

"Sorry. I'm thinking about things. We writers tend to do that. I forgot to ask you before, how is your book coming?"

Alicia smiled. "It's not really a book yet—only some musings."

"Keep at it. Writers need to practice writing as much as musicians need to practice their instruments."

"How long have you been 'practicing' writing?"

John grinned but then a shadow spread across his face, "Ever since...well, you know tragedies often spur deep writing."

Alicia knew he meant he started writing after his wife's death and was sorry she opened an old hurt by her question. He continued, "Actually, I suppose I've been writing all my life. Even as a kid, I entered all the Cobble Cove short story contests. When I got into journalism school, I was writing different types of material, but I was still writing. My dad always said it was my calling, but you don't always make much money from a calling.'

"Most writers need day jobs, at least to start."

John picked up his burger to continue eating. "That's the sad truth, Ali."

***

When they returned to the inn after dinner, Dora was there alone. She asked them if they wanted to eat, but they told her they'd already had a meal at Casey's. Alicia asked how Dora's day had gone, and she said she'd had a 'delightful' time at the theater.

"One other thing," Alicia said, taking the opportunity after John left for his room to work on his book. "Do you have a washer and dryer here I can use? I need to do some laundry tomorrow."

"Come this way." Dora led her behind the breakfast nook and down some steps into the basement. Alicia hadn't seen this part of the inn. The basement wasn't totally finished, but it contained a washing machine and dryer along with some storage boxes.

"I always meant to put a pool table or something down here," Dora said. "But other expenses got in the way."

"Have you known Charlie long?" Alicia changed the topic.

Dora smiled. "I met him when he came to town to look at houses. That was about a year ago. He moved in a couple months back, and we've been—" she blushed, "—I guess you would call it dating."

"Good for you. He seems like a nice man."

"He is."

Alicia didn't know if she was being forward when she asked, "Would you marry him if he proposed? Maybe the two of you could run the inn together."

A light came into Dora's gray eyes. "I'm not rushing things, but I would consider it. John may have told you I once had a crush on his dad. It wasn't serious. I've never met the right man. Charlie might be the one, and it's better late than never, I guess."

"I wish you luck."

Alicia should've expected the question Dora threw back. "How about you? Would you marry again, Alicia?"

She considered the question, but she already knew the answer in her heart. "I suppose so. It's too soon right now, but if someone came along…"

Dora's eyes probed. "I know it's not my business and I've never done matchmaking before, but I think John is interested in you. He's had a rough time of it and lots of ladies have tried to mend his heart, but I think you two could develop something if you stuck around."

Alicia felt the same way. "I guess we'll both have to see," she said.

CHAPTER 6

Alicia was awoken from a sound sleep in which she'd been dreaming, but all memory of the dream was washed away by her ringing cell phone she'd forgotten to turn off the night before. By the time she reached for it on the nightstand, the message had gone to voicemail. She glanced at the display. It was four o'clock in the morning. She was tempted to silence it and go back to bed, but curiosity got the best of her. She checked the message and saw the call had been from Abigail Nostran, otherwise known as Gilly. She sat up in bed, fully awake now, and redialed her friend, not even bothering to listen to the message. What was wrong? Was Gilly or one of the boys sick? But why would Gilly call her if that were the case?

"Oh, Alicia, thank goodness you called right back," Gilly answered, her voice distraught. "I know it's early, and I apologize, but something awful has happened. There's been a fire at your house, and they contacted me because I told your neighbor I was watching it."

Mrs. Gorman, the old lady next door, knew Gilly well, and she was always looking out for Alicia. Like the Cobble Cove residents, though, her concern was mixed with gossip fodder. "Oh, my God! Was there much damage? How did it happen?"

There was a pause on the line, and Alicia thought her cell phone had malfunctioned, but Gilly continued after a breath. "You need to get back here as soon as you can. The police asked me some questions. They want to talk to you, and you'll need to make a claim with the insurance adjusters."

Alicia's head was spinning. "What did the police want?"

Another pause. "I'm sorry, Alicia. They think it may have been arson."

"Arson?" Alicia couldn't believe her ears. "How? Who would've…"

"That's what they're trying to determine. Come home, Alicia. You can stay with me until things are settled."

"I'll leave as soon as I pack my stuff and maybe grab a cup of coffee. Thanks for contacting me so quickly."

"Of course. Be safe driving." Gilly clicked off, leaving Alicia wishing this had just been a nightmare.

After she'd showered, dressed, and packed her suitcase, Alicia scribbled a note on the Cobble Cove Inn stationary and left it on her bedside table,

Emergency at home. Will be back after all

is settled. Thanks so much for your hospitality.

She signed it,

A.

Attempting to exit the inn quietly so as not to disturb Dora or John, her plans were thwarted. She had her hand on the doorknob when a male voice said, "Where are you going at five-thirty a.m.?" John was standing there in the clothes he'd had on last night. They were slightly wrinkled, as if he'd slept in them. His hair was mussed and his cheeks stubbly, but both made him look sexier.

"I didn't want to wake anyone. I have to go home. My friend called on my cell. There's been a fire at my house."

"Oh, no!" John was concerned. "I'm so sorry, Ali. Look, if you give me a few minutes, I can make up some coffee and a few eggs for us. You shouldn't leave on an empty stomach."

"I was planning to hit a McDonalds or a rest stop on my way home."

"I guess you thought of everything except telling us."

"Sorry, I didn't think there'd be time. I didn't want to wake you or Dora. I left a note upstairs."

"Well, a few more minutes won't make a difference, and you don't want to get stuck in Monday morning rush-hour traffic going into the city. That would delay you, anyway. Come to the kitchen with me. I have an idea."

Alicia followed him into the dining nook. "You're usually a late sleeper. Did I wake you?"

John started the coffee. "No. I didn't sleep well last night. I'm blocked on my book. I think I dozed off around two, didn't bother to change." He glanced down at his clothes. "I should take a shower after we eat and put on new clothes." He turned on the stove's burner. "I'm surprised Dora isn't up too. She's a light sleeper and usually rises early."

"Did I hear my name?" Dora stepped through the alcove wearing a robe and pink fuzzy slippers.

"Come join the club," John said, taking an egg carton from the refrigerator. "I'm afraid Alicia's had some bad news from home, Dora. There was a fire at her house. She has to drive back ASAP, but I told her to wait until traffic slows on I-87."

"That'll be hours," Dora said, walking to the oven. "You sit, John. I'll finish preparing breakfast. Both of you are guests, after all."

John didn't argue with her but sat across from Alicia. "Thanks, Dora." He turned toward Alicia. "Here's my proposition, Ali…" She was hypnotized by his eyes and the way he spoke her name. Her stomach was doing flips, and she wasn't sure it was from the adrenaline still racing in her veins or something equally stimulating. Her mind kept trying to ignore her treacherous heart to no avail.

"Proposition?"

John smiled. "I think that's the right term. You know us journalists, always looking for the perfect word. Anyway, I'd like to accompany you. You'll need someone to navigate you through all the paperwork and questions."

"My friend is there," Alicia said, thinking of Gilly, but the thought of John at her side was even more comforting.

"I'm your friend too. You can never have too many."

The coffee machine began perking, and Dora brought them both a hot cup. "John's right. I can spare him for a few days until you return."

Alicia was thinking it might take longer. "I'm not sure how much time this will take, Dora."

"If it takes too long, I'll return on my own," John said. "I want to make sure you're okay and have things settled first."

Alicia felt cornered, but it was nice knowing people were looking out for her. "Okay," she said. "Now I have someone to carry my bags." John laughed, and she could tell he was relieved by her reply.

They waited until nine. John showered and changed into jeans and a blue sweatshirt that emphasized his eyes. Alicia sat talking with Dora and then made her promise to send her apologies to Wilma about the makeover. She would be sure to have one when she returned.

Once behind the wheel, she asked John if he was able to take over the driving if she grew tired. "You must be out of practice since you walk all over the place after coming home to Cobble Cove."

"It's like riding a bicycle, you never forget. And I do drive my truck occasionally. If you want to share the driving, just let me know when you're ready for a break."

"Deal."

"You do realize the true reason I came along?" His blue eyes were quizzical, a bit mischievous.

"What is that, Mr. McKinney?"

Now the smile spread across his face. "I want to make sure you return, Ms. Fairmont."

***

They hit traffic crossing the Throgs Neck Bridge. John took over the driving after the tolls onto the Grand Central Parkway. Alicia pulled the car over, and he got behind the wheel adjusting the seat a little to fit his taller frame. She was becoming tired after the three hour drive and was thankful she'd agreed to have him join her on the ride.

"Tell me the directions to your house as we get closer," John said. "Or maybe we should visit your friend first."

Alicia checked the time. It was a little after noon. "That might be best. I can call her on my cell phone."

John kept up with traffic. "Lots of memories on this stretch. Before I settled at Columbia, I was driving back and forth from Cobble Cove to set up my dorm. Then, when we got the apartment…" He paused. "I still came back to visit Dad. He really liked Jenny. I think it hurt him a lot when we lost her."

The sadness in his voice saddened Alicia too. How many times had she come this way with Peter? It seemed ages ago, not just six months, but everything that had happened before her trip to

Cobble Cove already seemed part of another life.

***

When they arrived at Gilly's house after Alicia let her know they were on their way, Gilly greeted them before Alicia even undid her seatbelt.

"Oh, honey," Gilly said, racing to the car. Alicia got out and they hugged. "I've been so worried. Thank goodness you're back." Alicia felt guilty about the way Gilly looked—more frazzled than usual with her hair a mess and makeup smeared.

After John parked the car on the street in front of Gilly's home, she ushered them into the house.

"Come in, both of you," she said. "I have coffee or tea on if you'd like some. The kids are at school, and I called in sick to the library today."

As they entered the house, Gilly cleared artwork, toys, and baseball cards from chairs where they were piled. "Sorry about the mess. I really have to get those kids to clean up after themselves."

"Gilly has three boys," Alicia told John.

John smiled. "No need to apologize, Mrs...."

Alicia had forgotten to tell him Gilly was divorced, but Gilly just shrugged, "Call me Gilly. Any friend of Alicia's should be on a first-name basis with me."

John extended his hand. "Nice to meet you, Gilly, although not under the best circumstances. I'm John McKinney. You can call me John." He smiled, flashing his dimple, and Alicia knew her friend would have some words with her later about the hunk she'd brought home.

Gilly smiled back. "What do you take in your coffee, John? I already know Alicia likes milk in hers."

"I'm fine, but thank you."

"Me too," Alicia said. "Please sit down, Gilly. I'm so sorry for all you've gone through with the police and everything. Tell me exactly what happened. I checked everything before I left, and I know I didn't leave anything on."

Gilly sighed but remained standing. She seemed more fidgety than her usual hyper self. "No, honey. It wasn't anything you forgot. They say it was arson. They found a can of gasoline. They asked me if I knew who else was aware you were away. They wanted to know…" She started to choke away tears. "They wanted to know if you had any enemies."

Alicia got up and patted her friend on the back. "Gilly, please don't cry."

"It was so terrible. There's nothing much left of your house. Luckily, the fire didn't spread to the neighbors. They were able to contain it after Mrs. Gorman called. She said she had gotten up to feed her cats when she heard this loud noise and smelled smoke. She looked out her windows and saw your house ablaze. I'm glad she didn't have a heart attack and thought to call the fire department so quickly."

"It sounds like you all did the right things," John said. "Did the policeman who handled this leave his card or a phone number?" He turned to Alicia. "You'll need to contact your insurance carrier. I'll help you."

Alicia was thankful again John was there. She imagined Gilly was relieved, knowing he would help.

"Yes," Gilly replied, scavenging around in the pocket of her sweatpants and then handing a card to John.

"Detective Michael Faraday," John read. "Do you mind if I call him, Alicia?"

"No, of course not. We need to do that as soon as possible." She still liked the way they were both using the word 'we' as if they were on the same team. It made her feel less afraid to face what she knew would be extremely difficult.

"Can I use your phone?" John asked Gilly. "My cell needs to be charged, and I'd rather talk on a landline." She nodded, and he got up to dial the phone mounted on the wall by the refrigerator, which was covered with artwork and sports schedules hung by magnets.

Both women waited while John was connected with Detective Faraday. John identified himself as a friend of Mrs. Fairmont's and said he was with her at another friend's house. The two of them could come to the station to talk when Faraday was available. He agreed to whatever the detective said and hung up the phone with a "See you then."

"We need to be there in a half hour. He was waiting to hear from you," John told Alicia. "Are you ready?"

Alicia swallowed a lump in her throat. "I think so."

"Do you need me to come?" Gilly offered.

"No, thank you. You need to be home when the boys get out of school. I have no idea how long this will take, and John will be with me. You should rest. You've had a tiring morning."

Gilly didn't protest. "All right, honey, but can we speak alone before you go?"

Before Alicia could answer, John said, "I still have your keys, Ali. I'll go start the car. You two ladies take your time together."

After he left, Gilly turned toward Alicia. "That's one handsome guy you have there. If they're all like that in Cobble Cove, I'll join you."

Alicia laughed, and it felt good to release some pressure. "I knew you'd have a comment about him. But, no, most of the citizens are around thirty years older than John."

"Rats! Oh, well. Good luck with the cops, sweetie. Don't let them confuse you. Faraday is okay, but I didn't like his partner, Ramsay. You have nothing to be guilty about. In my opinion, this was some teenage prank that got out of hand."

"I hope you're right," Alicia said, but she didn't really believe some teenagers had set fire to her home and destroyed it.

***

"Don't be nervous," John told her as she got in the car after hugging Gilly one last time.

"Are you kidding? Why would I be nervous? I'm just about to be interrogated by the police."

He touched her shoulder. "Remember, I'll be with you, and you're the victim, not the perpetrator."

She wanted to make light of the situation. "And how much practice do you have with the police?

Cobble Cove doesn't even have a sheriff."

"Nor a jail. But I did take a year of law at Columbia before I switched to journalism."

"You did? You never mentioned that."

"Wasn't worth mentioning. I didn't pursue it. Now let's just think of this experience as something we can write about in our books."

Yes, it would help to make it feel fictional and not really happening, Alicia thought. "I'll try. It sounds like this Faraday guy is the good cop and his partner, Ramsay, is the bad one."

"That's the way the police teams usually work— at least in criminal procedurals, but we'll see." He keyed the address of the police station into Alicia's GPS.

"John?"

"Yes."

"Before we go to the station, can we stop by my house? It's only a few blocks away. I need to see it."

He turned to her. "I don't think that's wise, Alicia. From what Gilly says, it may be traumatic for you to view it."

"But I need to." She had to see with her own eyes that the home she'd shared with Peter was truly gone.

He nodded. "Okay, we can drive by. We shouldn't be late for the police, though."

She gave him directions and when they turned her corner, she drew in a deep breath. It was an eyesore with yellow police tape around it, a huge gaping burnt structure.

"I want to get out."

John didn't argue. He pulled the car over and followed her as she stood before what was once her home.

"Don't get too close," he warned. The police tape stopped her. She could still smell ash on the light wind blowing over the remains.

Her eyes filled with tears. "Why would anyone do this?"

John had no answer. He put his arm around her. "I'm sorry, Alicia. The adjusters will be able to help you replace your lost belongings. We'll contact them later. Did you have a fire safe box or anything for your policies and important papers?" He figured the police may have already confiscated those types of items, but she shook her head. "No. I think Peter had one at the bank, but I'm not sure."

"It's okay. Let's go to the police station now." He guided her gently back to the car.

"I just feel so violated, John," she said when they were seated. "That was my home, the first place I lived after being with my parents. I still remember how Peter and I found it after house hunting for months and how we decorated the rooms together. I'm hurt, I'm mad, and I'm scared because it's all gone." Her voice broke, and she punched the dashboard.

"Be careful," John said. "Hit me if you want, but don't hurt yourself."

Her hand throbbed as she pulled it away. She didn't mind the pain, but the fight was out of her. She put her head on his shoulder and cried until her eyes were red, strong racking sobs that shook her body and bellowed through the car. When the storm of her sorrow subsided into hiccups and sniffles, he let her lay against him until she said, "I'm ready to go now, John. Please take me."

CHAPTER 7

A young officer led Alicia and John into a small room that reminded Alicia of a jail cell. It featured a beaten up desk on which stood a lamp, phone, and computer. The officer pulled out a chair for her in front of the desk. Since the only other chair was behind the desk, John stood by the door.

"Detective Faraday and Detective Ramsay will be with you soon," the officer told them on his way out.

Alicia realized she was holding her breath and clenching her hands in her lap.

"Try to relax," John said, sensing her mood, "I know it's hard, but being nervous won't help anything."

Alicia nodded. "Thanks for staying. You didn't have to."

"Yes, I did. I need to give you a character reference." He smiled and she felt a little calmer.

She was hoping they wouldn't have to wait long, so was glad when the two officers strode into the room. Both wore badges, so she could tell them apart. But even if they weren't identified, she could see by their expressions they were indeed playing good cop/bad cop. Faraday, taller than John, smiled as he came in the room and extended his hand to her and then John. "Detective Faraday, glad to meet you, and thanks for coming down."

Ramsay, who stood behind Faraday, was a shorter, stockier man. His expression, behind thick eyebrows, was wary and calculating. He didn't shake hands with them but simply nodded when Faraday introduced him as his partner, Detective Ramsay.

John thanked them. "Nice to meet you, Detectives." Alicia stayed silent.

Faraday remained standing next to John while Ramsay sat at the desk across from Alicia. This made her uncomfortable. The man's dark, squinty eyes seemed to follow her and ignore John.

"Let's start with a few basic details," Faraday began. Ramsay booted up the computer and poised his thick fingers over the keyboard. "Detective Ramsay will be taking some notes while we talk."

"Okay," Alicia said. Her voice sounded small and young. John was watching her with a different expression than Ramsay. He seemed to be cheering her on, while she thought Ramsay was ready to catch any mistake she made.

"Your name is Alicia Fairmont. Is that correct?" Faraday began.

She nodded.

"We need a verbal answer," Ramsay said.

"Yes. I'm Alicia Fairmont," she replied a little stronger, avoiding eye contact with Ramsay.

"Thank you." Faraday looked at John. "And you're a friend of Ms. Fairmont's?"

"Yes. I'm John McKinney from Cobble Cove, New York. Alicia was visiting there when she had news of her house fire, and I drove back with her."

"Please answer one question at a time," Ramsay said, typing on the computer.

Faraday waved his partner's words away with his hand. "That's okay, Ron. Mr. McKinney was simply elaborating on their relationship. It isn't relative to our report. Let me continue with Ms. Fairmont."

It almost looked as though Ramsay pouted. Alicia guessed he didn't like being chastised. "Go on," he told his partner.

"Ms. Fairmont, I understand you were married to Peter Fairmont, who died in an accident six months ago?"

"Yes. My husband was hit by a car in May."

Ramsay interrupted. "We know all about that. We have a copy of the report."

"No need to go into that right now," Faraday said. "But Ms. Fairmont, do you believe there might be any connection between the fire at your house and your husband's death?"

Alicia hadn't even considered this. "No. I mean, I heard the fire was a case of arson, but they said the driver who left the scene of my husband's accident was driving fast and probably didn't see him in the fog."

John was quiet, standing against the wall. He seemed to be listening intently to the conversation.

"That's correct," Faraday agreed, "but let's

108

continue with the fire for now. Your neighbor and friend both told us you were not home at the time. Did anyone else know you were going on a trip?"

Alicia thought a moment. "No. I'd been on leave from work, so I didn't bother telling my employer or any other co-workers besides Gilly."

"What about Mrs. Nostran?" Ramsay asked, pausing in his typing. "She said she works with you. Could she have told anyone?"

"Gilly wouldn't do that. Maybe someone came by and noticed my car wasn't in the driveway."

"That's possible," Faraday said, "but we're also pursuing the possibility that someone thought you were home." His thin eyebrows lifted.

John broke his silence. "Are you trying to say you think Alicia may have been the target of the fire?"

"I'm afraid we have to consider that. Luckily, the house was empty. Furniture and knick knacks can be replaced, but not people."

"So what do I do now?" Alicia asked.

"We need you to think of anyone who may have had a cause to hurt you or your husband. We'd like to reopen his case file. The officers in charge will be contacted. We know it's a hard time for you, but we ask you stay in town until we get some things straightened out. Do you have somewhere to stay?"

Alicia thought of Gilly and her house full of young boys. "My friend has offered to let me stay with her."

"That's fine, but we can put you up in a hotel instead if you prefer."

"That might be best if you think Ali's in danger,"

109

John said. "In fact, I need a place to stay as well, and I wouldn't mind paying for a room at the same place."

Faraday took a card out of his pocket and handed it to John. "It isn't fancy, but it's clean. Reserve your rooms, and save a copy of the bill." He turned to Alicia. "That's all for now. We'll be in touch to let you know when you can leave town or if we've made any arrests regarding the fire."

Ramsay finished typing. "I'm emailing you a copy of the notes," he told Faraday. He got up brusquely and left the room without a goodbye. Faraday shook their hands and then John waited until Alicia preceded him through the door.

***

The hotel was nicer than Alicia expected, but it wasn't the Ritz Carlton. John managed to get them adjoining rooms. Once she unpacked, she called Gilly and told her the police had wanted her to stay in town and she thought it would be easier if she stayed at a hotel with John instead of disturbing Gilly and her boys.

"Nonsense," Gilly said. "You wouldn't have disturbed us, but we probably would've disturbed you. As you know, this is not a quiet house." She chuckled. "But seriously, honey, I'm glad you're with John." She lowered her voice, as if she expected him to be listening in on the conversation. "Are you two, you know…?"

Alicia laughed. "We have separate rooms, Gilly. They're only separated by a door, but they're separate."

"I see. Well, sleep well, sweetie, and call me tomorrow. I'm sick of those bodice ripping romances I pick up from the library. I need some real life smut to keep me going."

Alicia shook her head as she put down the phone. John was standing in the doorway that connected their rooms. She nearly jumped.

"Sorry. I just finished putting away my stuff. Was Gilly angry you won't be taking her up on her offer to stay at her house?"

"No. I think she was relieved. I didn't tell her what the police suspect. I don't want to worry her. If I stayed there, it might be dangerous for her and the kids."

"That's what I was thinking. Mind if I come in?"

"Of course not."

He came over and sat in the chair next to the bed. "I think you should call your insurance company and get the ball rolling about what you need replaced or at least what they will cover. It may take some time. I brought some cash with me, and I also have a credit card, just in case you need anything before then."

"Thanks, but I still have my credit card in my purse. Thank goodness I brought it with me. I didn't leave any cash in the house either. Most of my clothes were there, though, except what I brought to Cobble Cove, and Peter's stuff. I still hadn't gotten rid of many of his belongings."

"You'll need to make a list." He reached in the nightstand and took out the hotel's note pad and pen. "You should start doing that as soon as you can. List everything—the furniture, appliances, jewelry, any collectibles you might've had."

"I didn't collect anything but books, but I'm glad I returned all the library ones before I left."

"The police didn't mention they took anything. They'll probably let you into the house once they complete their investigation."

Alicia nodded. She felt like she was dreaming. It was hard to believe this was really happening, that she was homeless and someone might be trying to kill her.

John came over to sit beside her on the bed. "It's going to be okay, Ali." He put his arm around her, and she looked into his eyes. Her heart stopped beating for a moment and then his lips were on hers. This wasn't the light peck on the cheek he had given her in the town hall. This was a warm, deep kiss that engulfed her, body and soul. She was momentarily paralyzed. She couldn't think. She couldn't move.

She wasn't sure if she felt regretful or thankful when he was the one who pulled away. "Gosh, Ali. I'm sorry. I know this isn't the time." He stood up. "You've lost your husband only a few months ago and now your home. And some cop with an attitude is making you think someone is out to get you. I don't want to take advantage of our friendship by complicating it at this time, but I want you to know I care for you. I've been pining for my wife for years and not getting on with my life. You come along, and I suddenly see a reason, but I can't rush things. It wouldn't be right for either of us."

Alicia found it hard to answer, but it seemed

John wasn't seeking a reply.

"I'll leave you for now," he said. "If you can, call your insurance company and make that list of lost items. But rest too. You had a long drive and a police interrogation. I'll be back before dinner. We may want to try the hotel restaurant and compare it to Casey's." He winked.

He was gone before she found her voice again.

***

Alicia wasn't much in the mood for food, and John seemed more in the mood for talking. Between them, they hardly touched their dinner entrees at the hotel's small restaurant. Alicia had ordered a hamburger, and John teased her she really was trying to compare the food to Casey's. He ordered the fried chicken basket and said it was standard hotel fare.

They both had a glass of wine with dinner. John insisted. "I'm not a drinker, but I occasionally like a meal with a nice lady and good spirits." Alicia wondered how many 'nice ladies' John had dated since his wife died. In twenty years, she was sure he must've seen some women, although the Cobble Cove residents were a bit older than he. She thought of Sheila for a minute and then brushed that thought aside again. However, even though John lived in the senior-populated Cobble Cove, he could travel to other nearby towns for entertainment and company.

"A penny for your thoughts," he said, snapping her back. Alicia felt bold suddenly and wondered if it was the wine because she wasn't a drinker, either.

"I was just wondering how many ladies you've known since moving to Cobble Cove?"

"You mean since I lost Jenny?" His eyes looked sad, and she was sorry she'd brought it up, but then he smiled. "Do I detect some jealousy, Ms. Fairmont?"

She laughed, but it was more to cover her embarrassment than because she found the comment funny.

"To be honest, there have been a few one-night stands, but no one I'd even consider taking Jenny's place."

"Would you ever consider remarrying? Starting a family?" Her questions were not meant to give her hope, but she was interested in his replies.

"I'm not sure." He paused and took another bite of his chicken. After he washed it down with a sip of wine, he said, "I think I'm getting too old to consider being a father. But yes, if I found the right lady, I'd like to be a husband again. What about you? If you found someone you loved as much as Peter who could give you a good life and raise your kids, would you marry again?"

Alicia wasn't happy he'd turned the tables on her, but it was only fair. "I liked being a wife. I also always wanted kids. I guess I'm too old to think about that now myself."

"That's not exactly an answer." Neither of them spoke again until John added, "I'm sorry. This isn't a topic we should be discussing when your life is in such upheaval right now."

"Actually, I think it's taken my mind off the upheaval, and I was the one who brought up the topic in the first place."

"True."

"By the way, I called my insurance company. You were right—they need a list, and I'm working on that. I have an appointment to see the adjuster tomorrow."

"Good. Would you like me to come along?"

"Thank you for the offer, John, but I don't need you to take me everywhere and act like my protector. I've been thinking about what the police said about someone trying to kill me, and I don't believe it. Gilly said the fire might've been some teenagers playing a prank that got out of hand. I'm not sure she's right about that, but I don't feel like I'm in danger. Peter's death was just an accident. There's no connection with it and the fire."

John shook his head. "I hope you're right, but it's better to be safe than sorry. I don't mind looking out for you. In fact, that's why I came along."

"I thought it was to bring me back with you."

His smile widened, showing his dimple. "That too. I can write here as much as I can write in Cobble Cove. But I don't like leaving my dad for so long. I know Dora will keep an eye on him, but at some point, I won't be able to stay here. What I'm hoping is you'll be able to come back with me so I can keep looking out for you. But I'm also aware some things about Peter's death don't add up. We started searching for his family. We're closer to finding them here than we were upstate if they still live in Brookville."

Alicia had considered that. "But what would finding them prove now?"

"Don't you know the prime suspects in any investigation are the relatives? As a fellow writer, I'm surprised you don't."

"Are you saying you think one of Peter's relatives killed him?"

"Stranger things have happened. What was he doing jogging to work, anyway? Did he do that often?"

Alicia sighed. "The police considered all this, John."

"And as you also know, from crime novels and real life, the police aren't always right. But I'm sure they're taking a closer look now."

"And you think we should too?" Alicia followed his train of thought. "I'm not into playing amateur detectives, John."

"Even if it means getting the closure you need? Even if it could save your life? Even if it might give us a chance to be together?"

Alicia couldn't meet his eyes. "Oh, John. I'm so confused."

He reached out and touched her hand. "There I go again, putting too much pressure on you when what you need is some time alone to think this all through. I'm sorry, Ali."

She looked into his blue eyes and felt her heart tumble. His hand was warm in hers.

"Thank you," she said. "I do need time to think about all of this, and I'd be glad to have you come with me to the adjuster's tomorrow."

***

After dinner, Alicia and John went back to their rooms. John walked to the connecting door. "I want you to make sure your outside door is locked tonight but the door into my room isn't. Don't worry about waking me up if you're afraid. I'm a light sleeper, even though Dora always accuses me of sleeping late. The truth is I get up a lot during the night thinking and then I end up oversleeping." He smiled. "I'm only a few feet away, a stone's throw, you might say." He laughed at his favorite joke, but Alicia knew he was serious.

She wondered what he lay awake thinking about. Was it his dead wife and child? Could that be the real reason he wasn't making serious moves on her? She wanted to ask if she could come to him when she wasn't afraid. If she could go to his bed out of need and not fear? But something told her it wouldn't be the right thing to do. If John still wasn't over his wife after twenty years, how could she be over Peter after six months? Or was she? She knew there'd been a change in her feelings in Cobble Cove. Some questions John raised about her husband had caused them. And when they'd been so close to finding out about Peter's family, the fire had brought her home.

As John went back to his room, he told her he had some writing to finish and wanted to call his dad. Alicia settled down with the book she'd brought to Cobble Cove and tried to read, but her mind wouldn't focus. She didn't get far when she nodded off to sleep, exhausted by all the activity of the day.

***

Alicia woke to light tapping at the adjoining door. "Ali, are you up?" John called.

"I am now," she replied groggily.

"Sorry if I woke you. What time is the adjuster appointment?"

"Not until ten." She glanced at the hotel alarm clock on the nightstand. It said seven a.m.

"Okay, then we can have some breakfast on the way out there. Come in when you're through getting ready. Don't rush. I've been up for an hour and have already showered and changed."

So much for oversleeping, Alicia thought. There was a coffeemaker in the room, so she plugged it in and made herself a cup. A half hour later, she knocked on the adjoining door to let John know she was ready.

"Come in," John called. He was sitting on the bed with a newspaper spread out in front of him.

"I see the Cobble Cove newspaper man is checking out the local papers."

He turned and smiled at her, closing the paper. "Nothing here but bad news and ads. Are you ready for breakfast? You look nice."

Alicia had put on the last item she packed for her trip. It was a wine pantsuit accented with a multi-colored scarf. She was glad it hadn't gotten wrinkled in her suitcase, but she'd hung it up as soon as she'd checked in. She thought it might be a nice idea to dress decently for her appointment.

"Thank you. It's my last clean outfit. I guess I should find out about laundry service here or do some shopping later today."

"I'd do the latter, if I were you. Shopping always perks up ladies, and you may need it after the adjusters."

"I actually hate to shop unless it's online. But maybe you're right. It might boost my spirits today."

***

They had breakfast in a Starbucks in a strip mall. Both of them ordered cafe lattes and oversized chocolate chip muffins. Afterwards, they chatted a bit. John warned her again the claim would take time and the adjusters would need a lot of information.

They ended up with some extra time on their hands. John noticed a store selling women's clothes next to Starbucks. It was called The Casual Woman and wasn't one Alicia had heard of. From the outfits modelled in the window, it looked like her style.

"Go on in," John urged. He opened his wallet and passed her two $50 bills. "Buy something for yourself from me for Christmas."

Alicia laughed. "There's another month for that, but if you insist."

The clothes weren't inordinately expensive. She bought another pantsuit in a neutral tan shade and a few undergarments with John's money.

"Feel better?" John asked as she joined him where he'd been waiting for her on a bench outside the store.

"A little. Thanks. I'll need to buy some other

things, but at least I have something to wear tomorrow."

He smiled. "There's a laundry service at our hotel. You can pay for it or do it yourself. Just talk to the front desk. But if you like this store, I'll take you back after we're done at the adjusters and you can buy something from me for New Year's."

She laughed. "People don't buy each other New Year's gifts. John, I'm okay for now. Don't worry."

He stood and took her hand, "Where you're concerned that's easier said than done. Come, Ms. Fairmont. You don't want to be late for your appointment."

***

The meeting with the adjuster was frustrating. Although Alicia had tried to be as descriptive as possible with the contents of her house, she couldn't remember brands, models, prices, or styles. The adjuster also informed her, in a case of suspected arson, the insurance coverage might be void. This angered her. "Are you saying I burned my house down on purpose? I wasn't even home."

The adjuster, a man in his fifties with horn-rimmed glasses and white hair, nodded at her. "There have been cases where homeowners have done just that to collect money, and they haven't had to be home to accomplish it."

John gave Alicia a look, and she knew it was meant to calm her. "Ms. Fairmont understands," he told the adjuster. "She's under a lot of stress right now. Is there any way she can collect if the fire is determined to be a case of arson?"

"Sure," the man said. "If the police make an arrest and the perpetrator is found to have no connection with Ms. Fairmont, then our agency will pay the full coverage."

"And right now?"

Mr. Everett, the adjustor, shook his head. "Right now, nothing, I'm afraid."

Now John was the one getting mad. "Baloney. This woman is homeless. She has no clothes but the ones on her back and a few she brought with her to travel. She's living in a hotel on credit. The police could take years to solve this case or may not solve it at all."

Mr. Everett closed the black, leather-bound book in which he had been jotting down notes. "I'm sorry, but all that information was in the policy she and her husband purchased and signed. Good day, now." He stood, and Alicia noted he was much shorter than John and was secretly glad John wasn't going to let him bully either of them.

"Excuse me, Mr. Everett, but I can be crude and tell you where to stick that policy, but I'm a gentleman and, unlike you, I'm considerate of ladies. C'mon, Ali. We're out of here. Good day, sir."

Alicia followed John back to the car. "I can't believe that guy," he said, starting the engine. "Unfortunately, I don't think we have much ground to stand on. I'm sorry, Ali. We just have to hope the police catch whoever did this as soon as possible."

"I don't have much faith in Ramsay. If it was up to him, I'd be behind bars, and I don't think Faraday is much better."

"Let's see what happens. I know it's hard to be patient in your situation. I'd ask if you want to do some more shopping but, after that encounter, I think I'd better offer you a drink instead. Want to hit the hotel bar?"

"Thanks, but I think I just want to go back to my room, John. I was thinking of calling Gilly, but I don't want to upset her further. I wish I could do something productive right now."

"I have an idea." They were stopped at a light. "What if we drive up to Brookville and check out Carol Fairmont and her daughter?"

Alicia sighed. "John, we don't have an address. And even if we find them, what would I say? 'Hello, there. I'm your long-lost daughter-in-law and sister-in-law and, by the way, in case you didn't catch the obituary in *Newsday*, your son and brother died six months ago'."

John smiled. "That's a good start. Ali, I have a feeling about this. Call it a journalist's sixth-sense. At the very least, we'll have a nice ride up the Gold Coast and marvel at the mansions. And if we locate them, the worst that can happen is they slam the door in our faces or their butler slams the door in our faces." He grinned.

She had to laugh. "But where do we start looking?"

John pulled the car over onto a side street and took out his cell phone. "I never finished our Google search, and I have some additional apps on this that might do the trick."

Alicia sat while John worked his magic, but the

rabbit never came out of the hat. "Sorry. I can't find anything," he admitted after a few minutes of tapping in different search terms. "I need a different kind of database, like the one I used at journalism school. Wait a minute..." Alicia saw the lightbulb switch on in his head. "I have the passwords to those databases. I could probably get in on my phone, but it's easier on a computer. I know our hotel has a business center. We can log on from there."

He started the car again and they drove back to the hotel.

CHAPTER 8

It took another hour, but John finally found what they were seeking. There was an address for P. Fairmont in Brookville. Even though Peter's dad was dead, John figured his mother might live there.

They drove in silence. Alicia pondered what they would find at the Brookville home and what they would say when they arrived. John seemed to be thinking too. She figured the reporter in him was preparing for this next chapter in their unofficial investigation.

When they turned onto Old Brookville Road, John said, "We have to keep our eyes out for Dorsett Lane. The streets here are not marked well, and the homes are set way back. It's likely the Fairmont place is the only one on the block."

Alicia nodded. John was following her car's GPS. The electronic map showed a flashing red arrow on the right a short way ahead. "I wonder if anyone will be home."

"We'll soon see." His eyes were intent on the road.

As John suspected, it wasn't easy to locate the street. He turned onto a narrow road with heavy shrubbery along its sides.

"The next challenge," John said, "is to find the house."

That wasn't as difficult as they both thought because, as John ventured, the Fairmont house was the only one on the block. The property spanned nearly the whole street. Although they couldn't see the house beyond the gated entranceway, there was a sign before the gate that read, *'Fairmont'*.

"Wow!" Alicia exclaimed. "I had no idea…"

"Impressive. I'm sure they have a top-of-the line security system, so it's probably best we park on the street." He pulled over and turned to Alicia. "Are you ready?"

She was too shocked to reply. All those years with Peter, struggling to make ends meet, and it looked like his relatives were millionaires. "I guess so," she finally managed to answer.

The entranceway's black wrought iron gate had an intercom button attached to it. John pressed the button. At first, nothing happened. The gate remained locked. But after John tried a second time, a woman's voice came through the speaker. "If you're selling anything, we're not interested. Otherwise, state your name and business."

The woman's voice didn't sound terribly old, although voices were sometimes deceiving. However, Alicia imagined Carol Parsons Fairmont, who would be around eighty-three at this time, would sound older than this woman. She considered it might be a housekeeper because surely they had one.

"Hello," John said into the intercom. "My name is John McKinney, and this is Alicia Fairmont. We're here to see Carol Fairmont."

The pause on the other end lingered until Alicia felt the woman was gone, but suddenly the speaker buzzed, and the gate opened. "Come up to the house," the woman instructed. "It's about time we made your acquaintance."

John gave Alicia a quizzical look. She knew he'd detected the same haughty tone evident in the woman's voice.

The path to the house was easily a mile long. It brought them through a wooded area around a curve before the white structure came into view. A barn and stable stood at the side of the house. A few horses grazed behind its white fence. The door of the house opened and a woman appeared there.

As soon as they climbed the long steps and could see the woman clearer, Alicia could tell the lady wasn't a housekeeper. She was probably in her early sixties. Her ash blonde hair was short with no traces of gray. She was tall for a woman, maybe an inch shorter than John, and thin. She wore a dark charcoal riding habit with wine-colored leather boots and held a riding crop in her hand. She must've realized she was aiming it at them because she lowered it to her side as they stepped into a foyer of polished wood floors and oriental urns.

The woman looked them over and then invited them down a few stairs into the vast living room with its white leather couch that seemed untouched and authentic appearing oriental carpet. Whoever decorated this home seemed partial to an Asian theme. The woman didn't invite them to sit but continued to stand an arm's length from them by the burning alabaster-fronted fireplace that shed no heat into the room.

"So," she finally said, "his wife has finally decided to visit. And you…" She turned to John. "Even if you hadn't said your name, I would've recognized you. You're the spitting image of your father."

"The question is who are you, ma'am?" John asked.

The woman smiled exhibiting perfect teeth. "I'm your long lost sister, Pamela, of course." She extended the hand without the crop. Alicia noted the French manicure.

John hesitated in taking it but then gave it a quick shake. "Is your mother home too?"

The smile froze on her face. "Mother passed away last year. I've planned on taking a trip to that small town where we used to live—Cobble Creek or something—to visit dear old Dad. I assume he's still around?"

"If you mean my father," John said. "Yes. He's fine. The town's name is Cobble Cove. You're welcome to come, but give us notice first."

"Like you've given me?" She raised a perfectly tweezed pale eyebrow.

"Sorry, but we didn't have the number. I guess it's unlisted."

"But you've found the address." She walked over to the couch. "You might as well sit, and maybe we can catch up on some things." She glanced at Alicia. "Our maid is off for the day, but I can whip up something. Tea? Coffee?"

Alicia finally spoke. "No, thank you. We don't want to take up your time. It looks like you were ready to go riding." The last thing Alicia wanted was to spend much more time in this huge, suffocating house, but she needed answers to some of her questions about Peter.

Pamela nodded. "Yes. It's great exercise. Do you ride?"

Alicia wasn't up to small talk. "I've never tried, but I think horses are lovely." She paused. "The reason I'm here is I have a few questions about Peter, if you don't mind."

"Not at all, although I doubt I can answer them. Why don't you just ask him yourself?"

So she didn't know, or she was putting on a convincing act of ignorance. Alicia looked at John. "That would be a little difficult. Peter died six months ago. I couldn't contact you. I thought maybe you'd seen the obituary, but no one came to his funeral."

Pamela seemed surprised but not upset. "Peter's dead? What happened? No, I didn't see any obituary. I don't read the papers much, and if it happened more than a month ago, I was in Europe with my daughters. They're both studying abroad."

"It happened in May. It was a hit and run accident. Peter was jogging to work." She was amazed she could now tell the story without breaking down as she had so easily in the past.

"I see. He was always quite the athlete, what good that did him. And yes, I was in Europe in

May. I actually just returned. I have a house there, as well."

It was frustrating for Alicia to hear this woman talk so coldly about her brother after learning he'd passed away. "Peter never talked much about you," she said, "but I understand you had a falling out before we married." She saw John give her a warning look, but he seemed to be letting her do the talking even if he didn't approve of her approach.

"Falling out?" Pamela gave a short laugh. "I guess you could call it that. I have to give my brother credit, though. He knew when to walk away."

"What do you mean?" Alicia asked. "I'm sorry. This is confusing."

Pamela got up and opened a sideboard cabinet. Alicia could see some whiskey and wine bottles inside. "I know it's early in the day, but I need a drink. Would either of you care to join me?"

Before Alicia or John could reply, Pamela placed a bottle and three glasses on a tray and brought it over to the table in front of the couch. "Red is best with dinner, but I'm in the mood for it now. Can I pour you some?"

Alicia didn't know whether Pamela's mood for wine had to do with discovering her brother was dead or, more likely, the questions she had been asked. "No, thank you."

John shook his head. "We can't stay much longer, Ms. Fairmont."

"Morgan," she corrected. "But my husband is gone. Departed, not dead." She poured the red liquid into a glass and tilted her head back as she drank. After she swallowed the wine, she said, "So, about Peter. He was my father's true son. I think you already know that." She looked at John, but he didn't reply. "When Dad found out I wasn't his true daughter, he was unhappy with Mom and also with me."

Alicia wanted to ask how Paul Fairmont had discovered Pamela was Mac's daughter, but she didn't want to interrupt the rest of the story.

Pamela took another sip of wine. "It happened years ago, and I don't want to bore you with the details, but when Dad found out, he rewrote his will. He left everything to Peter. Perhaps he was trying to teach my mother a lesson for lying and cheating on him, but I thought it was a bit unfair of him to deny me his fortune, as well."

John stopped her there. "Excuse me, Ms. Morgan, but it doesn't seem as if you're doing so poorly here, and, as I understand it, Peter and Alicia led middle-class lives. Also, what happened between your mother and my father occurred before Paul married her, so it doesn't exactly fit your definition of cheating."

Pamela's eyes lit up in fury. "That's where you're wrong, John. My mother was practically engaged to Peter's father when he went to war. She had no right to have an affair with your father."

John grew angry now. "From what my dad said, Paul Fairmont never contacted your mother while he was away. How could he have expected her to remain faithful?"

Pamela stood, and Alicia was ready for her to ask them to leave, but instead, she said, "Peter's father wrote many letters to her, and I have proof, but there's no need to bring that up right now. Peter was smart enough to give up the fortune and let my mother and I enjoy his father's wise investments."

"He gave up the fortune?" Alicia was stunned.

"After his father died, Peter met with a lawyer and deeded all the money to my mother and me on the condition we would not contact him ever again."

Alicia was speechless. *What had made Peter do a thing like that?*

"So there you go," Pamela said flippantly. "The story of the Fairmonts and McKinneys." She glanced at John. "Anyway, good to hear your dad is still doing well, and I must visit him one day when my schedule allows." She glanced at the diamond-encrusted gold watch on her wrist. "It's getting late, and I really do want to go on my ride. Please come back again, but call first next time."

Alicia didn't appreciate being dismissed when she had so many questions, but John got up and motioned to her. "C'mon, Ali. We need to get going too."

Pamela walked them to the door. "Good day, then," she said and the relief was evident on her face.

In the car, when John had turned around and driven back to Old Brookville Road, he said to Alicia, "I don't know how much of that was true or if you might actually have any claim on that money, but I think you need to see a lawyer."

Alicia didn't agree. "I don't care about the money. I'm glad you didn't say anything about the fire at my house. I don't think she was involved, but

131

who knows? I can't believe how heartless she is, but calling in a lawyer may make matters worse. With her money, I'm sure she can get the best one."

John didn't argue with her, but she could tell he thought she was wrong. They drove the rest of the way in silence.

***

Back at the hotel, John saw Alicia to her room to make sure everything was safe. The red light on the hotel phone was blinking with a message. John waited while she played it back. After a few yeses and I sees, she hung up the phone and turned to John, who was watching with a questioning look. "That was Faraday. He says we're free to leave town if we want. It seems I'm no longer a suspect or intended victim. He still thinks I should be careful, although he seems to be buying Gilly's theory about teenage vandals setting my house on fire."

"They're taking the easy way out. Something needs to be done about the house, but first we should decide what we're going to do. I want to return to Cobble Cove and speak with my dad again. I'd like you to come with me, but it's up to you."

The thought of returning to Cobble Cove and its quirky residents made her feel surprisingly good. Even though some of the people appeared rude when she first met them, she now felt they'd given her that impression because she was a newcomer. Such a tight-knit community probably had some reservations when strangers appeared among them.

Even Sheila, who was hard to fathom, probably meant well. She considered taking her up on her offer to work at the library. What was left for her on Long Island—a shell of a house, a rich bitch of a sister-in-law, and a job she had avoided for six months? Of course, there was still Gilly, but they could keep in touch. It might be time to start anew and, of course, there was John. Maybe they could both recover from their pasts and build something together. It was worth a try.

"I'll come with you," she said. "It will take months for the insurance people to process my claim, if they even do so, and I can't spend all that time in a hotel or intruding on my friend's family. I'm going to submit my resignation at the library today. I don't think they'll be surprised."

A light came into John's eyes. "Does that mean you're moving to Cobble Cove and accepting the job offer at the library?"

"Yes," Alicia said, making her decision. "There'll be lots of details to iron out, but I have a feeling it's for the best. You said your dad always told you things happen for a reason. I believe he's right."

John came to her then and wrapped his arms around her. "I'm so glad this is what you want to do, Ali. I'll feel better knowing you're in Cobble Cove. But one step at a time. We can leave tomorrow if you're ready by then. I'm going to pack now and make some arrangements. I'll let Dad know we're returning, but I won't say a word to him about what Pamela told us yet or about you working at the library. We'll take care of that when we get there."

Alicia remained in his embrace. "Sounds like a plan. I'll be ready by tomorrow. I don't have much to pack."

John smiled. "Remember, I still owe you a New Year's dress, and they have a nice shop in Cobble Cove, or we could go to some of the boutiques in New Paltz." He loosened his arms from around her. "Let's plan a nice dinner somewhere tonight before we leave and then hit the road after breakfast tomorrow."

***

They had dinner at an Italian restaurant. John seemed quiet after they were served their fresh mozzarella and pepper slices with balsamic vinegar appetizer. He divided it on two small plates so they could split it. When he handed her a serving and she noticed his bare left finger bore a tan line of his wedding band, Alicia recalled Peter kept his wedding ring in a men's valet keeper she had given him the Christmas after they married. When she teased him about not wearing it, he said he sometimes had a reaction to gold, and he didn't believe in jewelry for men. *"Don't worry, honey,"* he said, *"if any other woman comes near me, I'll make sure she knows I'm married. I just don't think I need to advertise it."* His words hadn't made her feel better because she had seen the rings they wore as a symbol of their union. She looked down at hers now and wondered if Peter's had been destroyed in the fire. She was told she would have to come back to the house to complete the adjuster's report of damaged items even though it was unlikely they would be replaced anytime soon. John said he would go with her when she was ready.

"Is something bothering you?" she asked John as the silence between them continued.

John looked up from his plate. "Sorry, Ali. I've been meaning to tell you. I called Dora and Dad earlier to let them know about our return. It seems Dora just got a honeymoon couple at the inn, and she thinks its best we stay elsewhere at least for the next week. I'll stay with my dad, and I'm sure he won't mind you staying with us, but I checked with Sheila. She has the room above the library available and would love to have you there if you're interested. I know it's rushing things, and you haven't even given your resignation to your current employer, but maybe making a new start quickly will be beneficial. You don't have to begin work at the library immediately. Sheila could start training you since you would be on the spot, as it were. I hope you don't mind I didn't ask you about it first. If you aren't happy with this idea, you can stay with me and Dad."

Alicia looked across into his blue eyes she now noticed were almost the same shade as Pamela's, although his seemed warmer—a bright summer sky, while Pamela's had been a frozen lake. She wondered again why Pamela hated her brother so much even when he had given up his rightful inheritance to her.

"No, I don't mind at all, John. In fact, I think that will work out best. I'm eager to put the past behind me, and I planned to write my resignation tonight after dinner and give it to Gilly. I want to stop by her place before we leave tomorrow. I already called her and told her I would, if that's okay with you. I need to say goodbye, although I know I'll be back soon to deal with the details of the insurance claim."

John nodded. "Sure. It's fine with me for you to see Gilly before we head back." Just then, the waiter came by with their entrees—lasagna for John and baked ziti for Alicia. He placed the piping hot plates next to them. "Enjoy your meals."

"Thank you," John said.

They spent the rest of dinner talking about the meeting with Pamela that afternoon and all the questions they both still had. "It seems to me this alienation between Peter and his family had to do with my dad's fling with Carol Parsons," John said. "My dad is usually very upfront with things but, as he's growing older, he's starting to forget. I don't want to grill him, but I think he may have some answers for us."

"Maybe the answers no longer matter, John. I mean, Peter is dead and his sister doesn't even care. I've lost my husband and home, but I have an opportunity to start over away from all of it."

John frowned. "I know how you must feel, Ali, but what if Peter's death wasn't a simple hit and run because someone couldn't see him in the fog and panicked? What if someone killed him on purpose and set fire to your house to kill you, as well?"

Alicia moved her plate aside, suddenly losing her appetite. "Please, John, you sound like you're

136

creating a plot for one of your mysteries. The police were following that track too, but now they realize the fire was probably a prank that got out of hand with no connection to Peter's accident."

"I hope you're right, but I still want to talk to Dad. I think there's something more here, and whether it's connected to Pamela or is simply an unfortunate set of coincidences, I need to know for your sake. If you really don't want me to proceed, I'll stop, but I think you would feel better knowing the truth."

Alicia sighed. "You're right, John."

He reached across and took her hand again, and the warmth spread through her. "I'm sorry I ruined your meal. Let's talk about some pleasant topics. When I spoke to Sheila, she suggested some nice clothing stores that aren't too far from Cobble Cove. I made her promise to take you shopping. I've always thought she had great fashion sense."

"Thank you. I guess I really should replace my wardrobe, especially if I'll be working again."

The rest of dinner passed quickly as they talked about the continued nice weather, Thanksgiving, and the upcoming Christmas holidays in Cobble Cove, and how decorations would be put up shortly as the town went all out with lights and open houses. Although there weren't many kids living there, visitors came from nearby towns for the week-long Cobble Cove Christmas Fair. John told her he often played Santa Claus to visiting children in the town square, and Alicia started feeling excited about the upcoming celebrations as she hadn't felt in many months.

CHAPTER 9

That night, Alicia tossed and turned in her hotel bed, unable to take her mind off the trip back to Cobble Cove. She wondered if John was having the same problem, but he seemed quite resolved about the way things were turning out except for the questions he still had for his dad.

Finally, in the early hours of morning, she fell asleep and had a strange dream. She knew she was dreaming but, at the same time, could not rouse herself. It was like she was an observer at an accident who couldn't tear her eyes away from the scene.

A pearly gray dawn-like light shone around her. Underneath her feet, she felt sand. She thought she was at a beach on Long Island—Jones or maybe Roosevelt at Oyster Bay where she'd spent summers with Peter. But when she gazed at the seashore, she saw Cove Point where John had taken her before they'd left town. She watched her footsteps in the sand as they led her forward. Suddenly, another set

138

of footprints joined them. They were a man's. She felt his hand holding hers, warm and comforting. She saw his silhouette but not his face. He was a tall shadow in the sand.

A memory from the past invaded the dream. She was sitting on the beach on a towel in the sand writing wedding invitations. Peter sat nearby sipping a piña colada in a beach chair. She asked him if he was sure there was no one he wanted to invite from his family. At twenty-seven, this was her first marriage, and she wanted everyone to share in her happiness. Peter put his drink down, rose from his seat, and joined her on the towel. Putting an arm around her, he said, "To tell the truth, honey, after forty years, I think my relatives expected me to remain a bachelor the rest of my days. I doubt they'd be too disappointed not to receive an invitation. Let's just have a small party and then spend what we saved on a fun honeymoon."

The scene changed again to the one of her dream. A cool wind gusted her back. The shadow man next to her disappeared. The sand shivered, covering their footprints but revealing a gold circle hidden under a small mound. She reached down and picked up a wedding band.

As she attempted to figure out if it was John's or Peter's, she was woken by a tapping at the connecting room door.

"Ali, it's almost eight, are you awake?"

Alicia jumped out of bed and threw on her robe. "Sorry, John. I couldn't sleep well last night. Come in."

"I didn't mean to wake you," he said, entering the room. "I checked us both out online. We don't have many bags, so I think we can manage them ourselves. We can have breakfast first and then come back for the bags when we leave our keys. Then we'll go see Gilly and head back to Cobble Cove."

Alicia nodded. She didn't think it was necessary to share her dream. "I'll be ready soon."

When he left, she showered and dressed quickly and then called Gilly. She'd already written the library resignation letter the night before but hadn't yet had a chance to tell her friend of her plans. She had to admit she was a little nervous about doing that.

Gilly answered in her usual rushed breath. Alicia realized she might be disturbing her just as she was getting the kids out the door for the school bus, but Gilly said they'd already left. "I was writing my grocery shopping list. What's up, hon?"

Alicia felt her stomach drop. It would be hard leaving Gilly, but they could keep in touch. "John and I are going back to Cobble Cove today, Gilly. We'll stop by your place on the way, if that's all right with you?"

Gilly paused. Her voice changed to one of concern. "What about the fire investigation? Did they find out how that happened?"

"No, but we were told we could leave. It may take a long time. They may never find out, but they're thinking you were right about the teenagers."

"What if I wasn't? The more I think about it,

140

Alicia, the more I'm wondering if Peter's death may be connected. I don't want anything to happen to you."

"Oh, Gilly, please." She tried to sound confident. "I'm fine. I'll be with John. I actually wrote a letter to the library. I want to move to Cobble Cove and make a new start. I think its best."

She expected her friend to argue with her. Instead, Gilly said, "I think that will be good for you, hon. I like John. You know I do." She could almost see the wink through the phone.

"I'll keep in touch and visit when I can."

"Of course. Come over when you're ready. I'll put out more cookies. I baked another batch yesterday."

Alicia laughed. "We'll call when we're on the way. Thanks."

***

Gilly kept her promise about the chocolate chip cookies, and John had two despite the fact he and Alicia had eaten a quick breakfast at the hotel restaurant. Alicia helped herself to one but had a hard time finishing it. She was nervous about returning to Cobble Cove, but more from excitement than fear. She didn't feel she was in danger but still believed the sooner she escaped her old life, the better.

"You take care of my friend," Gilly told John as they were leaving. Her eyes were moist, as if she were about to cry.

"Yes, ma'am. I'll protect her with my life," John

vowed.

"I know you will." Gilly hugged Alicia. "Don't worry about the job. I'll hand in your letter. I think they were expecting it. Things won't be the same without you, but you'll call and visit and make sure I'm not killing my kids." She wiped a stray tear from her eye.

Alicia found herself crying too. "Thanks, Gilly. We'll stay in touch. I promise. I swear."

***

Their drive back to Cobble Cove was quicker than expected with little traffic. John offered to drive, and Alicia let him. They stopped for lunch at a highway rest stop and arrived in town a little after four. It was growing dark. A few raindrops tapped the windshield.

"I'll drop you off at the library and then walk home. I don't mind a bit of rain. I told Sheila I would when I called her last night. She's straightening up the guest room. I hope you don't mind staying there alone, but Sneaky Cat will probably keep you company. Dad also usually starts work early, so don't be alarmed if you hear him fiddling around with books downstairs before you're out of bed."

Alicia was thinking of the living area Sheila had briefly shown her, although they hadn't gotten as far as the bedroom. The rain was falling harder as John pulled into the library parking lot.

"Here we are. I'll take your bag if you like."

"No thanks. It's not heavy, but please come in

with me."

"Of course." He parked the car, got out, and opened the door for her. Sheila was already waiting for them.

"Welcome back, you two," she said, unlocking the door. "I closed the library early today, so I could get things ready for Alicia."

Alicia stepped into the library's front hall. John followed, shaking off his jacket. "It's starting to rain. We made good time and missed most of it."

"Would either of you like some coffee or tea? I can put some on upstairs."

"I'm okay, thanks," Alicia said.

"Me too. Actually, I just came to drop Ali off. I want to get back to Dad and cook him some dinner tonight."

"I used my crock pot for the first time this season and made a stew," Sheila said, turning to Alicia. "It's in the refrigerator upstairs for you to heat up later in the microwave."

"Thank you. That sounds wonderful."

John took his wallet out and removed a card. He jotted something down on it with a pencil from the table near the computer terminal. "If there's anything you need, here's my home number on the back of my business card." It seemed he figured it was the right time to make his exit. "You're in good hands with Sheila, Ali. I'll call you in the morning."

"Okay. I'll be fine. Thank you both."

After John left, the rain started in earnest. Sheila led her upstairs and showed her the rest of the apartment. Sneaky, the cat, was curled on a quilted blanket on the iron-posted queen bed.

"Looks like you have a friend staying with you." Sheila seemed affectionate toward the cat as she smiled. "He used to always hang out up here with Tina. I stayed here myself during a few snowstorms, and he was my constant companion."

"He looks quite comfortable." Alicia was somewhat relieved she wouldn't be sleeping above the library alone.

"Cats are masters of comfort. By the way, Mac usually feeds him when he opens the library in the morning, but if you'd like to put out some kibble tonight or when you wake up tomorrow, the cat food is kept in the bottom drawer of the microwave cart. You may have noticed Sneaky's water and food dish in the kitchen. His litter box is in the storage area where we keep books that need to be processed. Mac is in charge of that."

"The storage area?"

"Here, let me show you." Sheila led Alicia from the bedroom to another room in the back that had a cat door installed so Sneaky could enter and leave at will. Sheila switched on the light as they walked into the room. Books were piled in stacks around the space and a few were scattered on an old desk containing labels, tape, a mug full of pens, and what appeared to be a manual typewriter. The room smelled somewhat musty, and there was a strong, unpleasant odor emanating from the corner.

"Mac is in charge of cleaning the litter box also, but I have to remind him sometimes," Sheila said, explaining the foul smell. "It's not that he forgets, but he doesn't really enjoy the job. Tina used to do it when she was here, and John helps occasionally. I can't deal with it. Even when I had my Siamese, I left that chore to my husband. The problem is somebody has to do it. Cats don't tolerate dirty boxes well. If it isn't clean enough, Sneaky might go to the bathroom elsewhere."

"Oh, gosh," Alicia said. She'd had cats as a child and was aware of this offensive behavior.

"Yes, well, Mac forgot for a few days once, and Sneaky urinated on the jacket he left on the back of the chair. It taught him a lesson, so Mac's been cleaning the box more often. The dust from the litter sometimes gets on the books too, so they need to be dusted regularly."

"I can take care of everything," Alicia said. "It's the least I can do since you're letting me stay here."

"Mac will be happy to hear that, but please don't feel like you owe us anything." Sheila smiled again. "Once you start working here, you'll earn your keep. You can stay here as long as you like as part of the perks of being an employee, but you may want to get your own place in town. The rents aren't high but, then again, neither are the salaries."

Alicia didn't feel like talking about her employment yet, so she was glad when Sheila said, "But we have time to discuss that and your training later. Why don't you unpack and settle in first? Like I told you, there's food in the refrigerator for you to heat up. My contact number is attached to the mini fridge with a magnet, and John gave you his home number. Mac usually gets in around six-thirty in the morning. He knows you'll be here, so don't worry about him disturbing you."

Sheila walked Alicia back to the bedroom where

she'd placed Alicia's suitcase. "I'll leave you now. Have a good sleep. I arrive around eight-thirty, and I'll bring some breakfast up to you."

"Thank you."

"You're very welcome. I'm so glad you've decided to take the library position." Then Sheila was off, clicking her boots down the stairs. Alicia heard her lock the outside door and wondered if she would give her a duplicate key while she stayed there.

***

After Alicia unpacked her things, heated up Sheila's stew that turned out to be quite tasty, and changed into pajamas. She wanted to continue her story, but couldn't concentrate on the plot. She turned off the light and tried to sleep, but the heavy rain against the window kept her up, as did the loud purring of Sneaky Cat, who snuggled against her, happy to have company again. She thought about Tina, the girl who'd stayed here last. From what Alicia knew of her, Tina was a young library school graduate who'd been hired by Sheila as quickly as Alicia had. She'd lived over the library in this space as well, taken care of Sneaky, and left to care for her sick mother in Florida.

Sneaky dug his paws into the quilt at her back. It had been a long time since she'd had a cat, but she recalled the kneading sensation both male and female cats practiced to comfort themselves. Maybe it would comfort her too. Had she done the right thing by returning to Cobble Cove? Would she be bored in this small town with only a handful of people patronizing the library each day? Sheila had mentioned the large number of homebound patrons, the seniors of the town who needed books delivered. She might enjoy that. She liked reader's advisory work, selecting books that would interest people. Sometimes it was a challenge, but she always learned through the experience and even found new authors and books for herself.

After a few hours of restlessness, Sneaky finally got sick of her tossing and left the room. She felt strangely deserted. She decided it might be better to get up and do something than spend unproductive time in bed. She turned on the light and went out into the hall. All was quiet from downstairs except the continuous downpour. She didn't plan to go into the library, but she considered checking some of the unprocessed books Sheila had mentioned Mac was working on in the storage room. Perhaps she'd find something more interesting than her current reading that could help her fall asleep.

When she entered the storage room, she didn't see Sneaky, although she thought he might've headed there to use his litter box. Cats can be quiet and liked to sleep in the strangest spots, so he could be there in some corner. Mac's jacket was still draped across the chair by the desk. She laughed recalling the story about what Sneaky had once done to it out of spite, so typical of an angered cat. She sat in the chair and perused the stack of books on the desk. A few were from James Patterson's 'Private' series. She didn't read too many series and had only read a few of Patterson's standalone titles.

As she was about to choose a book from the pile, she heard scratching in the corner. She jumped. Hopefully, that was Sneaky and not a mouse he hadn't caught, for this place probably attracted them. She walked cautiously to the corner where she'd heard the noise. It wasn't coming from the litter box under the window but from the opposite side.

Since the one bulb in the room was dim, she could hardly see in the dark recesses of the room. She wished she had a flashlight. As she approached the area where she heard the noise, she saw a bunch of boxes. She was relieved to see Sneaky scratching the side of one, cardboard pieces scattered at his feet. "Oh, Sneaky," she said. "You scared me, but you're only using a box for a scratching post." The cat, caught in the act, stopped mid-scratch and scampered away through his cat flap. Alicia made a note to speak to John about helping her find a real scratching post for Sneaky, but before she left the room, she went over to the boxes. She figured they contained more books, but when she looked inside the one Sneaky had been scratching, she saw a few papers bundled together with rope. Newspapers? They weren't that thick. She realized as she picked up the first bundle, they were a stack of letters. She felt uneasy snooping through them and was about to toss them next to the other two stacks in the box when she caught the name on the top envelope, Miss Carol Parsons. Her heart thudded in tempo with the rain. Were these the letters Mac wrote to Peter's mother all those years ago? If so, how had Mac gotten them back?

She dug deeper, despite a growing unease, and pulled out all the bundled letters. She brought them to the desk. While the first two bundles were addressed to Carol in different handwriting, the second bundle of letters hadn't been opened. The last bundle was addressed to John McKinney in a flourished female hand. These looked as if they had been handled the most, and some of the letters spilled out of their envelopes.

For a moment, Alicia considered sitting down to read them. She could hardly go back to bed now. She knew they must be Mac's private property, so she put them back where she found them. Mac hardly had them hidden because the box they were in wasn't sealed. She decided to ask John about the letters the next day since he was already planning on questioning his father about the information Pamela gave them.

Surprisingly, after Alicia turned off the light and crawled back into bed, she fell asleep rather quickly next to Sneaky, who had rejoined her, a beige ball of fur purring a soothing lullaby that drowned out the rain.

CHAPTER 10

Alicia woke to the sound of whistling. At first, she thought it was her cell phone, although it wasn't the same pitch. Then she realized it was coming from downstairs in the library. She glanced at her cell phone—6:30 a.m.—and knew it was Mac, right on time. Sunlight filtered through the window's white curtains. The rain must've stopped while she slept. She quickly threw on her robe and descended the stairs, being sure to make a little noise so she wouldn't surprise Mac. The cat followed her, probably anticipating his breakfast.

Mac stood whistling by the local history section. He turned when he heard her and put down a book he was holding. Observing him in the morning light of the empty library, she was tempted to ask him about the letters but decided it was better not to say anything until she'd talked to John.

"Good morning, ma'am," he said. "I hope my whistling didn't wake you."

She smiled. "Not exactly. I thought it was my phone for a minute, but don't worry. I like to rise early."

"Lady after my own heart. My wife, let her rest in peace, was the same. The early bird certainly has more chances to catch the worm." He chuckled at his creative use of the common expression. "John said he'll be bringing us some muffins and coffee later. Sheila planned to do it, but he called her last night and offered to instead. I usually get here before Sheila arrives and the library opens, so I can have some privacy and start on the day's work because, as you know, I've pretty much had it by noon and am ready for a nap." He winked. "Ah, so you've made a friend of our Sneaky Cat." The Siamese wound around Alicia's bare legs and bumped his head against her calves.

"I think he wants to eat. I promised Sheila I would take over the cat care while I'm here, so I can go back up and feed him. I'll also change the litter box. I know that's a job you usually do, but I'm sure you won't mind taking a break."

Mac's gray eyebrows rose. "That's kind of you, girl. My back isn't what it used to be, and scooping that box is not so easy anymore. Now Tina's gone, I'm stuck with the job unless John takes it off my hands. Sheila won't do it. She barely tolerates Mr. Sneaky."

Alicia realized this might be a good opportunity to find out more about Tina. "I don't mean to take up your time when you want to start working, but do you mind if I ask you a few questions before John and Sheila arrive?"

A wary expression crossed Mac's wrinkled face for a second, and she wondered if she feared she was going to ask him about Carol or Pamela. She wasn't sure if John had broached the subject yet, so she quickly added, "I'm curious about that girl, Tina. How long did she work here?"

"Let's go into the reading room and I'll tell you as much as I know about Tina, but you might want to feed the cat first or he'll start meowing and begging."

Alicia knew Mac was right because Sneaky was still circling her legs. "Good idea. Sheila showed me where she stores the cat supplies. It won't take long."

After Alicia fed Sneaky and changed his litter box, she took a quick shower and changed into the pants set John purchased for her on Long Island as a Christmas gift. John hadn't yet arrived, and Sheila wasn't expected for another hour.

She found Mac at the table set inside the reading room's alcove by the local history collection. She joined him, and he put down the book he was stamping: **'Property of Cobble Cove Library'**.

"That was fast, ma'am. Have a seat. I'll tell you about Tina Deerborn."

Did she detect a hint of dislike in his tone? She waited while he gathered his thoughts.

"She came to us one stormy, wintry night. I'd say it was about two years ago. John placed an ad in the *Cobble Cove Courier*, and Sheila advertised the library position through the area's papers. I believe it ran as far as New Paltz. Tina was our first applicant. Sheila hired her on the spot. I have to admit I was taken with her too. She was a pretty young thing." His eyes, so like John's, twinkled at the memory.

"Sheila can tell you more. I never saw her application. I think she attended some library school further upstate. She wasn't too knowledgeable about the Dewey system, but she had a knack for working with people, especially the fellas." He winked. "We were sorry to see her leave. It was a bit sudden, but her mom took sick. That happens sometimes." For some reason, as he said those words, Alicia felt he didn't really believe them.

Mac waved his hands. "I'm not a nosy man. I've had my share of private business, but I told Sheila I thought Tina left with some guy. She probably got sick of this place, which is what most young people do, and why this town is so old, if you know what I mean."

Alicia nodded. Mac would've continued, but a few raps on the door interrupted him. "That must be John," Mac said, rising to answer it. Alicia followed him as he let his son in, carrying a tray of coffee and a bag of muffins.

"Good morning, Dad, Ali. I've brought breakfast."

"Hey there, son. Thanks for picking that stuff up, but I think you should bring it upstairs. You know how Sheila hates people eating in the library."

"That's my plan," John said. "Is that okay with you, Ali? I know it's your living space now. I brought an extra muffin for Sheila when she joins us."

"It's fine with me," Alicia said. "Would you like me to hold the muffin bag?" She knew it was hard to juggle the bag and the hot coffee up the stairs.

"Thanks." John handed her the bag as he started upstairs. Alicia followed, and Mac drew up the rear. She expected the cat to come along too, but Sneaky had already finished his breakfast and was curled up in his basket by the local history books.

Since the kitchen was small with a table and only two chairs, John insisted on standing at the counter while Alicia and Mac sat at the table.

"Sheila might be late this morning if she's still packing," John said, munching into his muffin. "That's why I offered to bring you guys breakfast."

"Packing? Is she going somewhere?" Alicia asked. Sheila hadn't said anything to her last night.

John took a sip of coffee from his Styrofoam takeout cup. "I'm surprised she didn't tell you. She's visiting her daughter and grandchildren in California for Thanksgiving."

Alicia suddenly realized Thursday was a holiday. "I forgot all about Thanksgiving."

"Well, you've had your mind on other things, young lady," Mac said, starting on his second muffin.

"Whoa, Dad. I thought you were saving one for Sheila."

"Sorry, but I skipped breakfast this morning, and these muffins are great. Are they from Claire's Bakery?"

"You bet."

"Don't worry, I only want one," Alicia said. "But about Thanksgiving, how do people celebrate it here in Cobble Cove?"

John laughed and almost choked on his muffin. "You make it sound like we're aliens, Ali. We eat turkey like everyone else. In fact," he paused, "I was about to mention Dora has invited you to the inn with Dad and me on Thursday. She's cooking a full-course Thanksgiving dinner with all the trimmings."

"How nice," Alicia exclaimed. "I'd love to go, but what about the honeymooners?"

"They left yesterday. It seems they're touring the Catskills and were only passing through Cobble Cove."

"Does that mean I can go back to the inn?"

"That's up to you, but I think Sheila wants you here for a while, especially since she'll be away for the week. If you get lonely, Dad and I are only a phone call away and a stone's throw by foot." John laughed at the familiar joke that was beginning to grow stale.

"I don't mind staying here. I have Sneaky for company."

"Alicia is even doing cat duty," Mac told John. "She's saving my back."

"That's one job I don't admire."

Alicia thought of the conversation she had with Mac. "John, you told me you didn't know Tina well. I was talking to your dad about her. I was curious since she stayed and worked here before me."

The look that passed between John and his father caused Alicia to regret mentioning her discussion with Mac. John's reply was noncommittal. "I really have nothing to add about Tina except I spent a few days in the city at a library conference for Dad back in the spring. She left shortly after I returned. I heard her mom in Florida got sick."

Mac was the one to change the subject. "If you two don't mind, I want to get to work downstairs. Sheila should be here any minute, anyway." He turned back to John. "Thanks for the breakfast, son. Will you be home for lunch today?"

"Not sure. I'd like to take Alicia to lunch and maybe to do a little shopping. She still needs to replenish her wardrobe. I was hoping Sheila would take her, but I'm sure she's too busy preparing to travel."

Mac laughed. "It's casual dress here at the library and in Cobble Cove in general. But I know the ladies like to dress up from time to time, especially near the holidays."

"I should get something for Thanksgiving," Alicia said.

"I was talking about Christmas. Has John told you how fancy things get around here? Edith and Rose are on the Christmas Committee. They'll recruit you too." He winked.

"Don't scare her, Dad. Sheila is on the Christmas Committee too, and puts up a tree and decorations in the library. It's festive."

Mac got up. "You came at a good time, Alicia. While Sheila's gone, I can train you a little if you're interested. You might be able to help me with the cataloguing."

"Sure," Alicia agreed.

"Okay. See you two downstairs later." He grabbed his cane, and they heard him thumping down the stairs.

"Too bad you don't have an elevator," Alicia

said.

"Expensive to install, and Sheila prefers to keep the place homey."

"And an elevator would make it less so?"

"I don't argue with the boss."

Alicia wanted to ask John more about Tina, but a part of her was wary. Instead, she whispered, "I found something last night that might interest you. I wasn't nosing around or anything, but Sneaky started scratching a box in the storage room, and I noticed the box was open and full of letters."

"Letters?" He seemed surprised. "I don't spend much time up here, but I thought the storage room only contained books and assorted library supplies."

"The letters were from your dad to Carol Parsons, and there were return letters too. Some weren't even opened."

"How strange. I'd like to look at those. I haven't spoken to Dad yet about our encounter with Pamela, but I still mean to do that after Thanksgiving. I could come back here after the library closes tonight, and you could show them to me."

"All right." Alicia stood and began clearing the table. She placed the last muffin back in the brown bag. "Let's go down and wait for Sheila. She may have some things for me to do before you return at lunchtime."

John's blue eyes lit up. "So you're coming then?"

"You bet," she said, but a part of her still wondered about his expression when she told him she'd spoken to his father about Tina.

157

***

After John left, Sheila breezed in. "I hope you had a pleasant sleep," she told Alicia.

"Yes. Thanks. The bed is quite comfortable, and Sneaky makes a great pillow."

"We saved you a muffin, Sheila," Mac said, handing her the bag Alicia left on the reading table.

"Thanks, but I'll grab a bite later. I want to start training Alicia before I leave. Did you fill her in on that, Mac?"

The old man looked slightly guilty. "John did."

"Good." Alicia noticed Sheila still had her coat on.

"I was planning to ask Mac to show you how we process books, but he can do that while I'm gone. I'd rather take you to visit the homebound patrons. I hope you're up for a little walk around town." She eyed Alicia's pumps.

"Sure. It's not raining today."

"Yes, but it's getting chilly. You should wear a jacket."

"Will we back by lunchtime? John was going to meet me here and take me out today."

Alicia raised a red brow. "We should, although some of our homebounds love to talk. They don't get much company. In addition to book deliveries, we often act as a social service, if you know what I mean."

"Gilly used to say the same thing happened at our library, even with patrons who came in. Many of them are lonely and only need someone to listen."

Sheila nodded. "Get your jacket and we'll be on our way."

Alicia went upstairs and grabbed her raincoat. As she descended, she heard Mac say to Sheila, "She was asking about Tina. It's up to you what you want to tell her."

When Alicia got to the bottom of the stairs, the two stopped talking. Mac continued stamping books on the reading table, and Sheila turned to her. "Okay, let's go. Our first stop is Mable's house. She's ninety years old and reads large type mysteries. Her favorites are Agatha Christie books, but she also likes those written by M.C. Beaton." She walked to the mystery section and took some books off the shelf that she placed in a library bag with 'Cobble Cove Library' printed in brown letters above the logo of a book sitting among cobblestones. Alicia had seen the same image on the sign outside the library.

"You take these, and I'll get the others. Luckily, we only have three houses to visit today. I keep a list of each homebound's reading interests. Some of them prefer you select their books. Have you had any experience with reader's advisory work?"

"Yes. I enjoy helping patrons choose their books."

"Perfect."

Sheila finished gathering the rest of the books and walked toward the door. "Bye, Mac," she said. "We should be back before you leave and," she looked at Alicia, "before John comes by to take you to lunch."

Alicia thought of the conversation she'd heard

between Sheila and Mac when she was upstairs. She wondered whether she should broach the subject of Tina to Sheila while they walked to the homebound houses. She decided to play it by ear and wait for the right opportunity.

***

Mabel the mystery reader lived right off Bookshelf Lane. Sheila told Alicia she had sorted the homebound deliveries for that day in distance order. Mabel's house was one of the stone ones popular in the area. It was small with a *'Beware of Dog'* sign stuck in the front lawn. The gate creaked when Sheila opened it.

"Don't worry about Gigi," Sheila said when she saw Alicia eyeing the sign. "She's a little pup whose bark is worse than her bite."

Sure enough, as the women approached, a tiny yipping terrier ran to the front door. Mabel, trailing behind with a walker containing a tray, took a bit longer.

"Oh, my goodness," she said, catching her breath, "My librarian is here with books." It sounded like she was speaking to someone in the house, although Alicia had heard she lived alone. Then Alicia realized the old woman was talking to her dog. "Books for us, Gigi. How wonderful!"

"Hello, Mabel," Sheila said. "I've brought the new librarian with me. This is Ms. Alicia Fairmont."

"Fairmont? That name sounds familiar." The white-haired woman opened her door and squinted at Alicia. "Come in, both of you. I was just starting to knit, but I can put on a pot of tea if you'd like."

"No, thank you," Sheila said as they entered the house. "We're making the rounds for deliveries this morning and don't have much time." She dropped the book bag on a nearby table.

The dog had quieted down and taken a place by Mabel's rocking chair where a ball of red yarn and knitting needles lay in a basket. Alicia wondered if Mabel remembered Peter's family, but the woman had gone into a back room to gather the books from her last delivery.

"I liked all of these," she said, reentering the room after a few minutes. Reaching into the walker's tray, she handed Alicia a library bag that contained her returns. "Beaton is such a good author. Her Agatha Raisin mysteries are interesting but funny at the same time. What I like best is there's no bad language and sex that are in a lot of books today."

Sheila smiled. "I know you like cozy mysteries, so I try to stock up on them, Mabel."

"How sweet of you. Are you sure you and your friend wouldn't like some tea?"

"Not today, but thanks. Enjoy your books."

Mabel stood at the door waving to them as they left the house.

"Next on the list is Georgiana," Sheila said when they were past Mabel's house. "Unlike Mabel, she adores what we call bodice rippers."

Alicia knew the term. Gilly used it frequently. "Yes, most of those are usually paperbacks written by authors like Johanna Lindsey, Julia London, and

Sabrina Jeffries. Many are historical."

"I knew I hired you for a reason," Sheila said. "Georgie's house is right down this block."

They had turned Mabel's corner onto Pebble Place. Sheila strode up a long driveway to a ranch house. A woman sat outside on a porch swing.

"Hi, there, Georgie," Sheila hailed her. "I've got some books for you, and I've brought along the new librarian for you to meet."

Georgiana stepped off the swing. It continued to rock in the slight breeze. The lady was tall and wore a long, blue-flowered skirt and high-collared matching blouse. She looked younger than Mabel but when Georgiana walked over to take the books, Alicia noticed she had a slight limp.

"Thank you, Sheila. I've been missing my dukes and ladies." She winked. "I heard you were hiring a new librarian. I miss Tina. Have you had any word from her?"

"I'm afraid not. I'm sure she's too busy caring for her mother to contact us, but Alicia here is a godsend."

"Alicia. What a pretty name," Georgiana said, offering her hand. "Nice to meet you, dear."

Alicia noticed the woman's hands were bony and arthritic-looking, so she shook the extended one gently. "Likewise, ma'am."

"One moment." Georgiana went in her house. She was back quickly with her bag of book returns and a box of Whitman's chocolates.

"Please share these with Alicia," she said, handing the chocolates to Sheila.

"Thank you. Have a good day. I hope you like

the books." She passed the chocolates to Alicia and took the return bag.

"One more stop before we bring these back to the library," Sheila said. "Do you think you can handle the next bag?"

Alicia nodded. "I'll manage. I can carry two if you want."

Sheila didn't seem burdened. Alicia observed she was quite fit to carry two book bags and walk up the hill without needing to catch her breath.

"The homebounds are so nice, and the street names are charming," Alicia commented as they arrived at the top of the hill and turned up Copper Penny Lane.

Sheila smiled. "Most of our homebounds are sweet old ladies. This last one is a bit surly sometimes. Her name is Betty, and she isn't always happy with the books selected for her. She likes popular authors—Patterson, Clark, Roberts."

Alicia tried to take some mental notes to remember each person and their book preferences, even though Sheila said she recorded them.

"Do you have any male homebounds?" Alicia asked as they approached a brick house with closed curtains.

"There are two, but I'll give you the complete list when we return to the library. I made sure all the deliveries were taken care of while I was away, so you wouldn't need to worry about them. I just wanted to get you started meeting some of the homebounds since you were here."

"Is Betty home?" Alicia asked.

"Oh, yes. She likes to keep her house dark

because she doesn't trust strangers. We'll have to be insistent on who we are to get her to answer."

As Sheila warned, it took several knocks until Betty, after peering at them through her curtain, decided it was safe to open the door.

"You're from the library, aren't you?" the small woman in black asked. Her face was twisted into a grimace.

"Yes. It's me, Betty," Sheila said. "I know I haven't delivered books to you in a while, but I hope you remember me."

Alicia thought for a moment the lady was going to request identification. Instead, she turned her beady eyes on Alicia and asked, "Who is she?"

Alicia saw what Sheila meant by Betty being "a bit surly," but remembering her initial issues with Dora and Casey, she tried a friendly approach. "I'm Alicia Fairmont, the new librarian," she introduced herself without expecting a handshake.

The woman huffed. She made no motion to let them in.

"You have my books? I hope they're better than the last batch."

Sheila handed over the remaining books of the delivery. "I'm sorry you didn't like our last selections. Was there something in particular that displeased you?"

Betty grabbed the books. "They all stunk, that's all. Let me get them if you still want them." She closed the door behind her.

Sheila glanced at Alicia with the expression, 'I told you so,' written on her face. "Don't mind Betty. She has her moods."

Alicia wondered what the woman was like on a good day. Before long, Betty opened the door again and dumped her return bag on the step.

"Here you go. I'd get my money back for these if I were you." With that, she closed and locked the door.

Alicia picked up the bag. "I'll take this."

Sheila nodded. "Thank you. Sorry about Betty. I should've warned you."

"You tried."

Sheila smiled. "Patron psychology should be a subject taught in every library school, but as you and I know, it's mostly on-the-job training. I'm just glad we visited Betty last. The library is right around the corner. We made a circle. When we get back, I'm going to need you to check in those books. I'll show you how we do it. There'll be plenty of time before John comes to take you to lunch."

As they walked back, Alicia decided to broach the subject of Tina. "Sheila, I asked Mac about Tina, and he said she worked here about a year and a half before she had to leave to care for her mother, who became ill in Florida. Is that where she came from?"

It took a few minutes for Sheila to reply. "I assume so."

"You don't know? Didn't she fill out a job application?" As she asked the question, Alicia realized she herself hadn't filled one out yet.

"We do things a little different here, a bit more casual." They turned the corner, and the library came into view.

"But surely you checked her credentials, library school, references...?"

Instead of answering, Sheila said, "I'm afraid we aren't fully automated yet. I know you've seen the computer for patrons, but our circulation system is still manual. You check the books in on a sheet and record their title, author, and return date. First, you need to go through them and make sure there are no damaged or missing pages. Our homebounds sometimes drink coffee or eat while they read, so the books incur water or food stains."

"The same type of things happened at my home library," Alicia told her, recalling how many books came back torn, crumpled, and stained. They'd arrived at the library then, and Alicia noted Sheila had effectively dodged her question about Tina.

When they walked in, Mac was busy at the reading desk stamping books, but Alicia also saw the newspaper crossword puzzle on his other side. It seemed he was multitasking between stamping and puzzle solving.

"Hi, there," he said, looking up as they entered.

Sheila dropped the bag of books she was holding on the chair next to him. "I have some errands to run to prepare for my trip. I'm leaving Alicia with you, Mac. She needs to check in the books. Would you mind showing her how we do it?"

"No problem," Mac said. He took a blank, columned sheet from a desk drawer and placed it next to him. "I'll be glad to train our new recruit."

"Thank you. I'll be back after lunch and will bring food for your dinner, Alicia."

"That's very kind of you. Are you sure you don't

mind? I have leftover stew from yesterday I could heat up, or I can do some grocery shopping. I'll need to do that when you're away, anyway." She hated having to rely on people, especially those she was just beginning to know.

"I really don't mind, but if you're sure you have leftovers, I'll be busy packing tonight, so that might work better." She turned to Mac. "Don't overwork her," she warned as she left the library.

"Well, then." Mac moved Sheila's book bags to the floor and patted the chair next to him. "Come sit, young lady, and I'll give you a check-in lesson." Alicia recalled he had been a tutor, and it was obvious he enjoyed teaching by the way his eyes sparkled, so much like John's, as he instructed her.

She took the offered seat and placed the returns from Betty on the table. A few James Patterson books and a Mary Higgins Clark fell from the bag as she emptied it. "I guess we should start with these."

"Righto." Mac pushed aside his crossword puzzle and the book he was stamping. "You need to check every page. I know that seems time consuming, but it's important. I was about to take a break, so I'll go upstairs for a few minutes while you do that. When I get back, I'll finish your lesson. Be sure to check every page and, if you see anything wrong, mark that page with a bookmark or scrap of paper or jot the page number down somewhere."

After she heard the tap of Mac's cane ascending the stairs, she opened the first book and began paging through it. Everything was fine until she got to page 105. When she turned to that page, a small slip of folded paper fell out. She was going to throw it away, but she figured she'd read it in case it was something important Betty left in the book. When she opened it, she caught her breath. In dark black letters, as if the person had pressed deeply into the paper, were the words:

I know what you did. I saw you with him.

Alicia thought it was a prank, but aimed at who? Sheila? Or perhaps, it was just a note Betty wrote while reading the book. It was even possible the note had been left there from a previous reader. For some reason, Alicia decided to keep the paper, but she thought it was better not to mention it to Mac or Sheila. She placed the note in her pants pocket and went on to the second book. She wondered if she'd also find something on page 105 of that one, but she didn't. The next note was on page 216. It was the same white square of folded paper with the same deep writing, and this message said exactly the same thing. The last of Betty's returns contained the identical cryptic message on page 375. Alicia kept all three papers in her pocket and continued with Mabel and Georgiana's returns. Neither of them contained any notes.

When Mac came back downstairs, she tried to act casual. "These are all fine, Mac, but can I ask you something?"

He thought she was asking him about the check-in procedure. "Sure. All you do is write the date in the return column next to the book's author and title." He passed her the check-in sheet and a pencil. Alicia noticed the sheet wasn't blank after all, but was full of a list of books checked out along with their check out dates and the name of the homebound to whom they had been checked out. The writing was fancy, like calligraphy.

"In the notes column, you indicate if anything was amiss. Sheila keeps a log of these in the homebound loose-leaf binder on that shelf." He nodded toward the stack containing the local history books, at the foot of which Sneaky napped in his cat bed. The upper shelf contained a series of black binders she figured were the ones he was referring to.

"That wasn't exactly the question I wanted to ask," she said. "I was wondering how often homebound deliveries are made."

"Depends. When Tina was here, they were done quite often, usually on a weekly basis. When she left, well, Sheila hasn't had much time to devote to them. That's why she's glad you're here now."

"The homebounds I met today seemed quite friendly except for a lady named Betty."

Mac laughed. "Betty Harpin, that old crone— pardon the expression. She hates everybody and everything, so don't imagine you can befriend her."

"Thanks for the warning. Sheila gave me one too, but I see her last delivery was several months ago." Alicia had scanned the dates next to Betty Harpin's checked out books.

"That's correct. Sheila was putting it off. I know Tina made a delivery there right before she left.

That was back in the spring some time."

"Didn't Betty complain? I mean that's a long time to go without new books."

Mac smiled. "Betty is not only rude, but she's senile. She'll read books over and over again without remembering them. I'm no example. I forget things I read too."

"Yes, but she told us she disliked them. She seemed to know what they were about, and why would you allow her to keep popular titles out so long?"

"She may like popular authors, but we don't bring her their latest titles, and we make sure we have extras. As far as her not liking them, she dislikes everything. We only bring her books to humor her. I know that sounds kind of cruel, but she never leaves that house. It's a way of checking up on her, although the mailman does that daily. Old Luke tells me he looks for her peering from behind her curtain and makes sure she's moving. The mail disappears from the box, but she won't open the door until he's out of range. She's been doing that for years, even when I was at the post office."

"You worked at the post office?" Alicia knew Mac worked at the school and then she thought he became the town's library director, giving up the position to Sheila when he grew too old to work a full day.

Mac nodded. "Indeed. It was great exercise. I worked there both in the sorting room and on the Cobble Cove route, volunteering while I was in high school. I gave it up to help my father at the library in 1955 and have been here ever since."

"And then Sheila took over?" Alicia was checking her facts.

"Correct again. Sheila took the reins about ten years ago when I semi-retired. She worked for me first as a reference librarian."

"So the only employees at the library all this time have been librarians? You've never hired any clerks? That seems rather strange, and I meant to ask about it sooner."

"Cobble Cove is a small place, so we don't need a large staff," Mac explained. "When there were still young people in town, my dad occasionally asked one to help shelve books, but we manage fine today without extra help, especially now that you've joined us."

"I see, but back to Betty. How does she eat or shop for food if she doesn't leave her house?" Alicia knew many seniors became shut-ins for fear of the outside world. Even though the woman was nasty, she pitied her.

"The grocer delivers to her once a week. She makes Duncan leave the bags outside too. Weird lady, if you ask me, but I'm not one to judge. I like being among people. That's why I work with the public. I can't understand those who prefer their own company so much."

Alicia nodded. Maybe the notes were the result of an unstable mind, but what if they weren't?

CHAPTER 11

John arrived in his pickup at noon and told Alicia and Mac he was treating them to lunch at Casey's. Alicia didn't object, although she was somewhat disappointed Mac would be joining them. She had hoped to discuss the notes she found in Betty's books with John alone at lunch, but she knew she'd have another chance that night when John came to see the letters in the storage room.

Lunch went well with the two men talking about football, the unseasonal nice weather, and the upcoming Thanksgiving meal at Dora's. Alicia kept quiet most of the time, concentrating on her food and the many questions she was saving to ask John later.

After John dropped Mac off at home, he asked if Alicia wanted to go shopping. Although it might've presented an opportunity to talk about the notes earlier, she declined. She told him she was a bit tired. John thought the homebound deliveries were the cause and said, "You'll get used to all the walking around here. It's great for your health and your waistline, although yours doesn't need much help." He winked. "By the way, you look pretty in that pantsuit I bought you."

"Thank you."

"I actually have some writing to do this afternoon," John said as he pulled up to the library, "I'll let you off here. I see Sheila's car, so she must be back. I'm sure she'll have a few more things to show you before she leaves." As she opened the car door, he added, "I'll be by around seven tonight."

"See you then."

He waited while she entered the library before driving off.

Sheila was reshelving the returns. "Hey there," she said as Alicia walked in. "How did the check-ins go?"

Alicia tried to act natural but then decided it wouldn't hurt to comment about Betty's returns without mentioning the notes directly. "Everything went well, Sheila, but do homebounds ever leave things in books?"

"Things? Oh, you mean bookmarks or paper clips? Patrons leave all sorts of things—gum wrappers, photos, recipes, you name it." She furrowed her red brows. "Did anyone leave anything today?"

"No, I'm just curious," she lied. "Did Betty ever leave anything?"

"Not that I know of, but Tina did most of her deliveries and check-ins."

Tina. Could the note have been directed at her? Alicia suddenly remembered the way John's face changed at the mention of Tina's name and Mac's conversation with Sheila when Alicia was upstairs. She decided she would have to ask John about Tina again tonight after she showed him the letters and notes.

Before Alicia and Sheila could talk further, a patron walked in. She didn't recognize her at first but then realized it was Dora. She wore a hooded poncho and brown, knee-length boots. "Good day, ladies. I need a cookbook. Can one of you help me?"

"Hi, Dora," Sheila said. "I'll let my new librarian find one for you. I'm actually leaving for the day. I have an early morning flight to San Francisco."

"How nice," Dora said. "It must be wonderful seeing your daughter and granddaughters for the holidays." She looked a bit wistful. "I wish you a good trip."

"Thank you," Sheila said, gathering up her coat and purse. "If you have any problems the rest of the day, Alicia, call Mac or John. I'll check in with everyone after Thanksgiving." She fished in her pocket and pulled out a bronze key and a piece of paper. "This is the key to the library and some instructions I've prepared for next week."

"Don't worry. Enjoy your time away," Alicia said, taking the key and paper. Without reading the instructions, she noted the handwriting was neat but not fancy or dark. It didn't match those of the notes in her pocket or the ones in the homebound ledger. She walked to the cookbook section as Sheila left the library.

"The cookbooks are here, Dora. What type are you looking for?"

The cookbooks spanned a wall in the corner they referred to as the "Cookbook Nook." The choices ranged from breakfast, lunch, and dinner recipes to ethnic dishes of Italian, French, and other countries to appetizers, desserts, and holiday meals.

"I need a holiday cookbook. I have several recipes, but I also like to try new ones. Are you coming to the inn tomorrow?"

"Oh, yes," Alicia said. "Thank you for inviting me. I'm looking forward to my first Thanksgiving in Cobble Cove."

After Dora left with a book on appetizers and desserts, the library was quiet for an hour except for a few unfamiliar people who sat reading or using the computer. They didn't even come to the desk. At five, an hour before closing, Edith and Rose arrived. They nodded to her and mumbled to themselves as they gazed at the holiday display books Sheila set up near the reference desk.

"Can I help you ladies?" Alicia asked.

Edith answered for both of them. "No, thank you. We were just looking for some Christmas decorating books. We like to get ideas early."

Alicia walked out from behind the desk. She was sick of sitting. "This one is nice," she suggested, pulling out a book called *Holiday Trimmings: Great Ideas for Christmas Decorating*.

"Yes," Edith agreed, taking it and browsing its pages of full-color photos. "I think this one will do." She reached in her purse and withdrew her Cobble Cove library card, a simple cardboard square handwritten with the number 77 and the library's name and logo.

"By the way, Alice, is it?"

"Alicia."

"Sorry, Alicia. Would you be interested in helping us decorate around town this year for our Christmas Fair?"

Alicia had been warned. "I think so. It sounds like fun. What would I need to do?"

"We're having a planning meeting the day after Thanksgiving at noon. "It'll be in the church. You're welcome to attend."

"I'll be there," she said, not sure what she was signing up for.

"Wonderful!" Edith put the book on the counter, and Alicia wrote it down on the day's checkout sheet along with Edith's card number.

"Have a good day," Alicia wished the cousins as they left.

"You too," Edith said. Rose just smiled and nodded. She walked next to her sister but slightly behind her. The two were mumbling as they walked out the door.

***

By the time John showed up at seven, Alicia had locked up library, put out the *'closed'* sign, eaten Sheila's leftover stew, fed the cat, and cleaned off the kitchen table. She had gone down to the reading room to wait for him, even though she knew he had a key. When she heard it in the lock, she stopped reading a book she had checked out from the mystery section and eagerly went to the door. She had been feeling lonely after the last patron, a man who had asked for a book on setting up birdfeeders, had left at 5:30, according to the clock over the reference desk that featured numbered books around its face. It was an item Sheila told her she'd picked up from a gift shop on a shopping trip a few years ago.

John smiled when he saw her, and her heart took a leap. He looked handsome in his brown corduroy jacket and jeans.

"Hey there, beautiful. How was your day? I hope Sheila wasn't too tough on you."

"No, she was fine. I wish the library was automated, but I guess a circulation system would be expensive to put in place."

John nodded. "What are you reading?" He had seen the mystery she'd chosen from a shelf.

"Nothing great. Just something to pass the time. By the way, Dora was here for some cookbooks for tomorrow and the cousins came for some holiday decorating books."

"Did they recruit you?" He grinned, displaying his dimple.

"Yep."

"I told you so."

"And everyone else did too. Do you want to see the letters?"

John had thrown his jacket over a chair and the brown plaid shirt underneath accented his chest muscles. "Yes. Please show them to me."

He followed her up the stairs to the storage room.

Alicia walked to the back of the room to the box in the far corner. She realized Sneaky was behind them, ready to scratch his makeshift post again.

"Right here," Alicia said. "See the scratch marks on the box? Sneaky's prepared to add more claw prints. You might think about getting him a real one in the future."

John laughed. "Dad's good at woodworking. I might ask him to make one. It probably would be a lot less messy than having Sneaky tear up cardboard." He walked over to the cat and gave him a quick scratch on the head. He reached into the box and withdrew the letters.

"Let's look at them over here." He took the three packages to the desk and switched on the lamp. "Have a seat, please."

Alicia sat in the desk chair while John untied the first pack. As she'd observed the night before, the letters were unopened and addressed to Miss Carol Parsons. She now realized they weren't from Mac. The Cobble Cove address they bore was for Carol Parsons c/o Madeline Parsons.

"These aren't from my dad. They're sent from different army bases by Peter's father, I think."

"Oh, my God. Pamela insisted Paul Fairmont wrote to Carol while he was in the Army, but she denied receiving any letters."

John fingered the yellow envelopes. "Are you thinking what I'm thinking?"

"I'm afraid so. Your dad told me today he worked in the post office a short time when he was young. He may have prevented the delivery of those letters because of his feelings for Carol."

"Possibly, but I want to talk to him before I jump to conclusions. Let's retie these letters and put them back."

"What about the second pack?" Those were obviously the letters written from Carol to Mac, many of which were separated from their envelopes.

"I don't want to trespass on dad's privacy by reading those, open or not."

Alicia helped John replace the letters in the scratched box. Sneaky looked on guiltily but kept his paws off the box.

"What now?" John asked when they were done.

"Well, there is something I wanted to ask you. What do you make of this?" Alicia withdrew the three notes from her pocket and lay them on the desk under the lamp.

"Hmmm," John raised his eyebrows. "Where did you get these?"

"In a homebound's books. Do you know any of them? Her name is Betty, and she's weird—hostile in fact."

John thought and then replied, "I don't think so. Even though I know most of the people in town, she doesn't sound familiar."

"But what do you think of what she wrote? Do you think it was intended for Sheila or Tina?" Her voice choked on the name. "I checked the homebound list, and Betty hasn't gotten books for several months. I thought that was odd, but Sheila said Betty forgot when she had books delivered and kept re-reading the same ones."

"Poor lady. Dad's forgetful also, and it worries me." He touched Alicia lightly on the shoulder. She felt a tingle where his fingers pressed through her sweater. "Please don't read too much into those notes. I know we writers have creative imaginations, so it's easy to make up mysteries, but I think that woman just had too much time on her hands and decided to play a prank on whoever opened those books. Unfortunately, it was you."

"Maybe you're right." Alicia threw the notes into the wastebasket next to the desk.

"Since that's solved, would you still like my company here tonight?" John turned a bit red, and Alicia wondered if he were blushing, but then he continued. "I could sleep on the couch downstairs."

Alicia knew the moment had arrived for her to ask the question that had been nagging her. "Yes. I get a little lonely all by myself here, but there's something I need to ask you, John. Maybe we can talk in the kitchen. I'll make some coffee, or tea if you prefer."

"No coffee at this hour, but tea would hit the spot." John followed her into the kitchen. She put the kettle on to boil while he selected an herbal tea from the variety Sheila stored in the cabinet. He chose peppermint while she picked the soothing chamomile vanilla to help her relax.

They sat across from each other at the small table. Alicia found a box of tea biscuits Sheila left on the counter and brought them over. John opened the box and took one. He offered a cracker to Alicia, but she declined.

"What's up?" he asked, his blue eyes quizzical.

"I don't know how to phrase this."

John reached over and took her hand. "Just say it, Ali."

She felt the buzz again. It prompted her to

continue, but she couldn't look him in the eyes. "Were you ever involved with Tina?"

John exhaled deeply. "If you're asking if I was sexually involved with her, the answer is yes. If you want to know if it went deeper than that, then it's no. I've never come close to being emotionally involved with anyone else after Jenny until I met you."

Alicia remained silent. "I already told you I saw some women after I returned to Cobble Cove. I wasn't serious about any of them. I was trying to forget, but it didn't help."

Alicia looked in his eyes and saw the truth and the pain. She pressed his warm hand. Without thinking, she let her heart take control. "Would you like to stay upstairs with me tonight, John?"

"It's about time you asked." He grinned, lightening the situation. "It will almost be as naughty as making out in the stacks." His face shadowed as he realized what she might be imagining. "No. I never did that with Tina here— downstairs or upstairs. It was always at my place. I had a small house at that time. I gave it up when Dad began having memory lapses, and I figured it would save me money and allow me to keep a better eye on him. Then, in case we started driving one another crazy, I started helping Dora at the inn for some extended weekends. It gave me and Dad some breathing space."

When he finished his explanation, Alicia stood, still holding his hand, and they walked to the bedroom. Their tea was left to cool on the counter.

***

They made love into the morning. It had been the first time since Peter, but Alicia felt no guilt. She was in love again, and it was wonderful. Her heart and mind were now in sync, knowing she'd made the right decision to turn her back on the past and start anew in this town with this man.

John turned and looked at her. She could see the love in his eyes. "We need to get some sleep." His grin was wide and affectionate. "Actually, I should go—not that Dad would notice me missing. He goes to bed early but rises at the crack of dawn. Just the same, it might be awkward his finding me up here with you when he opens the library."

Alicia smiled. "He'd be happy for us."

"I'm sure, but he's my dad, and it would make me self-conscious." He sat up. "I think I'll go home, take a short nap, and then pick us all up some breakfast like I did yesterday. When I bring it over, we can have that chat about those letters you found."

Alicia thought that was a good idea. She wanted to be in on that discussion. John kissed her goodbye, dressed, and then kissed her again. "I'll lock up when I leave. Dad should be here in, oh, gosh, two hours or so. Get some rest, Ali." His final kiss was on her forehead, light and tender.

CHAPTER 12

After John left, Alicia had trouble falling asleep. She understood John's explanation about Tina, although she still had questions about the girl. She was also confused about Mac's letters and hoped he wouldn't be offended they'd invaded his privacy when they approached him later. The main thing that kept her awake were the notes she'd found in Betty's book. She even retrieved them from the garbage and put them in her purse. John hadn't made much of them, but she had an unsettled feeling he might be wrong.

After an hour of trying to sleep with Sneaky rolled up at her feet, Alicia heard a key turning in the door followed by the sound of someone's footsteps. She checked her cell phone and saw it was only 5:30, an hour before Mac was due to arrive. However, it was possible he'd come earlier, or maybe Sheila, who was leaving on a morning flight, forgot something at the library and came back for it. Alicia threw on her robe and rushed to the top of the stairs. "Who's there?" she called.

"Mac? Sheila?" There was no reply. She waited a few breaths. The front door opened, and the footsteps retreated.

Alicia ran down the stairs, nearly falling on the hem of her robe. By the time she reached the door and looked outside into the dark morning, whoever had visited was gone. There was no sound of a car starting, so the person must've walked and disappeared into the shadows. She wasn't about to run after them. She went back inside and surveyed the library to see if anything was missing, but she theorized it couldn't have been a thief because the person who'd entered used a key. She stopped in her tracks when she saw the paper on the reading table. It was a white sheet of copy paper across which someone had typed in capital letters:

GO HOME

The door behind her creaked open, and she jumped as Mac strolled in whistling. "Sorry I frightened you. I know I'm early, but I had a hard time sleeping. I see you did too."

Alicia held the paper.

"What's that?" Mac ambled over to her. She handed it to him. Her hands were shaking. "Someone was just here and left this. I heard them come in and leave. You didn't see anyone on your way in, did you?"

Mac's face turned serious. "This looks like it was typed on our typewriter. See where the O's are nearly missing the top of their loop?" He gave the paper back to Alicia. "I've been meaning to change that ribbon forever. Sheila's wanted me to upgrade to a computer for the longest time, but I didn't think it was necessary for the work I do up in the storage room." He balanced on his cane. "When I got here, I thought you left the door unlocked by accident. I didn't see a soul except the morning birds. I wish I'd arrived a few minutes earlier. I don't know who would've done this."

Alicia took some deep breaths to help her calm down. She was almost sure she'd heard a key turn in the door, allowing the intruder to enter, but could John have forgotten to lock it on the way out? She didn't want to mention their night together to his dad, so she said, "The door was locked. I heard someone open it. Besides you, John, and Sheila, does anyone else have a key?"

Mac considered her question a moment. "The only other person I can think of is our cleaning woman, Gladys, but she only comes on Thursdays. Since that's Thanksgiving this week, she'll probably come Friday."

Another idiosyncrasy of the Cobble Cove library. At Alicia's, a custodian was on duty daily and a cleaning service at night. "Could she have tried coming today instead? Maybe she realized someone was here and left, but why would she leave a note like that?"

"She wouldn't. It doesn't make sense. Also, you were sleeping upstairs. If this really was composed on the typewriter in the storage room, they would've had to have it typed beforehand and then brought it in with them today. When John gets here with breakfast, we'll see what he makes of this. Sit down a minute and relax, Alicia. You've had a shock."

Alicia did as she was told, almost dropping onto the couch near the cookbook nook, the one John originally offered to sleep on before she'd invited him to her bed. Sneaky, who had followed her down, had already taken a spot on it, and she noted clumps of his beige fur decorated the dark upholstery. Cats tended to shed seasonally. It was fall, and he would be acquiring his winter coat soon. She wondered if anyone brushed him regularly and made a point to consider doing that in the future, if she was still around. At that moment, she had her doubts.

"Good girl. I wish I had something to offer you to drink. I can go up and make some tea."

"That's okay." She didn't want Mac making the trip with his cane. "I can wait for John."

"It'll be a while. I think John was out late last night. I'm a light sleeper, and I heard him come in during the wee hours."

Alicia felt a blush burn her cheeks. "I'll be okay. You start on your work, Mac."

"All right. I'll keep an eye on you. If you're still tired, you can go back to bed. I'll be at the reading desk."

Alicia didn't want to leave the old man alone down in the library in case the person who wrote the threatening message came back, although the note seemed aimed at her. "Thanks, but I can't sleep now. I'll feed the cat and change his litter and then come back down to wait for John. I might do some reading. I need to keep my mind off this."

Mac nodded. He had already put some books and his stamp supplies on the desk.

She wondered why Mac wasn't more concerned, but she tried to put that thought aside. There was no reason for Mac to wish her harm or want her gone. Was there?

***

When John arrived carrying bagels and spreads, he immediately sensed the atmosphere. Mac was still at the desk working, but Alicia was up and pacing.

"Hey, what's wrong?"

"Let's talk upstairs."

John's eyes fell on the typed paper Alicia had left upright on the table. "What's this?" He picked it up and frowned. "Where did this come from?"

Mac answered his son's questions. "Alicia was holding it when I came in today. It seems someone broke in and left it. Must be some prankster, but I can't imagine who."

"They didn't break in," Alicia corrected. "They used a key. I heard it turn in the lock, but they left the door open on the way out. Your dad didn't see whoever it was, even though they left only a few minutes before he arrived. I didn't hear or see a car, so they must've been on foot or parked farther away from the library."

John's frown deepened. He gripped the paper tighter. "No one else except me, Dad, and Sheila has a key."

"And Gladys," Mac added.

"Yes, but she wouldn't do something like this. Neither would any of us. Wait a minute." John's look changed. "Did Tina ever give Sheila back her key?"

"Tina's gone," Mac said. "I have no idea if she gave it back it to Sheila, but Sheila's already on her way out West, so we can't ask her."

"Does anyone have Tina's mother's number in Florida?" Alicia asked.

"Sheila would have that too," John replied. "Why would Tina come back and leave that note? I think Dad's right. This was the work of a prankster."

Alicia grew angry at how both McKinney men were taking this so casually. "Were those notes in Betty's books by the same prankster?" She forgot she hadn't told Mac about the messages she'd found going through the homebound's returns.

"What notes?" Mac asked, looking from Alicia to John.

"Alicia found some papers in the homebound return books yesterday," John said. "They said something about knowing and seeing something. It was gibberish."

"Gibberish!" Alicia didn't have a temper most of the time, but when she got mad, she exploded. She found herself close to doing that now. She tried to calm down. "What it said was *'I know what you did. I saw you with him.'*"

"Something's going on," Mac said. She couldn't look at John.

"Let's go upstairs and have some breakfast while we talk about this," John said. "I don't like it any more than you, Ali. I thought you were safe here, and I still think you are, but these messages need to be addressed. We don't have a police department here, but I can call the precinct in the next town. Tomorrow is Thanksgiving, but if you don't want to wait until Friday, I'll call today."

"No. I don't want to ruin the holiday."

John nodded. "Are you sure? We can contact Sheila on Friday and ask about Tina, but I can't see why she would return from taking care of her sick mom and do this."

Alicia agreed, but she still had unanswered questions about Tina. "Let's eat, and then we can talk."

"Sounds good. I'm starving," Mac said. Alicia had no appetite, but she had to concentrate on something else.

John laid the food out on the upstairs table and offered to stand at the counter again. Since he hadn't brought coffee this morning, Alicia plugged in the coffee maker, added a filter, and opened a can of Maxwell House.

"I overslept and didn't want to be late, so I skipped my stop at Duncan's," John explained. "I knew Sheila kept some coffee up here, anyway, but I'm sorry for the extra trouble of having to make it." Alicia felt heat rise to her cheeks recalling why John overslept.

"You did get in mighty late," his dad said, taking an 'everything' bagel and spreading it with cream cheese.

John turned bright red. Alicia tried to hide his embarrassment by changing the subject.

"Mac, there are some things we wanted to talk to you about." She decided to be blunt. "I found some of your letters in the storage room and showed them to John. We're curious about them."

Mac looked embarrassed now. "Oh, dear. I should've kept them in a more secret place, but they're water under the bridge now. Carol has been gone quite some time."

John put down the coffee mug Alicia handed him. "Dad, we can understand why you have the letters Carol wrote you, but we don't understand why you have some that were never opened and didn't look like they were written by you."

Mac's eyes clouded. He stopped chewing his bagel and slowly swallowed a piece. "I guess it's time to confess. I did something mean when I was young. Remember I told you I used to work in the post office, Alicia?"

"I do."

"I worked there when Paul mailed those letters to Carol. She hadn't given him her New York address at first because she wasn't sure where she'd be staying, and he had already gone to war. I assume he asked her for her address in one of his letters and never got a reply. I expected him to just stop writing, but he continued. I took all the letters. I'm not proud of that."

He glanced down at his half-eaten bagel. "When Paul returned, he told Carol he wrote to her at her mom's address, but she didn't believe him. Her mother denied getting any letters and, of course, she hadn't. They made up, as you know, despite my tampering with federal property." He turned to his son. "Your mother, rest in peace, never knew about Carol. I hid the letters in the storage room because I didn't want her to find them at home. Why I saved them, I don't know. I've always been somewhat of a hoarder. They're basically all I have left of Carol now." Silent tears fell down his cheeks. "Don't ask why Paul never called Carol's mother to check why Carol wasn't answering his letters or to ask for her phone number. Things were different in those days. Communication overseas was more difficult. There was no Internet, cell phones, or email. I never served in the military, but I know it got crazy out in the field and people lost touch." His tears were falling more freely now.

"I kept Paul's letters because I wanted to give them to Carol one day and explain. I almost did before the family moved away, but I was afraid it would change her opinion of me. I wanted good memories between us. I was already married to your mom by then, John, so I hid the letters and focused on my new life." Mac stood up. "If you don't mind, I'd like to get back to work now. I'll have a bite later when I take a break." His confession had clearly taken a toll on him.

"That's fine, Dad," John said. "I'll stay up here with Alicia a little while longer." He took Mac's seat as his father headed cane first down the stairs.

***

"I'm sorry," John said once Mac was gone. He tilted Alicia's chin up with his finger and looked into her eyes. "I know you're frightened about the notes, and I'm not discounting your fears. Believe me, I'm taking this seriously. For the first time since Jenny died, I think I'm in love again, and I would never forgive myself if anything happened to you."

Alicia saw the sincerity in his eyes and heard it in his voice. John let his finger drop. "I have a plan for today and tonight, if it works for you," he said, taking a few bites of his bagel and swallowing them down with coffee. "You and Dad open the library at nine. He'll help you until noon, and then I'll be back to take you to lunch. This afternoon, you'll be here by yourself, but you can call me if you need anything. I'm putting out the newspaper today, so I'll be at the office. I'll leave you that number." He paused. "Tonight, I'll stay here the whole time but—" his face was reddening again, "—if you care to spend time with me again, I'll sleep on the couch downstairs afterwards so Dad can find me there in the morning. I'll let him know I'll be staying here to keep an eye on things."

"That sounds perfect. And yes, I'd like very much to spend time with you again, Mr. McKinney."

He smiled. "I'll look forward to that." He checked his watch. "I'd better be going now. I promised Dora I'd do some cleaning at the inn this morning to get it ready for tomorrow and then I have to spend some time on my book."

"How's it going?" Alicia hadn't been able to write one word of hers.

"Actually, it's coming along well. I may even use some of the notes you found in it but take some poetic license with them."

"I just hope this isn't a real life mystery. I don't mind reading and writing them, but I'd rather not live one."

"Don't worry, Ali. After Thanksgiving, I'll take you to the closest police station, but I'm not sure what they'll think."

"Talking about police, I've been wondering what Faraday and Ramsay are doing about my case. I also need to call Gilly to wish her a happy Thanksgiving. I should do that today. She usually goes to her mom's with the boys for the holiday."

"Say hi for me. I really like her." John got up. "Okay, let's start our day." He took a card out of his pocket and handed it to her. "This is my office number in case I forget to give it to you later. I think I gave you one before, but here's an extra you can carry."

Alicia glanced down at the business card. "John McKinney, Jr., *Cobble Cove Courier*."

"Thanks, and good luck with the paper. What's the big story this month?"

"Thelma Perkins broke her shoe heel on the church steps and twisted her ankle two Sundays ago."

She laughed. As the morning sun streamed through the upstairs window and John looked at her in that dreamy special way, her fears began to fade.

CHAPTER 13

The morning passed quickly. Hardly any patrons came in, and Alicia figured they were all home getting ready for Thanksgiving. The ones that did come by, a Mrs. Quigley and a Mrs. Graham, asked for cookbooks like Dora had the day before. Mac showed her a few things, but he kept mostly to himself stamping new books and repairing those with broken bindings. She could tell he was uneasy around her after their discussion about the letters, so she avoided the topic and stuck to library business when they talked. She also managed to read some pages in the book she'd chosen off the shelf and, on her break, had a chance to call Gilly.

"I wanted to wish you and the boys a Happy Thanksgiving," she said when her friend answered the phone. "How are things going there?"

"Hectic as usual. I'm so glad Mom is cooking again this year. The house is a total mess, and I could never handle it."

"You could bake."

"I already have. I'm bringing dessert—chocolate

chip cookies, of course." Her laugh made Alicia homesick. "What are you up to, girl? Any action with hunky man?"

Alicia wondered if Gilly was psychic or just optimistic. "Well, we are, how can I say—a couple now."

Gilly's scream made her hold the phone away from her ear.

"I knew it. Is he a good lover? I bet he is."

"No comment. Has there been any other news?" She wasn't about to mention the strange, threatening messages she'd found.

Gilly paused. "I was going to call you after Thanksgiving. I heard from Detective Faraday and, by the way, he's pretty hunky himself. Too bad I saw a ring on his finger. That ugly Ramsay is probably single or divorced."

"What did Faraday say?"

"He asked about you and how you were doing and then he said they'd officially reopened Peter's case."

Alicia was stunned. "What? I thought they determined the fire wasn't connected with Peter's death."

"I don't know. Faraday said something about new evidence or another witness coming forth. He mentioned he might be contacting you soon. I gave him the library's number. I hope you don't mind."

"Of course not." Alicia's head was spinning. "I'm not at the inn right now, anyway. The library has a room upstairs I stay in at night. They even have a resident cat who sleeps with me."

She regretted relating that information when her

friend exclaimed, "Even with John there?"

"Gilly, is that all that's on your mind?"

"Has to be because I don't get any otherwise."

"I wish I could help you there, but I know there aren't many good men our age around who are available."

"Well, I'm glad you found one, honey. I have to go now. If you hear from Faraday, let me know."

"I will. Bye, Gilly, and take care. Have a great Thanksgiving."

"You too."

After she hung up the phone, she stood wondering a few moments about what new evidence Faraday might have found.

***

John arrived exactly at noon. He had a smile on his face and was carrying a large picnic basket. "How was your morning, dear?" he asked, coming over and kissing Alicia on the lips right in front of his dad.

Mac didn't comment. She was sure he'd already been apprised of their relationship.

"It's been rather slow, even for Cobble Cove."

John must've noticed something in her expression because he asked, "What's wrong? Did something else happen?"

"No, nothing." She didn't want to speak about it while he'd made plans for a nice lunch for them.

"Good, because I've booked us a spot on Cove Point for a picnic feast. I made all the sandwiches myself, and I even ordered the nice weather. It's unusually warm for this time of year, so we should take advantage of it."

She smiled, feeling better already. "Sounds wonderful." She grabbed her jacket and said goodbye to Mac.

"Have fun, you two," he said, looking up from this work. "I'll hold the fort until your return."

***

When they got to the top of Cove Point, John laid out a large plaid blanket and placed the picnic basket on it. I've even brought a bottle of champagne," he said, taking it out of the basket along with two glasses. He popped open the champagne with a bottle opener and poured them both some of the foaming liquid. "Let's make a toast."

She felt the warmth of the sun on her back and her hair lifting in the mild breeze. She could almost believe John had ordered this beautiful day before Thanksgiving. The town lay below them, all the houses, trees, and paths glittering like tiny jewels in the sun.

He handed her a glass.

"What would you like to toast to?"

"Us," he said, his eyes wide. They clinked glasses.

"To us."

John put out the sandwiches he'd wrapped in aluminum foil. "My special PB&J sandwiches for this special occasion."

She couldn't get over his playful mood, and she

started to catch it too. All her earlier fears took a back seat as they sat together in the sun eating, drinking, and enjoying one another's company.

When they finished the food and emptied their glasses, Alicia teased him she would be going back to work drunk, and he said he'd save some of the champagne for that night. Then he asked her to lay down, and he put her head in his lap and began brushing her hair with his fingers. "Ali, I don't want to spoil our day, but I've been thinking about a few things, and I need to ask you a few questions."

She was relaxed, but alert at the same time. "Of course, John. I need to tell you something too." She figured she might as well mention her discussion with Gilly."

"You go first."

"I spoke to Gilly this morning. I called to wish her and her family a nice Thanksgiving, and she mentioned she'd heard from Detective Faraday."

He was still stroking her hair. "Go on."

"Gilly said he contacted her and told her they'd officially reopened Peter's case and that they would probably be calling me after Thanksgiving."

John stopped abruptly. "I thought they determined there was no connection between what happened to Peter and the fire at your house."

"That's what I thought too, but it seems they've found some new evidence or heard from a new witness."

"How strange. I wonder what that's all about."

"John, they'll probably ask me back. When I returned to Cobble Cove, it was because I'd decided to put things behind me. Sure, I'd like to know what happened to my husband and our house, but I'm just getting settled here."

"It won't be permanent."

"That's not what I mean. I'd rather they not start digging things up again. For so long I wanted answers. Now they don't matter as much."

"Ali, you may have no choice." He exhaled a breath she hadn't realized he'd been holding. "What I thought about this morning while I was cleaning at the inn was the stuff that has been happening here might be connected to what happened to you on Long Island. It seems too strange a coincidence for things not to be connected. If we go to the police in New Paltz, they'll surely contact Faraday and Ramsay. What I suggest is we talk some stuff over and try to figure out what's going on ourselves first."

Alicia sat up and faced him. "John, I don't want to play amateur detectives. It could be dangerous."

"Hear me out a second, Ali. I'm not saying we become Nick and Nora or another mystery solving couple. What I'm saying is we try to sort some of this out together. I think we should start with Peter."

"Okay. What do you want to know about him?"

"The police asked you this before, but can you think of anyone who would have anything against Peter, you, or both of you?"

"No. Even though he wasn't talking to his sister, you saw Pamela. She has everything she wants, and she looked genuinely surprised when we told her about his death."

"Some people are good actors, but I agree. I can't see her motive. Did Peter owe anyone money?"

"I don't think so. He handled our finances. I was never good with math."

"So, you're not sure?"

"I took in the mail most of the time, and I never saw anything from debt collectors."

"I'm talking personal here. People who wouldn't send bills."

"I still don't think so, and yes, the police did ask me about our financial situation."

"Okay," John said, changing track. "I hope I can be delicate here. Did you ever suspect Peter of cheating?"

Alicia let out a halfhearted laugh. "That's not so delicate, but neither were the police. Peter traveled a lot. He took business trips without me and, as you know, his job itself involved visiting different libraries around the tristate area to sell products. That's how we met."

John nodded. "I'm trying to cover all bases here. Did you ever see or hear anything that might indicate he was involved with another woman?"

"No, but he was very private. Looking back, I can say I never had a feeling, though. Women have intuition about these things. I didn't. Maybe I wasn't looking. Maybe I trusted him too much, but I never saw lipstick on his collar or any woman's card in his pants when I laundered them."

"What about old girlfriends? Did he have any?"

"A few. He talked about one, but she was married and lived in another state."

"Hmm. Married doesn't always count, and neither do locations in this digital age. Did they keep in touch through email, Facebook chat, or Messenger?"

"I doubt it. John didn't even use Facebook that I know of. I have no idea who he emailed."

"Are you on Facebook?"

"Yes, but I use it for work. I'm not on it often."

"Doesn't matter. Someone could find you. Are you strict about the friendship requests you accept? Most people aren't."

"I try to be." Alicia was impressed by John's thoroughness. He would make a good lawyer or a detective if he wanted to change careers.

"Were you connected with Peter on Facebook?"

"No. Like I said, I don't think he had an account."

"I can check that out later." John paused. "Did he exhibit any strange behavior before the accident? Did anything happen to him or you that seemed odd around that time?"

Alicia thought back. "There were a few things I told the police about. I don't think they made much of them."

"Tell me."

"About two weeks before his accident, Peter came home very late. He was tipsy. I think he was drunk."

"Was he a drinker?"

"No. That's why I found it strange. I asked him what was wrong. He acted angry. He said it was just some problems at work. He went in his bedroom and fell asleep. The next day, he seemed fine."

"He had his own bedroom?" John looked surprised.

"Peter liked to stay up pretty late, and I snore in my sleep sometimes. I don't know if you've noticed?"

"No, but go on," he prompted.

"We both agreed separate bedrooms would be okay. He didn't spend much time in his. He visited with me…you know."

John nodded. "I understand. If my questions are too personal, just tell me. During those two weeks, I guess they were in April or early May…I think you said his accident was in May…did you—" he paused "—how can I put it?"

"Had our sex life changed? No. It was good. It was regular. When he returned from being away, we picked right up. He seemed to miss me."

John changed the subject. "You said Peter had been jogging to work that day, so I assume he worked nearby, but you also told me he traveled a lot."

"He had an office. All the company reps have one. A few of them may have shared the same one, I don't know. I never visited him at work, but I knew his company's building was close to our home and may have been why he was interested in our house when we were shopping for a home. The company paid his travel expenses and even gave him a company car when he went to tradeshows and various libraries to showcase new products or support them with ones they already owned. He saved a lot by being able to walk or jog to the office. That's why we only had one car. If the weather was especially bad, I'd drive him to work or he'd get a ride with a co-worker."

"I see." John had his "Thinker" look on, concentrated brows, straight lips. "Besides Peter acting mad and getting drunk two weeks before, what other strange things happened?"

"I fell. I told the police this too. A few days before the accident, I was going downstairs to check something I thought I heard in the basement. I don't know how it happened, but I ended up at the foot of the stairs. My shoe must've caught on something. Luckily, I wasn't injured."

"What time did it happen? Was Peter home?"

"No. It was a Friday during the day. I was home because I sometimes had Fridays off when I worked Saturdays at the library. I was also off the morning Peter was killed the following Wednesday because I worked a later shift that day."

"What did you think you heard in the basement?"

"I'm not sure. I might've thought it was a mouse. We didn't have a cat, so that was a possibility."

"Did you or Peter check afterwards to see if there was something on the steps that caught your shoe?"

"I didn't tell him. I was fine. I saw no need."

John nodded. "Can I ask another personal question?"

Alicia shook her head. "Why stop now?"

John laughed. "Sorry, honey. I promise this is it. Why did you guys never have kids? Did either of you have any problems in that area?"

"We didn't have any problems, not that I know of. Peter just didn't want children. We decided it was probably best since we both had careers. I think his home life had an impact on him, and he felt he wouldn't make a good dad. I'm sure that wasn't true, but I couldn't change his mind."

"So you wanted kids?"

"I thought that was the last question."

"Give me a break, Ali. That was part of the last."

"Okay. I think every woman wants a child. We argued about it early in our marriage, but I gave up eventually. I figured we had a good life without children. I saw what Gilly was going through with three boys and a man who deserted her."

John looked at Alicia with something like pity and then he glanced at this watch. "Ali, it's almost time to get back. I hope you enjoyed the lunch despite my interrogation."

"I did. Thank you, John. I know you're trying to help." As she spoke those words, she realized her mood had soured. Maybe it was because John's questions had her looking back at things she never should have ignored.

She got up. "One thing, John. Do we have a quick minute to stop by Betty's, the homebound's, house? I want to ask her about the notes I found."

"From what I heard, she's not an easy person to talk to, but sure, I'll go with you."

Alicia recalled the route Sheila had taken to Betty's house, and they arrived there in a few minutes.

When they came upon the small dark house, John said, "Are you sure that's it?"

"Positive." There was no mistaking the gloomy residence.

"That's a coincidence."

"What is?"

John was eyeing the house next door. Alicia hadn't noticed it on the previous visit. It was also small but looked more like a cottage. It was painted white and had a few wildflowers around its gated path. "That's the place I rented a few years ago."

"What?" Alicia was shocked. "You said you didn't know Betty."

"I only stayed there to sleep."

Alicia remembered he'd brought Tina there too. It made her think of the second part of Betty's notes, "I saw you with him." Was the 'him' John? She tried to put that thought out of her mind for the time being. "Is anyone staying there now?"

"Doesn't look like it." The house seemed closed up, the windows shuttered like Betty's.

"Who rented the place after you left?"

"I have no idea. Dad might know, though."

"Why would Mac know?"

John laughed. "It's Mac's rental. Sorry I didn't mention that before. Dad takes care of some of the real estate in Cobble Cove."

This was news to her. "Your dad seems to be a jack-of-all-trades."

"I guess. For years he strived to live up to my Grandpa Kurt's image." He started up Betty's path. "Shall we talk to that homebound lady now?"

Alicia had to knock on the door several times before she saw a dark shadow peering through the closed curtain. Finally, Betty opened the door. "You again? What do ya want?"

"Sorry to disturb you," Alicia said, trying to be civil. "I had some questions about the books you returned yesterday."

John stood within range of the old woman, but she didn't acknowledge him. If he was the man she mentioned in her notes, Alicia assumed she might say something, but maybe not.

"Books? Oh, those awful ones. These are no better, if you want them back."

Alicia was surprised Betty had already finished them because Sheila told her the woman had trouble recalling the books she read and ended up rereading them. It was possible Betty had skimmed the back pages or parts of the books and already formed an opinion about them.

"You can keep them for now, but I was just curious about some notes I found in them. I was wondering if you left them in the books by accident." Alicia handed over the three papers still in her jacket pocket. She waited for a reaction, but the woman didn't even look at them.

"I know nothing about notes," she said, but there was something in her voice that indicated otherwise. Her tone was high-pitched and echoed with guilt.

John put an arm out to Alicia. "Let's go, Ali." Was he rushing her because the woman might identify him if they stayed longer? Alicia didn't want to believe that, but she couldn't leave without more information. She tried another tactic. "Betty, do you know who's living next door to you now?"

"No one lives there," Betty said. "He's gone, and good riddance to him. Making all that noise with her." She put hands over her ears as if she still heard the two people interacting. *Shouting at one another or making love?* Alicia wondered.

"Who?" Alicia asked, but John still had his arm

on hers urging her to leave.

"What business is it of yours?" Betty's eyes grew small and angry. "You should go home. Go, go, go!" she screamed and then slammed the door.

Alicia was startled. She knew there was no way the old woman could've gotten into the library, typed a note to her, and left it there yesterday morning. However, Betty's words seemed as threatening as the typed message she'd received.

"C'mon, Ali. That old woman is crazy. Let's get out of here."

Reluctantly, she allowed John to lead her back to the library, where Mac was whistling behind the reference desk. When they entered, he said, "Welcome back. You had a call earlier, Alicia."

A call? Could Faraday have changed his mind and decided to interrupt her Thanksgiving, or was Gilly calling back? No one else had her number in Cobble Cove.

Mac handed her the name and number of the caller. It was indeed Faraday. Her fingers trembled as she dialed his line.

"Faraday here."

"Detective Faraday, it's Alicia Fairmont returning your call."

John stood there listening, his hands in his pockets. Mac had gone somewhere to finish shelving books.

"Ms. Fairmont. I'm sorry to bother you right before Thanksgiving, but there's been a breakthrough on your case."

Alicia didn't realize she had a case. She wasn't about to tell him she had spoken with Gilly and was expecting his call after the holiday. She waited for him to continue. John remained standing by her side, but he backed up to give her a little privacy.

"I don't like using the telephone to deliver confidential information, but the reason I called is I need you to come back here as soon as possible. I'm off tomorrow, thank goodness, or my wife would kill me. She needs me to carve the turkey. Can you come on Friday?"

"I don't know." She looked at John. *Would he accompany her back?* "How long do you need me?"

"It depends, but it shouldn't take long. An overnight should be sufficient."

"Hold on." She signaled to John and covered the receiver. "Faraday wants to know if I can go back to Long Island on Friday to see him. He's found something related to the case."

"I'll come with you," John said immediately. "I'm finishing the newspaper this afternoon, so I'll have time."

Alicia picked up the receiver again. "I'll be there," she said. "Thank you."

***

The afternoon was quiet, but Alicia couldn't stop all the questions and concerns circling her mind. What did Faraday need to tell her that she had to see him in person? Was John the man Betty saw with a woman despite the fact she hadn't seemed to recognize him? Was that woman Tina? Were all the signs leading up to Peter's death signals she shouldn't have ignored? She sat behind the reference desk after Mac and John left and couldn't concentrate on her work. She halfheartedly helped the few patrons who came in, pointing them in the directions of the books they requested instead of getting up to help, breaking one of the cardinal rules of good librarianship.

By the time she closed the library, it was only her and Sneaky, who was perched on the window seat in the reading area looking out on the early darkness. She knew John would be arriving soon, so after she locked up, she called Sneaky upstairs with her and fed him dinner. The cat was now responding when she called his name. They'd gotten pretty close. She used to tease Gilly about the way she talked to her dog, but Alicia now found herself in conversation with Sneaky.

"So, boy," she said as she opened his can of Friskies Chicken in Broth. "What do you think of all these mysteries? Mac will probably have to feed you while I'm away Friday night, but I'll be sure to bring you some leftover turkey from Dora's tomorrow." The cat looked up at her with wide blue eyes. She put the food down and he ran to it.

A few minutes later, John unlocked the door and called out to her. "Alicia? Are you upstairs?"

She hesitated a minute, wondering if things would be strained between them after their earlier conversation and some of the questions she still had. Her concerns were alleviated when she went downstairs. John was holding a bouquet of beautiful fall flowers, bright orange and yellow mums interspersed with yellow roses and baby's breath.

"For you," he said, handing her the bouquet, "to

cheer you up."

Her heart melted. "Oh, John. Thank you. Is there a vase around here? I can put them out for patrons to admire."

He smiled. "Forget the patrons. Bring them upstairs. I'm sorry they may not last until we get back, but you can enjoy them tonight and tomorrow. I borrowed a vase from Dora." He turned around and picked up the wide bottomed, clear container he had left on the table behind him. "I used to always bring flowers home to my wife, so I know it's nice to provide a vase. Dora said you can keep it as long as you like."

"I'll have to thank her tomorrow."

John followed her as she took the vase and flowers upstairs, cut the bottoms of the stems with a scissor from the kitchen drawer, added some fresh water, and arranged the flowers inside. She brought them to the bedroom and placed them on the bureau.

"Beautiful," she said, admiring them.

"Like you." His arms closed around her. "Now would you like to go to dinner? I know a nice place."

Alicia quickly agreed. She was starving.

***

They ate at an Italian Bistro named Giovanni's in a town a few miles away. They drove in John's seldom used blue pickup. The restaurant featured murals of gondolas on its light green walls and candles on the table. Waiters dressed as gondoliers served heaping bowls of pasta while singing. It was corny, but Alicia loved it. She began to relax. "Where did you find this place?"

"I took Jenny here for one of our anniversaries. It was fun." She noticed he no longer spoke with pain when mentioning his dead wife. She hoped she was the reason.

After they finished their meal of a family-style lasagna they shared along with some red wine and fresh warm Italian bread, John looked across the table at her. "Ready for dessert?"

Alicia picked up the dessert menu. "I think I'm too full, but I'd love to try a piece of the Napoleon."

"Then I'll take the cheesecake." He signaled the waiter.

Alicia was glad neither of them brought up any of the stuff they were worrying about during dinner but had spent the time together in pleasant conversation. She found John witty and well-versed in many of her interests. He had read many of her favorite books from the classics to popular mysteries and literary novels. They also spoke of writing and each of their own methods for overcoming writer's block, editing their drafts, and creating plots and characters.

As their talk grew more personal, John spoke of his parents. In his eyes, she saw the love and pride he had for his father and the deep loss he'd suffered when his kind, nurturing mother passed away. She told him about growing up with devoted but somewhat stifling parents and her struggle for independence as a sheltered, overprotected child until she left the nest in her late twenties. She didn't mention Peter, and neither did John say anything about Jenny.

When they returned to the library, she asked him, "Do you think we should check to see if anyone left more notes?"

John switched on the lights. "Let's not get paranoid over this, Alicia. I know that's easier said than done."

Alicia couldn't help but look around the library. Everything seemed in place. She noticed Sneaky curled up in his bed under the local history books.

John saw her scanning the room and added, "I honestly can't imagine how someone could get in here, use the typewriter, and leave messages. Maybe we'll get to the bottom of this when we speak to Sheila on Friday. We can still call from Long Island."

Alicia nodded. "I'll miss the Christmas Fair decorating meeting Edith invited me to at church."

"Don't worry about that. Sheila's missing it too. I'm sure they'll catch you up and find some task for you. Those ladies love to assign jobs to people. By the way," he took a paper out of his jacket pocket before hanging it on the coat rack in the library foyer, "I meant to show this to you at dinner."

Alicia shook off her jacket. He exchanged it for the paper. It was the December edition of the *Cobble Cove Courier*.

"I'm proud to say it's a little early this month, but I didn't want to work on it over Thanksgiving."

They walked to the reading room, where she unfolded the paper and began reading. Sure enough, the front page story was Mrs. Carlisle falling outside church and twisting her ankle. Next to it was a photo of the twins holding holiday wreaths with the caption:

Edith and Rose Carver, members of the Cobble Cove Christmas Fair Committee, Organize the First Holiday Planning Meeting.

Below the photo were the date and details of the meeting.

"Who takes your photos?" Alicia asked.

"I do. That one's actually from last year. I keep a file of stock photos on hand."

She turned the paper over and read the other side. Most of it was full of ads. One of them was for Wilma at Cobble Cove Beauty, and she immediately felt guilty at missing her appointment again. "I have to get to the salon soon. I keep promising poor Wilma I'll show up for an appointment."

"I think you're lovely enough," John said. "When you're done reading that rag, I'll meet you upstairs."

She put down the paper. "I'm pretty much finished, and I'd say it's much better than a rag, considering it has a staff of one."

"You got that right, Ali. I'm editor-in-chief, publisher, and printer all in the same handsome body." He laughed as she tapped his arm.

"And I mustn't forget how modest you are, either."

"Modest and impatient. Are you joining me?" He sounded like an eager little boy.

"Yes, Mr. McKinney. I think I will."

CHAPTER 14

Their lovemaking was passionate, yet gentle. They fell asleep afterwards wrapped in each other's arms. Alicia woke around midnight. John was sitting up, looking down at her. "Did I wake you?"

"No. I was dreaming, but I can't recall about what."

"I hope about us." John smiled. "I hate to do this, but I'm going to head downstairs. I've been sleeping, but I've also kept an ear out for intruders. I'm sure it's safe, but I also want to be down there when Dad arrives. I know that sounds silly for a grown man, but it would be awkward for me, even though I've spoken to him about us."

"You have?"

"Yes, and he said he already knew. I guess it's obvious." He bent down and kissed her lightly on the lips. "Let me go before I won't be able to leave. Tomorrow, we have a Thanksgiving meal at the inn and the library is closed, but Dad said he still wanted to get here early to finish up some work. I can't argue with him. Dora wants us at the inn by noon. She's another morning person and she'll have the turkey in the oven early."

Alicia watched John get out of bed, marveling at his strong body and lean muscles. Sneaky, knowing there was now room for him, jumped up next to her.

"You already have someone to replace me."

"He probably just wants to be fed."

The Siamese purred and meowed as she petted him. "I left out enough dry food for you overnight, Mister. Now let me sleep, please."

John laughed. "You can snuggle Mr. Sneaky while I go down and keep guard to protect you. Dad promised to bring breakfast this morning, and I think he's preparing it himself."

Alicia had a hard time going back to sleep after John went downstairs. After an hour or so, she decided to get up and read more of the book she'd started. She hadn't gotten far, but she liked the characters and thought the story would be interesting once she delved deeper into it. She turned on the lamp next to the bed. Nudging Sneaky away from where he lay against her, she reached for her book. Her fingers touched it, but the book was a bit too far from her grasp. It fell to the floor. "Darn it!"

She stood in her bare feet and checked under the bed where it probably landed. Sneaky jumped up, circling her legs. "It's not breakfast time yet, cat. I just dropped my book." Her cell phone read one a.m. She wondered if John was asleep or up watching the door.

She peered under the bed where Sneaky had scuttled. It was dark, and the bed lamp didn't illuminate much except the cat's blue eyes, gleaming as if he'd found a mouse. She didn't want to consider that, but she was afraid to put her hand under the bed nonetheless. Should she go wake John and ask for his help? His arms were definitely longer. No, if she did that, he would probably end up staying or consider her too much of a damsel in distress for his taste. She wouldn't mind his company or his thinking her a weak woman, but she wanted to get some rest at least for a few more hours. Then she remembered the flashlight kept in the drawer of the nightstand where she also kept her writing notebook. She took it out and shone it under the bed. She finally saw her book within arm's grasp. She also noticed another book next to it. She decided to pull them both out. Maybe the other book was from the library and might be more interesting than the one she was reading.

As she pulled the books out, Sneaky jumped back up on the bed. She put both books down next to him, pulled the bedcover over, and slipped in. She fluffed up her pillow behind her and gathered the books in her lap. When she opened the book she'd found, she realized it wasn't a library book. It was a diary. Her breath caught as she saw the large flourished handwriting on the front page that matched the entries in the homebound ledger.

Diary of Tina Deerborn

Her heart started to race. This was the diary of the woman who preceded her as librarian here nearly two years ago. She must've forgotten the diary in her rush to get to her sick mother in Florida. Alicia closed the diary, only to reopen it seconds later. Although she knew she shouldn't impinge on this woman's privacy, something compelled her to read the first page. The entries were short and irregular, about a month apart. Illustrations of flowers, hearts, and other squiggles appeared in the margins. Clearly, Tina had been more artistic than literary.

Monday, December 2, 2013
Okay, this is my first shot at diary writing. I don't even know why I'm starting, but I like to try new things. Maybe this is a good time to begin with my new job in Cobble Cove. I can't believe she hired me without any references. I had a bunch prepared just in case, along with a phony diploma. It's amazing how much you can fake these days. People like her are just too trusting.

Friday, January 10, 2014
Wow! I can't believe I've been here a whole month. It's so booooorrrring. The only thing that excites me is seeing him. I know he's much older, but who cares. I think he can give me what I need in case things don't go the way I hope.

Friday, February 14
Oh, how sweet. This has to be recorded. He gave me the most beautiful flowers for Valentine's Day. I think he's fallen for me.

Wednesday, March 19
He's found a place for us. It's a cute little cottage. We can meet there in private away from that stuffy library.

Alicia paused before she turned the page to the next entry. Should she continue? It seemed Tina hadn't been a library graduate after all, so why had she answered the ad Sheila placed? She also wondered who the 'he' was that she referred to in the diary. Could the man who gave her flowers be John? But when she said the man who excited her was much older than she, Alicia pondered if it could possibly be Mac. Could both father and son have fallen for this young woman? Alicia had to keep reading to see if the rest of these vague entries would give her any answers.

The next page started several months later.

Saturday, August 30
I almost forgot about this diary. It's not that I haven't had time to write. This town is so boooring. I can hardly believe I'm still here, but I think I'm finally making headway. When he isn't around, I go to our love nest. It's nice to

get away from the library and into the world I create. The only downside to going there is seeing that nosy woman who hides in her house, the lady she makes me deliver books to. She's nosy and lazy too. I see her peering out of her window at us. I don't care that she hates the books I select as long as she keeps her mouth shut.

Friday, October 31
I don't know how much longer I can last here. I'm going crazy with boredom. They both dressed up for Halloween, even tried putting the cat and dog in a costume. I'm glad Sneaky clawed her when she did that. His stupid dog just looked silly. The only part I enjoyed was the candy she put out.

Thursday, December 25
Christmas. Those crazy cousins had me decorate the library with her. I try to stay away from there as much as I can now. He's given me a present. I didn't have anything for him, so I just gave him my photo. I'm sure he'll treasure it.

I've thought of a new idea for the New

Year, but it will take a while to plan.

Saturday, February 14, 2015
No flowers from him. I think he's sick of me, but I don't mind. I'm even sicker of him and this nowhere town. He doesn't even ask me to the love cottage much anymore. It's hard to see him every day and hide my disgust.

There was one more page of entries. Alicia still had no idea what Tina was describing, but the entries were now more often, only days apart.

Sunday, April 26
He finally invited me to the love cottage. I was surprised. I thought he was through with me, and I wouldn't care if he was. But he only asked me to the cottage to tell me he was going away for a while. I really didn't care, and our goodbye was not tender at all. I think that old lady next door heard us. She better mind her own business.

Monday, May 4
He's back, but I'm ending it with him. I have my chance now and am going to take it.

Friday, May 8
It didn't work, but it's made me face the facts now.

Tuesday, May 12
I'm leaving. I'll tell her my mom's sick. Will he miss me? I won't miss him or this boring library and town. I can do much better. If my plan works, it'll all be worth it.

Wednesday, May 13
I told her, and I feel no regret.

Thursday, May 14
I asked him to meet me at the cottage. I'm almost packed. Everything's in the car except a few things and this diary. No sense in writing anymore. It's over, but if things go well today, everything will work out fine. If not, I have a backup plan.

Alicia put down the diary. How strange. Should she share this with John? He was obviously in it, although his name wasn't mentioned directly. She had to trust her intuition and not say anything about it yet. She put the book on top of her nightstand with her library book and went back to bed. She knew it would be even harder to sleep now. Maybe, in the light of day, she could find a way to decipher the strange writing without showing it to anyone. They had planned to call Sheila for Tina's mother's number on Friday. If they contacted her and Tina was indeed in Florida, then the diary was likely a creative writing exercise and not a true journal. Otherwise, where was Tina? Who were the he's and she's she wrote so angrily about? Only Sheila, who was almost definitely the she, and Betty were clearly identified. John had persuaded Alicia not to push Betty for information. Why? To protect Alicia, himself, or maybe even his father? How was all this tied to Peter's death and their house fire? She noticed Tina's last entry was the day after Peter's accident. What did that mean?

"Oh, Sneaky," she said, laying back down with the cat. "We have to figure this out." In her heart, she almost didn't want to for fear of what she might find.

***

True to his word, Mac brought a homemade breakfast. He arrived at seven. Alicia was already dressed and had joined John downstairs. She resolved to put what she'd read in the diary behind her for the time being and think about it after Thanksgiving.

"Okay, kids," Mac greeted them with a large basket, the same one John used for their picnic. "I have some goodies for us, but I know Dora is making a feast, so I didn't go all out."

Alicia was amazed how the old man balanced the basket in one hand and his cane in the other. John rushed to take the food as soon as his father walked in.

"Wow! This is heavy. Let me take it upstairs, and then we can see just how not all out you went, Dad." John winked at Alicia.

In the upstairs kitchen, Alicia helped John lay out the contents of the basket. There were warm biscuits and cinnamon rolls fresh from the oven and some assorted spreads.

"I'll put on the coffee," Alicia said. "This sure looks good, Mac."

"My pleasure. I have to admit the biscuits and rolls were from Pillsbury, but I did the baking, and the spreads are my homemade preserves."

As the coffee perked and she sat across from the old man, Alicia couldn't help think of the line in Tina's diary, *"I know he's much older, but who cares..."* She pushed that thought aside as she bit into a warm biscuit.

John poured the coffee. "It was quiet here last night, Dad. I doubt we'll be getting any further pranks, but I think I should stay again tonight. Alicia and I are leaving early tomorrow morning, anyway."

Mac was eating a cinnamon roll. "That sounds like a safe plan. I'll be able to take care of the library on Friday and Saturday. It'll probably be quiet over the Thanksgiving weekend. If we don't have many patrons on Saturday, I'll close."

John nodded. "We'll be back Saturday morning. If you decide to stay open, Alicia can take the afternoon shift if she's up to it."

"No talking business today," Alicia told the men.

224

"It's Thanksgiving, and I'm so thankful to have met you both." She hoped there was sincerity in her voice because she really meant it, and she wouldn't be able to bear either one of them being the 'he' in Tina's diary, although she already knew John had been involved with Tina.

"We are also very thankful you came into our lives," John said, bending down and kissing her cheek.

CHAPTER 15

Thanksgiving was a wonderful day. Dora decorated the inn with cardboard cut-out turkeys, cornucopias, and pumpkins. She asked John to move a dining table from downstairs to the breakfast nook. The long table seated all of them—Dora, Charlie, Mac, John, and Alicia. It also fit the huge turkey, a twenty-five pounder on a platter, and all the trimmings; chestnuts, green beans almandine, marshmallow sweet potatoes, creamy mashed potatoes, homemade stuffing with raisins, corn on the cob, two types of cranberry sauce, and steaming brown turkey gravy.

Alicia was overwhelmed. Since she had no family and Peter was estranged from his, their Thanksgivings normally took place either at a restaurant or at home with a small turkey breast she served up with some store bought sides. This family meal was amazing, and she enjoyed the food as much as she did the company, although she noticed Mac was unusually quiet. She teased John about his preference for plain cranberry sauce while she preferred the berried. He countered with mock criticism for the way she ate corn on the cob, slicing the kernels off with a knife instead of biting them off the cob.

When Dora wheeled out the desserts after everyone was stuffed and swore they couldn't eat another bite, all eyes widened. Dora had baked several pies—apple, pumpkin, and Alicia's favorite from the time she and Peter traveled to the Amish country in Pennsylvania—shoofly pie.

John patted his stomach. "I think I've gained ten pounds," he groaned.

"Is that shoofly pie?" Alicia asked, already knowing the answer.

"Sure is. I got the recipe from a friend I met on a tour in Lancaster once, and I brought it home with me. I make it as a special for inn guests once in a while and on holidays."

Despite everyone's protests of being full, all three pies were consumed, the men doing most of the honors.

After dinner, John, Mac, and Charlie went into the parlor and talked sports. Dora brought out a small TV so they could watch the game. Alicia stayed in the kitchen helping her clean up.

"You know," Dora said as she brought some dirty dishes to the sink to wash, "you're still welcome here anytime. I'm practically guest free right now, so there's lots of room."

"Thank you, but I'm fine at the library." She wondered if Charlie was staying at the inn. Dora looked different, happier. There was a pinkness to her cheeks.

Dora's next words answered Alicia's unspoken question. "If you ever change your mind, Charlie and I wouldn't object at all. I won't need John as much since Charlie is here, although his back gives him problems from time to time. I asked John to do the fall bulb planting, but I guess he never got around to it. It might be too late now."

"Are you ladies gossiping about me? I heard my name." John stood in the doorway.

"I was just telling Alicia I asked you to plant some bulbs a few weeks ago, but I forgot to remind you. The weather is still nice. Do you think you'd have some time this weekend?"

"I don't have plans for Sunday. I could get to it then. Maybe Ali can assist me."

Alicia recalled her small garden at home. Sadness washed over her at the memory of the burned out shell of her house. She pushed it away. This day had been too nice to ruin it with bad memories. "I'd love that."

"Wonderful!" Dora exclaimed. "I'm going to another play with Charlie on Sunday, but I can leave the bags of bulbs on the porch. You can come any time to plant them. I'll also leave out my gardening gloves and tools for you."

Alicia noticed Dora looked tired. She signaled John. "I think we should get going now. I have to finish packing for tomorrow."

They thanked their hostess and praised her delicious food. Alicia asked for a goody bag for Sneaky, but Dora had already prepared one. "I double checked for bones," she assured Alicia.

Mac told them he would find his way back home

as soon as he was able to move, and the walk would do him good.

John had driven to the inn in his pickup, and he groaned as he got in, struggling with his seat belt. "Looks like I put on so much weight I can hardly get this belt around me."

Alicia laughed, but she was having problems with her belt too. "I'd say it was worth it. Dora's a good cook."

"Now you know why I hang around the inn so much." He grinned. "I doubt either of us will want dinner tonight, but if we're in the mood for a snack, I put aside some biscuits and cinnamon rolls that were left from this morning."

When they got to the library, John went in first, switching on the lights in the main room and over the stacks. He scanned the entry hall and reading room. Alicia followed him, looking for any notes or signs of an intruder.

"All's clear to me," John said.

Sneaky appeared, and Alicia took him upstairs to feed him the turkey leftovers.

John followed them. "I'm pretty full," he said, "but I know some exercise that might burn off a few of the calories we just ingested."

He took Alicia's hand and led her to the bedroom. When she stepped in the door, she saw his flowers on the bureau and was reminded of the flowers Tina had written about in her diary. John saw her expression change.

"What's wrong, Ali?" He dropped her hand. "I thought those flowers made you happy."

She turned to him. "John, I know you said you

always gave your wife flowers, but when Tina was here, did you give her any?"

John became angry. "Why are you asking me this, Ali? I told you my feelings for Tina were nothing like the ones I have for you. If you're jealous of a woman you never met, that says something about the trust you have in me. I believe in honesty in relationships, so I'll answer your question. I gave Tina flowers the first Valentine's Day she was here because she was having trouble adjusting to the library and this town. I wanted to cheer her up."

"Sorry, John." Alicia knew she'd have to tell him about the diary now. "You're absolutely right about honesty and trust. I have some problems in that area. I either trust too much or not enough. I can't seem to sense when to believe someone and when to have doubts about them. The reason I asked you about the flowers is I found Tina's diary this morning under my bed. She must've forgotten it. It's not clearly written. It speaks about a 'he' who is much older but who she says may give her what she wants."

John's temper calmed as his curiosity increased. "A girl her age would refer to me as a much older man. She was twenty-five, almost young enough to be my daughter. Can I see the diary?"

Alicia checked the top of her nightstand, but all that was on it was the library book she'd been reading. "It's gone," she gasped. "I'm sure I put it on top of the nightstand." She checked the bureau drawers just in case, and John helped her look elsewhere in the room.

"Someone's been here and taken it," she said after neither of them found it.

"Don't jump to conclusions, Ali. Is anything else out of place or missing?"

"No. I don't think so. I was getting some stuff ready to pack, which I still have to do, but everything looks the same."

"Come sit here and tell me more about what the diary said," John implored, taking a seat on the bed and patting the area next to him.

Alicia joined him. "It was strange. There were only a few entries. She mentioned Sheila, but called her 'she.' Tina said she had a phony library degree and was surprised Sheila didn't even ask her for references. Why would she apply for the job knowing she wasn't qualified?"

John sighed. "Ali, I know in the city and on Long Island having a master's degree in Library Science is required, but here in Cobble Cove, anyone can pretty much run a library. I guess Sheila needed someone, and Tina was the only one who answered the ad. Why she answered it, I have no idea."

"There's more, John. It sounds as though Tina didn't go home to her mother. She may even be the one playing these tricks on us."

"I doubt that, but maybe we'll find out more after we talk to Sheila tomorrow."

"One other thing," Alicia hesitated to mention it, "because of the way Tina wrote the entries, do you think it's possible she was referring to Mac instead of you as the older man?"

"Dad? Nah. It's true he's been lonely since Mom

died, but he wouldn't fancy a fling with someone as young as Tina. Remember, he still seems to be carrying a torch for Carol. It's not that he didn't love my mom, but some men keep a special place in their heart for their first loves. I know Jenny will always be in mine, but it takes a special woman to share that space. You're that woman." He leaned over and kissed her. "Let's stop questioning for now and wait for some answers. I'm curious as to what Faraday has dug up back on the Island. I don't know if any of that is connected with the stuff happening here, but I wouldn't put too much weight into a young woman's diary."

Alicia agreed with him for the time being. She let him gently lower her onto her back as he kissed her more urgently.

***

The next day, Alicia finished packing her overnight bag and showered and dressed before John woke. She fed the cat and changed his litter box. Then she heated some of the leftover biscuits and cinnamon rolls in the microwave and made coffee. She brought the food on a tray into the bedroom. "Wake up, sleepyhead."

He murmured and opened his eyes. "Good morning, sweetheart. Aren't I supposed to bring you breakfast in bed?"

She laughed. "Next time, it's your turn."

John eyed her packed overnight bag by the door. "Looks like you're all set. I still have to drop by Dad's to grab my stuff."

"No problem. We should say goodbye to him before we leave. I took care of Sneaky, so he'll be fine until tonight."

The cat, as if hearing his name, jumped up on the bed and pawed a piece of biscuit. "He's still hungry."

Alicia picked up the cat and placed him on the floor. "Cats are always hungry. Don't worry, Sneaky. We'll only be gone for a day."

After their light breakfast, John dressed, and they locked up the library. It was only six a.m., but John said Mac would be up already. He was right. The old man was waiting for them when they pulled up.

"Good morning, son, Alicia. I've just put on some eggs. Would you like some?"

"No thanks, Dad. We already had some of your food from yesterday. I'm just going to get some stuff together and throw it in a bag for our trip."

While John packed, Mac invited Alicia to sit in the living room. The dog leaped up at her. When Mac tried to pull him away, Alicia stopped him. "Fido is fine. He remembers me." She petted the dog's head, and he shook it in pleasure.

John returned with a duffel bag. "Okay, all set. Thanks, Dad." He joined Alicia petting the dog. "Good boy. I'll be back soon."

Alicia told Mac that Sneaky was taken care of until that night.

"Don't worry. I'll feed him when I close the library and first thing tomorrow morning. I may stay over there tonight."

"Good idea," John said, but Alicia was thinking about the intruder who had twice been at the library.

"You might want to come home. Fido is here."

Mac seemed to read her mind, a trait he may have passed on to his son. "I would take him with me, but I don't think Sneaky would like that. He'll be all right on his own. So will I."

Alicia knew it was useless to argue with him, and John was nudging her out the door. "I want us to avoid morning rush hour traffic."

They waved goodbye to Mac and Fido.

CHAPTER 16

They drove in silence except for the light rock playing on John's car stereo. Alicia was lost in her thoughts, wondering what Faraday had to tell her and what Tina's diary entries meant.

John broke the quiet between them once they were on the Long Island Expressway. "I know you're worried, Ali, but it's best for you to know the truth. We'll listen to what Faraday has to say and then you should share with him what's been happening in Cobble Cove. I'm still planning to call Sheila about Tina. We have a nine a.m. appointment at the police station first. That's too early for Sheila if she's on West Coast time. We can try her after lunch. I've booked us at the same hotel we stayed last time. You can visit Gilly while we're here too."

"I'd like to do that. I should've let her know we were going to be on the Island today. I hope she's home. She has some Fridays off."

They arrived a little early for their appointment with Faraday. The same young police officer showed them into the room they'd occupied last time. They didn't need to wait long. Faraday arrived in less than five minutes, holding a coffee mug. He greeted them and sat behind his desk. Ramsay wasn't with him.

"Thank you for coming down. This won't take long, but I don't like doing business on the phone."

Alicia nodded. John sat beside her in a second chair the young officer had moved into the room.

"You said there's something new in my husband's case."

"Yes." Faraday glanced down at some papers on the desk. We conducted another interview with Mrs. Clemens, the woman who found your husband the day of the accident this past May. She was walking her dog when it happened."

Alicia swallowed the nervous lump in her throat. She urged him with her eyes to continue. John watched her as the detective spoke, alert to her discomfort.

"I'm afraid Ramsay was a bit rough on her. My partner tends to be pretty persistent." He looked across the desk at Alicia and John. "Mrs. Clemens admitted she hadn't told the complete truth about what she saw that day. It seems she actually witnessed the accident. She was quite a distance down the block when it happened, but she has good eyesight. With prompting, she recalled the make and the model of the car that hit your husband."

Alicia was startled.

"Why didn't she come forth earlier?" John wanted to know.

Faraday shook his head. "Some people are hesitant. She's a nurse. Her main concern was the

236

victim. She tried to administer CPR, but he was already dead when she reached him. The car she identified is quite common, and she couldn't make out the license plate from that distance. We don't even know for sure if she's right about the car. Witnesses are often unreliable, but I thought I'd call you in case you knew anyone who might drive that type of car."

"What type of car was it?" Alicia asked.

"A silver Toyota Camry. Mrs. Clemens said she had the impression it was an older model. She couldn't be sure from that distance."

Alicia knew no one who drove a Toyota Camry, but she heard John exhale a deep breath from beside her.

"Detective Faraday, if I may, there have been some strange happenings back in Cobble Cove after Alicia started her new job there, and I'm beginning to see a connection between those occurrences and what you just told us."

Faraday's eyes lit up. "Is that so? I'd be interested in that information, but I'd like another cup of coffee first. Would either of you want one?" When they both declined, he got up and left the room. Alicia had a feeling he was giving them some time to talk together.

"John, what's going on? I don't know anything about a silver Toyota."

"Sorry, Ali," he said in a low voice. "Tina drove one. It can't be a coincidence."

Before Alicia could recover from her shock, there was a commotion outside the room. She and John watched as Ramsay burst in, an angry look on his face. He approached Faraday, who had finished filling his coffee cup.

"They're here? I told you to wait for me. I have more information." He fluttered a manila folder in Faraday's face.

"Calm down, Ron," Faraday said in a composed voice. It seemed he was used to his partner's outbursts. "They just got here. They have something to tell us too." She noticed Faraday didn't offer Ramsay any coffee. He probably figured his partner was hyper enough.

"Fine," Ramsay muttered. Without greeting them, he walked in, sat at the desk displacing Faraday, and placed the open file in front of him.

Faraday followed, looking over Ramsay's shoulder. He pointed to something on the paper, and Ramsay nodded.

"Excuse us, folks," Faraday began, "Detective Ramsay has another report he wants to share with you. We're still interested in your information, but please let us finish first."

Alicia and John sat again. Alicia was on the edge of her seat.

"Of course," John said. Alicia nodded. She knew her voice would break if she spoke.

"It seems your neighbor, the one who reported the fire, also withheld information from us." Ramsay paged through his report. "When I questioned her again yesterday, she acknowledged to me she's seen a car in the vicinity of your house on several occasions. Although she couldn't verify the dates, she said she noticed it often back in the spring but didn't say anything to you at the time…"

"Ron, I already told them about the description of the car given by Mrs. Clemens, and you have that report as well," Faraday interrupted.

"Yes, I do. The description matches exactly. There was a late model silver Toyota Camry cruising the neighborhood last spring. The driver of the vehicle is unidentified, but your neighbor said there was a dark-haired female at the wheel." He looked over at Alicia with an expression that made her feel like the guilty party. "Do you know who this woman may have been?"

"She doesn't, but I do," John replied. "Her name is Tina Deerborn. She worked at the Cobble Cove Library before Alicia. She came there under false pretenses. I think she's back in Cobble Cove now causing some problems, although everyone thinks she's in Florida with her mother. If you're ready to hear what we have to say, Alicia and I can fill you in about what's been going on."

Faraday and Ramsay looked at one another.

"We'll have to do a search of her name in our online criminal databases," Faraday said. "We have an alert out for the car already, but as I said, it's a long shot with the number of Toyotas currently on the road. Now we know she may be in Cobble Cove, we can send a team up there." He took a pen and jotted something down on the pad next to his desk.

"Ramsay," he addressed his partner by his last name this time, "can you take notes on what Mrs. Fairmont and Mr. McKinney tell us?"

Ramsay grabbed the pen and pad from Faraday, abandoning the computer for some reason. "Yeah.

Go ahead." He glared in their direction.

Alicia told them about finding and then losing Tina's diary. She also explained about the notes left in Betty's books and the one she found in the library. When she started to falter, John picked up the story. He told about their visit to Peter's sister, although he didn't know if there was any connection between her and Tina. He left out the part about them discovering his father's letters and, by secret agreement, Alicia didn't mention it either.

When they were done, Ramsay looked up from his notes. "We'll have to talk to that woman in Cobble Cove and also to Pamela Morgan."

"I'll speak to Morgan, and you interview Betty," Faraday said. "Can you get up to Cobble Cove today?"

Ramsay nodded. "They should come with me."

"I agree. Why don't we make it tomorrow since they're staying overnight on Long Island. I'll interview Pamela Morgan first." He looked over at John and Alicia. "Why don't we drive out there right now? You can leave your cars here."

"We came in one car," John corrected him. He turned to Alicia. "Let's go."

She nodded. All she wanted was for this to be over. She hoped these police officers, the friendly one and the fierce, could solve this mystery.

***

Alicia had never driven in a police car before. It was more comfortable than she expected, but she wondered how many criminals sat where they were sitting. She and John were in the backseat of the cruiser. She observed Faraday, who put on his driving glasses. "How did you find Pamela Morgan's address, anyway?" he asked. John had given it to him to plug into his GPS.

"I studied reporting at Columbia and have some access to private databases."

"I see." He started the car and they drove off. After a few minutes, while voices on the police radio were garbling some APBs and other police jargon, Faraday said, "Ms. Fairmont, it's a strange story about your husband and his sister. I know it happens in families sometimes. I'm quite close to my own sister, but I have friends who haven't talked to some of their relatives in years. It's a shame. Life's too short for that sort of thing, you know?"

Alicia wasn't sure if he wanted a reply or was just talking to pass the time. Before she had a chance to comment, he continued. "I'll fill in Ramsay on what your sister-in-law tells us today. I also have some instructions for him on how to interview Betty. Ramsay comes across as pretty rough to people, but he's a good cop."

They were headed down Northern Boulevard, and Alicia knew they weren't far from Pamela's Brookville home. She wondered what Pamela would say this time, how she'd react to police at her door, or if she was even home and not back in Europe. What type of life had Peter's sister led, and why had he left her his inheritance? Alicia also worried Mac and Carol's story would come out and Faraday might find it worth looking into further, might even want to interview Mac. She recalled how John's dad reacted to their questions about the letters and knew it would be painful for him. She looked at John, who sat quietly watching the road. Was he thinking the same thing?

When they reached the gated entrance, Faraday whistled. "Looks like you have some rich in-laws." He got out of the police car and opened the door for Alicia. John came out her side. The three of them walked to the gate.

"How do you use this thing?" Faraday asked, looking at the intercom.

John smiled. "The buzzer is right below. See the black button? I hope she's home. She told us to call ahead next time."

"Police don't call. It's better to approach suspects by surprise."

Alicia didn't realize Pamela was a suspect, but she guessed they couldn't rule out anyone. Faraday pressed the black button. Again, it seemed to take forever for an answer. He pressed it a second time. Alicia imagined Ramsay impatiently jamming the button until it broke. She was glad Faraday was more patient than his partner.

Pamela's voice finally echoed through the speaker. "Please identify yourself and state your business."

"Detective Faraday, 2nd precinct. My business is to speak with Pamela Morgan." Faraday presented his police ID to the speaker, but Alicia didn't think Pamela could see it on the other side. This seemed like a voice unit, although it was possible it was also visual.

A pause. She could imagine what Pamela was thinking. No further word issued from the intercom, but the gate opened. The three of them filed in and walked the long drive to the house. On the way, Faraday muttered, "Nice place. Lots of land." A few Canadian geese gathered under a maple tree. As they came upon the house, Faraday added, "Horse stable too. Got to love this North Shore life. She's probably heading south to another house for the winter."

John nodded. "We're lucky to catch her between travels."

"Seems odd she stays here at all," Alicia said. "Doesn't the woman get bored?"

"I'm sure she belongs to a bunch of clubs, North Shore ladies, literary reading groups, similar ritzy groups," Faraday said.

They were at the front door. Pamela stood there, this time in a paint-spattered smock holding a paint brush instead of a riding crop.

"Good day, Officer, Alicia, John." She didn't seem surprised they accompanied Faraday. "Please come in. I was just in the studio painting. You can have a seat in the parlor while I clean up and change."

"Thank you," Faraday said. "We're sorry to interrupt, but there's some business we need to discuss."

Pamela held the door open for them as they entered. Her expression was neutral. She didn't seem nervous at all.

When they were seated in the large parlor on the white leather couch that looked as if it didn't have a speck of dust on it—Alicia figured Pamela had a good housekeeper—Pamela went upstairs to change.

Faraday glanced around, assessing the place. He got up and went to the fireplace. Above it hung a painting of a woman who looked somewhat like Pamela with the same blonde hair and blue eyes. Alicia was surprised she hadn't noticed it last time she was here with John, but maybe it had been added since then.

"I guess that's Mrs. Fairmont," Faraday said. "Striking lady. I wonder who did her portrait?"

"I did." The reply came from the stairs as Pamela rejoined them. She now wore an abstract-patterned caftan with wide-legged black slacks that looked like velvet. "It was hanging upstairs with some of my other pieces, but I decided to bring it down here the other day."

"You do nice work," Faraday complimented.

"Thank you. I've had art lessons for many years." She walked to the bar and opened it. "Would any of you care for a drink?"

"I don't drink on the job." Faraday declined. Alicia and John also said they were fine. Pamela smiled and poured herself a glass and then sat on the tapestry-covered armchair by the couch. Faraday remained standing by the fireplace.

"To what do I owe the pleasure of this visit, Detective?" Pamela asked after taking a sip of her drink.

"There have been some developments in your brother's case. I have a few questions regarding them."

Pamela lifted a light brow. "I didn't realize Peter had a case. I only recently learned of his death. I thought it was an accident." She looked over at Alicia.

"Up until now, so did we, but the witness who found Mr. Fairmont now recalls the car that hit him. We believe it belonged to a woman named Tina Deerborn. Have you ever heard of her?"

Pamela took another sip of red wine. "I can't say as I have, but surely, as my sister-in-law may have told you, I haven't been in touch with Peter for quite some time."

"And why is that?" Faraday turned to face her.

Pamela placed her glass down on the side table next to her. "I can't see what that has to do with anything, and I'm not in the mood to dredge up that sordid tale."

Alicia suddenly saw the tough side of Faraday as he approached Pamela and leaned over her. "Sorry, Ms. Morgan, but if you don't tell us that—" he paused, "'—sordid tale,' I will have to subpoena you and bring you to the station."

She smiled. "I have a good lawyer, but because you've brought along some relatives, I think I'll cooperate. Please, have a seat. This may take a while."

Faraday remained standing. Alicia looked over at John, who was still quiet but listening intently. She knew what Pamela was about to tell them would include his father.

Before Pamela began, John interrupted. "Excuse me, Ms. Morgan, but maybe I should give a bit of background here first."

Pamela smiled that strange smile Alicia found a bit perturbing because her teeth were so white and straight as if she had seen the best dentists and orthodontists. "Excellent idea, John. You can start with how your father—our father—betrayed Peter's father."

Faraday's eyes shot to John. He held a pen poised on the notepad he'd taken out of his uniform pocket.

John cleared his throat and glanced toward Alicia for support. "My father, we call him Mac because I'm a junior, was in love with Carol Parsons when he was young. He tutored her at my grandfather's school for a time. She was seeing Paul Fairmont then, and only thought of Mac as a friend. When Paul went into the army, he wrote Carol letters. She didn't receive any of them, so she thought he didn't care for her anymore or had been injured or killed in the war."

He paused and turned toward Faraday. "Before Paul returned, Dad told me he had an affair in New York City with Carol while she was attending dance school. He visited her there each summer. When Paul came back to Cobble Cove, Carol went back to him. They married and had their first child." He turned to Pamela. "And yes, people suspected Mac was your dad, and now we know it's probably true."

"Not probably, definitely," she confirmed. "I think I can fill in the blanks of the rest of the story."

"Please do," John urged.

"My mother never told Paul she had had an affair with John Fairmont while he was in service. It seems John didn't say a word either. He ended up marrying someone he met quite a few years later." She took another sip of her drink. "We were never a happy family to begin with. It felt like John's shadow hung over us because, even though it was never confirmed that I was another man's child, Paul couldn't totally ignore the rumors spreading through Cobble Cove. Nor could he ignore my mother's halfhearted affection. Peter's birth was their attempt to stay together. When Peter arrived, things changed but not for the better. Paul doted on his only son and grew even more distant from his seven year old daughter and wife."

"When Peter was in fifth grade and I was in my last year of high school, dad began to have new aspirations. He decided Cobble Cove was too small a town in which to raise his family and expand his wealth. He wanted to send Peter to a better school, an exclusive private one on Long Island that would give him an edge for college. He had no intention of paying for my college, though. He told me I would have to pay my own way if I wanted to continue school."

"We lived in several places after Cobble Cove. Woodbury was the first place we settled on Long Island. It was a nice area. Dad had invested in some stock and done pretty well. He went into business and made some more wise investments. Our family life finally started improving. As Dad saw his dream of bettering his son's opportunities come true, he actually started treating Mom and I better. That was until he found the letters."

Alicia gasped. She looked at John, who she imagined was shaking on the inside, although he seemed to remain calm.

"Letters?" Faraday asked. He jotted some notes on his pad.

"*The letters*," Pamela said, emphasizing the words. "The ones Mac wrote to Carol and she stupidly saved." She took another sip from her glass. Alicia noted it was almost empty. "We were moving to a larger home, and Dad was helping pack things up. He went into the attic and found them. He confronted Mom and they had a huge fight. Peter and I overheard them. Dad called Mom a whore. He accused her of throwing out his letters and lying that she'd never gotten them. He said she'd even convinced her parents to deny receiving them. He realized the rumors were true—I wasn't his daughter. Even though Mom insisted he was wrong, and why would she have married him if he was right, he ignored her." Pamela sighed.

"It might've been better if they divorced after that, but they didn't. Dad made us pay for it, me and Mom. Peter became his perfect son, and we were reminded constantly of how insignificant we were in his eyes. You would've thought Peter would treat his sister and mother differently, but he and Paul had formed a tight bond. Peter idolized his father and believed all the hateful things he said about us." She sighed again. "As a final insult, Paul changed his will so Mom and I wouldn't get a cent after he died."

Faraday glanced around the ornate room. "Seems you've done okay, Ms. Morgan, although I know your brother and his wife didn't fare as well financially." He looked in Alicia's direction. "What happened?"

Pamela finished her drink and placed the glass on the table next to the armchair. "Peter changed the will. When Paul died of a heart attack, Peter blamed my mother and me because we didn't call 911 when his father complained of chest pains. Mom insisted it was just a sour stomach from the pasta sauce she cooked that night and gave Paul some antacids. Peter was away at a sales conference when it happened. He'd already started working as a library vendor representative but still lived with my parents in a separate apartment Dad added to our house. I was with my daughters in my own home. Mark and I were separated by that time. When Mom called me about Paul, I agreed with her that it wasn't necessary to be concerned. Paul had no history of heart disease in his family and worked out regularly. He was prone to indigestion and acid reflux, so I figured he was just having another gastric episode. After I hung up the phone, Paul collapsed. He died before they got him to the hospital. Peter insisted he would've survived had we taken action sooner."

Pamela cleared her throat. "Peter would hardly talk to us after that and when he learned the details of the will, he said we could have it all, but he didn't want any future contact from us. He said he would rather have his father alive than a penny of the inheritance. He even accused Mom of seeing Paul's death as an opportunity to return to John McKinney. Mom tried to talk sense into him. She saw no reason why we couldn't split everything three ways, but he seemed to be a chip off the old block. Instead of viewing Paul's death as a way we could all become closer again, he saw it as a way of punishing us." Alicia thought Peter could've walked away with the money and that would've been a way stronger punishment, but it also occurred to her that he may have allowed his mother and stepsister to keep it out of guilt.

Pamela tapped her French manicured nails against the table with the empty wine glass. "Dad treated us like shit. He blamed Mom for cheating and me for being born. In my opinion, the money didn't make up for Peter's dad's jealousy and selfishness or Peter's turning his back on his family."

Pamela's last words lingered in the air and, as Faraday still wrote on his pad, John spoke again. "I have a bit more to add. We found those letters recently. I don't know how my father got them, but they were in the storage room in the attic. Alicia came across them and showed me the letters Carol wrote Mac as well as the letters Dad wrote to her." Alicia held her breath, wondering if John would mention the last batch of letters—the ones Mac hid from Carol, the ones Paul had sent her parents because he didn't yet have her New York address. He didn't, and Alicia wasn't about to mention them either. If the police knew Mac had confiscated federal property so Carol would turn to him, he would be fined at the very least. *John was smart to keep quiet*, she thought.

"Do you know how Mr. McKinney got those letters?" Faraday asked Pamela. She didn't blink an eye. "Of course. I mailed them to him. After Mom passed away, I came across them when going through her things. I thought Paul would've thrown them out or burned them, but somehow she must've found another place to hide them. I think she never got over Mac."

Alicia was reminded of what John said about his dad keeping a secret place in his heart for his first love, and she could understand why Carol may have kept the letters.

Pamela continued. "When I mailed the letters, I slipped in a little note. I can't remember exactly what I wrote, but I signed it *'from your only daughter.'*"

Mac hadn't told them that part. Alicia figured he'd omitted that from the story in consideration of John.

"I guess that about sums it up," Pamela said, standing. "Is there anything else you need, Detective?"

Faraday was finishing his notes. He looked up. "This is all quite interesting, but right now, I still don't see how Ms. Deerborn fits into all this."

"I'm afraid I can't help you there. I've never heard that name."

John reached into his pocket and withdrew a small photo from his wallet. "I thought I'd bring this along. I forgot all about it, but maybe this will jog Pamela's memory." He handed the photo to Faraday first. Alicia's heart sank at the thought John carried Tina's picture.

"Pretty woman," Faraday commented. Pamela walked over to him and took it. She examined it a moment. Her face changed. "She looks familiar. Let me think." It took her a few minutes, while everyone waited. "Yes. That's the girl, but her name wasn't Tina, as I recall. I think it was Maggie or Megan, something like that."

The detective perked up. "How do you know her? Do you recall her last name?"

Pamela paused again. "I only saw her once. She came to my library."

"Library?" Alicia's heart started beating fast.

"Let me show you. It's upstairs."

The three of them followed Pamela up the carpeted steps to the second floor. She walked down the hall and opened a door on the right. The room was lined with books. The tapestry throw rug on the floor looked as if it had been imported from Turkey. The red hues in it picked up the cherry wood of the bookshelves and the computer desk near the window. A world globe sat on the end of one bookshelf.

"Welcome to my library," Pamela said, leading them into the room. "Before they opened the Gold Coast Library, none of the homes on this part of the North Shore had a public library. Instead, most of them had home libraries like I do."

Alicia couldn't help herself. She examined the shelves and saw the complete works of Shakespeare in leather-bound volumes, a couple of first editions of Dickens, and many other priceless books. The books in this room alone were worth a fortune. She had an urge to reach out and touch the covers, but Faraday was speaking.

"What did this woman you've identified have to do with your home library, Ms. Morgan?" He withdrew his notepad again for her reply.

She glanced back at the photo in her hand. "She was a library vendor representative who came here to fill some of my orders. My regular representative was out sick that day."

Alicia's heart began beating fast. Peter was a library vendor representative. Pamela's next words confirmed her fears.

"Megan or Mary or Maggie or whatever her name was worked for a company called East Coast Publishing."

The room started to spin, and Alicia grabbed hold of John's arm as she felt herself falling. East Coast Publishing was Peter's company.

CHAPTER 17

When Alicia awoke, she was lying on a long white couch, a divan, she believed it was called. Her body sank into its soft contours. The room around her was also white, not stark white, but a soft creamy white that enveloped the walls, the bearskin rug on the floor, and the marble fireplace in the corner. It was a huge room. A bed with white silken sheets and a white lace bedspread took center stage. The paintings on the walls were soft pastels, flowers in a vase, a country garden, a spring gazebo. It had such a dreamy quality she almost felt as if she'd died and gone to heaven.

"You're up. I have some water for you," a familiar voice offered. John stood next to her holding a water glass filled with ice. He placed it on the white pedestal table to the side of the divan.

"I can get some cold rags for her head," Pamela said. "I also have some smelling salts in the medicine cabinet."

"Thanks, but I don't think that will be necessary now," John said.

"What happened?" Alicia thought she hit her head. Her memory was vague. She recalled Pamela showing them a room full of books and looking at a photo. Then it all came back—Tina and East Coast Publishing. She sighed.

"Are you okay? Should Pamela get you an aspirin or something? I caught you before you actually fell and walked you in here. Do you remember any of that?"

Alicia took a sip of water. Her mouth felt dry as a desert. "Vaguely. I remember about Tina." She shifted to sit up. "Where is Detective Faraday?"

"He's out in the hall. He's giving us some space. I think he's speaking with Ramsay on his cell phone. They want to run a check on that sales rep. He was able to copy the photo and text the image to his partner." John took her hand, "You really frightened me, honey." Pamela looked away. She had laid the photo down on the table with Alicia's glass. Alicia caught sight of a young woman with long dark hair and heavy mascara on her eyelashes.

Faraday stepped into the room. "Her name is Maura Ryan. She worked for the White Plains division of the company up until two years ago when she quit her job at East Coast. She left a forwarding address of some relatives in Florida, but it hasn't been verified. We put an APB out on her and are running some other checks. For your info, there's nothing on Tina Deerborn. The name must've been an alias. Ramsay said they may have identified the car. One meeting that description was found abandoned six months ago in the New Paltz area. It was registered to a Ms. Ryan, but because no one could contact her, it was impounded. It's not an unusual thing for an abandoned vehicle. You'd be surprised how many people run away each year and leave their cars."

Alicia was having trouble digesting all this new information. She didn't know if the dizziness she still felt was from all this strange news or whether she was still suffering from vertigo.

"Detective," John addressed Faraday, "I was going to contact Mrs. Whitehead, our library director in Cobble Cove, who has gone to her family in California for the Thanksgiving holidays. She may have the number for the relatives of Tina—Maura in Florida. That's where we were told she went to care for her sick mother when she left Cobble Cove."

"That sounds like a good idea," Faraday said. "I definitely would like to speak to Mrs. Whitehead if you can give me the number where she can currently be reached. It may be too early for West Coast time, but I'll make a note to contact her later today." He scribbled on his pad again. "If you're saying the woman who worked for Mrs. Whitehead was also the woman who worked at Mr. Fairmont's company two years ago, we need to find out what she was actually doing in Cobble Cove and, more importantly, where she is now."

Alicia spoke, her voice a little strained from dryness despite drinking water. "Peter never mentioned anyone named Maura. If she worked at the White Plains office, what involvement could they possibly have?"

Faraday gave her a look she'd seen on John's

face before. It seemed she aroused pity in these men for her trust in her dead husband.

"That's what we have to determine, Ms. Fairmont." He turned back to Pamela. "I have a few more questions for you, and then we'll be on our way."

"I don't think I can be of much more help. I only saw that woman once. She took an order for some books I wanted to add to the collection, and I never heard from her again. A few months later when I contacted my old representative, he apologized for the lost order. He said the woman who visited me was no longer with the company."

"When was that?"

Pamela waved her hand in a gesture of dismissal. "It was a few months after Mom passed away. I was treating myself to some new titles for my birthday, so it must've been the end of October two years ago. I heard from my representative, Joshua, in January, a week or so after New Year's. He said Ms. Ryan had left the company a month prior with very little notice."

Alicia recalled the first entry in Tina/Maura's diary. "That would make sense," she said. "The diary I found began in December when Tina, I mean Maura, first started at the Cobble Cove Library."

"Interesting," muttered John. "I think the library position was advertised around that time, as well."

"This has been quite informative," Faraday said. "I think we only need a few more pieces. Thank you, Ms. Morgan, Ms. Fairmont, and Mr. McKinney. I want to get back to headquarters and review these notes with my partner. I'll speak with

Mrs. Whitehead later too."

Alicia stood up, but her legs felt wobbly. John noticed and put out his arm. "Are you okay, Ali?"

"Not one hundred per cent, but I'll be all right. I think getting back outside in the air will help."

They left Pamela's bedroom, and John let Alicia walk down the stairs behind him in case she lost her balance.

When they were all downstairs, Faraday handed Pamela his card. "If you think of anything else that may help us, Ms. Morgan, please call me at that number."

"I shall," she promised.

***

In the police car, Faraday told them he'd drop them off back at the station and they should go back to their hotel and get some rest. Alicia knew he meant that especially for her. He also said Ramsay would meet them in Cobble Cove the next day at the library around noon. "Don't let him scare you. He's a good cop," he reiterated. "From how you describe Betty, that homebound lady, I think it's best he's the one who interviews her. She needs a bit of a rough approach. I'll be in touch with all of you regarding how the case is progressing up here. I think it's going to be quite easy to find Ms. Ryan, but I'd first like to know what crimes, if any, she has committed. I have a feeling faking a library degree and using an alias is not all she's guilty of."

"Do you think she killed Peter?" Alicia asked.

"Either her or someone who drove her car,"

258

Faraday said.

"And my house? Do you think she burned it down?"

"It's possible, but please don't drive yourself crazy. We're going to find the answers. You stay as calm as you can and let us do our job."

Alicia couldn't imagine why a stranger, this woman named Maura Ryan, would have wished Peter and herself harm.

"Detective Faraday is right," John said from beside her. "When we get to the station, let's go have some lunch and then settle ourselves at the hotel." He added in a low voice by her ear, "We have a single room this time. I hope you don't mind."

Alicia smiled and started to regain her composure. She didn't think Faraday had heard John's whispered words over the blasts from the police radio. "I don't mind at all," she said. "In fact, I'm looking forward to it, Mr. McKinney."

***

They decided not to go to lunch because Alicia was still feeling slightly woozy. Instead, they checked into their room and called room service. The room John booked was larger than the one with the connecting door, but it featured the same neutral color scheme of tan walls and green carpeting with a king-sized bed, television, desk with coffee maker, bathroom with hairdryer and shower, and a closet and bureau. There were several prints of the Montauk Lighthouse and Jones Beach scattered on the walls throughout the room. The room service attendant, after being admitted to the room, laid the tray of food on the desk while he handed John the receipt. He smiled when John tipped him.

After room service left, Alicia and John pulled up chairs by the desk and sat eating and talking. Alicia had chosen a chicken salad sandwich on whole wheat bread. John ordered a hamburger he said was twice the cost and half the flavor of Casey's. He'd also requested a pot of coffee for them to share, saying it would help revive her.

"So what do you make of everything?" Alicia asked him after she'd eaten half her sandwich. "What do you think it all means?"

John was munching the French fries that came with his burger. He swallowed and looked up at her. "I think Faraday's right. We can't jump to any conclusions yet. The way I see it, Maura—I can't call her Tina anymore—was involved with Peter. I'm sorry, Ali, but chances are they were having an affair."

Alicia expected to feel pain at this pronouncement, but all she felt was a strange relief. "I was stupid," she said. "I used to laugh at women who trusted their spouses when they were obviously cheating. I never thought I'd be one of them. I should've seen the signs. I should've questioned his withholding so much information from me." Suddenly, she was angry. "I was his wife. If he wanted her, why didn't he tell me? I would've let him go. I wasn't a stay-at-home housewife with five kids. I had my own means of support. I don't understand why he didn't ask for a divorce."

"For some men, a second woman on the side is the goal, not another wife," John said. "Peter may have cheated earlier in your marriage too. You said he traveled a lot and didn't wear his wedding ring."

"I thought I was a good wife, a good lover."

"You were, Ali. It wasn't you. It was him. There would never be anyone who could give him all he needed."

"Do you think she killed him?"

John took a sip of his coffee and considered. "We need to know more, and the police are working on motives, but yes, I think she may have wanted him to leave you, and he refused. Some women become possessive and that could turn dangerous, a crime of passion. This sounds more planned than that."

Alicia thought back. "He must've met her at one of the sales conferences he attended. I remember a big one a couple of years ago. It must have been early 2013, I think. He told me reps from all the divisions were attending. He was gone about a week. When he came home, he seemed distracted. I wonder where they managed to meet afterwards. I guess it doesn't matter." She pushed her sandwich away, unable to finish it. "She must've known about John coming from Cobble Cove. Why else would she apply for a job there and leave East Coast?"

"She probably figured it would be safer for them if she left the company, less gossip among co-workers that might get back to you. As for Cobble Cove, didn't you say you read something in the diary about a meeting place?"

"Oh, my God!" Alicia said, her face growing

pale again, "The house next to Betty's, the one you said your father rented to people and where you said you lived once…" She had trouble continuing.

"She had a key to that place," John said. "I was a fool. She seemed so innocent, so beguiling. I can see how Peter fell for her, although for me, it was purely physical. I'm ashamed of that now. She wasn't like my wife, nothing like you, but I needed someone then, and she was there."

Alicia's mind was racing in different directions. "It might've been Maura who got in my house and rigged one of my basement steps so I would fall and maybe break my neck."

John pushed his plate away as well. "Alicia, take it easy. I know you're eager for answers, but there's still more to this story. We have to be patient." He stood up and went to his unopened overnight bag and withdrew a yellow legal pad. "If it makes you feel better, we can sketch some of this plot out like we do for our mysteries."

Alicia tried to laugh but found she couldn't. "I outline all my book ideas in my mind."

"Different writers use different methods, but you want to give this a try? Since we both seem to have lost our appetites, why don't we go over to the bed and take some notes? It might make you feel better."

John got up and brought the pad over to the table by the bed. He fluffed two pillows, sat against one, and then grabbed a pen left with the hotel stationary. "I'll start with the characters—Peter, Maura, Pamela, you, and me."

Alicia joined him on the bed. "Don't forget

Sheila and your dad. They were in contact with Maura too, as was Betty."

"Yep." He added the names and drew circles around them. On the opposite side, he listed under settings, Brookville and Cobble Cove.

"Our house was in Syosset, and so was the division of East Coast John worked for. You might also want to include White Plains where Maura worked."

John wrote the additional locations. He drew a line under the characters and settings and wrote:

Timeline.

"Here's the hard part. I guess the timeline should start two and a half years ago when Peter allegedly met Maura, but it was before she moved to Cobble Cove, so let's say the spring of 2013. What month was that sales conference?"

"May."

"Okay." He drew the first mark on the timeline and set it at May 2013. Under it, he wrote:

Peter meets Maura.

At the next point, which he labeled October 2013, he marked:

Maura visits Pamela's library.

The next point was December 2013:

Maura leaves East Coast and Accepts Job at Cobble Cove Library.

"What else?" he asked. Alicia watched as he sketched in the details.

"I guess next would be Peter's accident. No, it would be my fall down the basement stairs. That was in April of this year."

John nodded and added at April 20151:

Alicia falls down stairs.

At May 2015:

Peter's hit and run.

"What else?"

Alicia reached out and took John's pen and added to the timeline:

November 2015, Alicia visits Cobble Cove Library and is offered job.

"The other things are only days apart—the notes Betty left in the book, the typed message in the library warning me to leave, and my finding Tina's diary. I mean Maura's diary."

"Also my dad's letters. We can't forget about those, although I can't see how they're connected."

"They were in the storage room," Alicia said.

"Maura was living up there like I am now. Maybe she found them too."

"Why would she care if she was just focused on Peter?"

Alicia didn't have an answer, but she jotted it down anyway under Miscellaneous Happenings.

"Now you've got the idea." John smiled, taking back the pen and writing:

Alicia's house fire.

Alicia winced. "How could I forget that? I also forgot to visit Gilly today. If I speak with her, I might cause her more worry. She didn't know I was coming, so maybe I should leave it for another time."

John nodded. "Good idea. Now I have one more project for us, and it doesn't involve writing." There was a gleam in his eye as he laid the pad and pen on the nightstand and turned to embrace her. "Are you up for this?"

Alicia had to admit she was feeling much better. Just the act of writing out all their questions had helped. "I think so," she said, and they spent the rest of the afternoon and night in bed.

CHAPTER 18

Alicia awoke to the ringing of the hotel phone. She turned to reach for it and was thankful it was on her side of the bed because John still slept beside her. "Hello," she whispered so as not to wake her sleeping lover.

"Good morning. Detective Faraday here. Before you head back to Cobble Cove, I'd like to invite you and Mr. Fairmont to breakfast at the station with me and Detective Ramsay. We've found some more information about Ms. Ryan we'd like to share with you."

"What time?" Alicia glanced at the room alarm clock. It read 6:00.

"Ramsay wants to get on the road early. Is an hour enough time?"

"Yes," Alicia said, worried it might not be. They hadn't packed yet, and both of them needed to shower and dress.

"Good. See you then." He hung up with a click.

Before waking John, she got up, showered, and dressed quickly. After throwing her stuff in her small suitcase, she roused John with a kiss. "Get up, sleepyhead. Detective Faraday wants us to meet him at the station in—" she glanced again at the alarm, "—twenty minutes." She'd taken longer than she planned.

"Twenty minutes!" John jumped up. "It'll take us ten minutes to drive there. I'll take my clothes in the bathroom and shower and change. I also need to shave. I'll be as quick as I can, but can you please do me a favor?"

Alicia raised an eyebrow, trying to avoid looking at his muscular nakedness but unable to help herself. "Depends on what it is. We don't have time for a repeat of last night."

John cracked a smile. "Now who has the lurid imagination? I was thinking you could help me pack. Most of my things are still in the overnight case, but please throw in anything else of mine you find around here, and remember the pad. We might need those notes."

"Sure thing." Alicia went through the hotel bureau and drawers while John got ready in the bathroom. She was checking for her stuff as well as his, although she knew she'd only unpacked her slippers and unused night gown along with some toiletries. After she'd double checked her suitcase, adding her dirty clothes from the day before in the bag she'd brought along for that purpose, she started on John's.

Alicia heard the water running in the shower and John whistling off key in the way Mac did upon arriving at the library in the morning. John's dirty clothes were rolled up in a heap by the bed where he'd dropped them last night. He hadn't brought a laundry bag, so she just stuffed them in his overnight bag along with the pad they'd used for their mystery brainstorming. As she did so, something small and hard pressed into her finger. It wasn't sharp, but she didn't expect it to be there among John's unpacked clothes. She put her hand around it and dug out what looked like a USB drive. At first, she thought it might have some files on it John was working on for the newspaper. Then she saw the drive had a handwritten label. She almost dropped it when she recognized the flourishes and swirls and read what the letters formed:

May 13, 2015.

The date of Peter's death. Below that was written:

Digital recording.

There were audio files on it. What was it doing in John's bag?

The shower water stopped abruptly. Should she call out to him and ask him about it? Maybe he had some evidence he was waiting to show the detectives, but why hadn't he told her? She made a quick decision and put the drive in her purse. If John noticed it missing, she wouldn't know what to say. Something told her she should listen to it alone first when she got to a computer.

John came out of the bathroom completely dressed in brown corduroys and a red and brown striped shirt. His hair was slightly damp. "I decided to skip shaving. Do I look okay?"

Alicia feared her voice would betray her guilt. "You look great." She turned away so he couldn't see her face. "The packing's all done, unless you want do a final check of the room."

"Why would I do that? I trust you."

His words stabbed her heart, but she needed to know what the drive contained.

"Is something wrong?" He came to her and put his arm around her.

"No," she lied. "We're just running late."

"I think we'll make it. C'mon." He grabbed his bag she'd zippered up and took the handle of her suitcase. "I can manage these. Just leave the key on the bed." He took out his wallet and left a tip for the hotel cleaning staff. "I paid at check in, so we're good to go."

When they arrived at John's pickup, he placed their bags in the back and then opened the passenger door for her. Glancing at his watch, he said, "If traffic cooperates, we should only be a couple of minutes late."

***

The breakfast Faraday invited them to turned out to be the old police officer staple, Dunkin Donuts and coffee. When they arrived at the station at 7:05, Ramsay was pacing back and forth with nervous energy outside the room they'd occupied the last two times they'd been there. "About time you showed up," he told them rudely, ducking into the

269

office where Faraday sat at the desk, the pink and white box of donuts open in front of him and four mugs of coffee spread across the desktop.

"Have a seat, Ms. Fairmont, Mr. McKinney," Faraday greeted them.

Alicia sat, and John took the chair next to her. Ramsay remained standing and pacing. The scent of donuts and coffee mingled in the stale air of the police station.

Faraday pushed the donut box forward after taking a jelly one. "Help yourselves," he offered.

Alicia's stomach was too upset for food or drink. John waved the donuts off as well. "Not right now, thanks," he said, but he did take one of the mugs. She figured he needed the caffeine for their long drive.

"Can we just get started?" Ramsay asked, still pacing impatiently.

Faraday glanced at the legal pad on his desk, similar to the one John used in the hotel room and Alicia had packed when she found the drive. Should she mention her discovery now? Without knowing what it contained, she hesitated.

"I've read the report you emailed me, Detective Ramsay," Faraday said. "Excellent job."

Ramsay didn't acknowledge the compliment. "My partner has found quite a bit of information on Maura Ryan aka Tina Deerborn. Before he fills you in on all that, I have some other good news."

Alicia didn't feel any news these officers would tell her would be good.

"The person who committed the arson at your house has been arrested. He's a seventeen year old juvenile. He was in the process of setting a fire at his school recently and was caught by a guard. When we questioned him, he admitted to burning down your house. He said one of his friends dared him to do it. Seems your house was chosen at random because no one was home at the time."

So Gilly was right. Her house was vandalized while she was away, and it had nothing to do with Maura Ryan.

Ramsay spoke then, picking up the story as he paced back and forth around the small room. "Although arson is one crime Ms. Ryan didn't commit, we found her in our crime database. She came from Florida originally, so that part of her story is true. Her mother was a single mom who, incidentally, worked as a cleaner for a library down there. She OD'd on sleeping pills and amphetamines when Maura was nine. After that, Maura was shuffled around to different foster homes. She left the last when she was sixteen and headed north to New York. There was some history of physical abuse, possibly with some of her foster fathers. She ran away to New York after stealing some money from her last foster father. He didn't press charges because of the abuse countercharge she threatened to file. In NYC, she worked at several places before landing the job at East Coast. Prior to that, she was arrested several times for shoplifting and once for prostitution. She seems to have cleaned up her act after that. She attended Nassau Community College for two years, graduating with an Associate's degree in Business and then took out a loan for her Bachelor's in

Business Administration that she received from Hofstra University. She defaulted on the loan, but she started paying it back slowly while she worked at East Coast. Her last known address was on Fisher Avenue in White Plains. She had an apartment there. Her landlord was a woman named Miller, a widow, who charged her a low rent. We interviewed Miller, and she has no idea where Maura went. She said the last time she was at the house was two years ago."

He paused, finally taking a cup of coffee and swishing it down quickly. "We also spoke with Mrs. Whitehead. She didn't have Maura's Florida number. She said Maura, or Tina, as she was known in Cobble Cove, told her she would call her with the number once things settled down because her mother's phone was being changed. She never called."

Faraday bit into his second jelly donut, swallowed, and wiped his mouth with a napkin. "So the question is, where is Ms. Ryan? From the information you both have supplied, she may be hiding out somewhere in Cobble Cove." He glanced at John and Alicia. "Ramsay is planning to speak to Mr. McKinney as well as Betty about that since the rental cottage mentioned in some of the interviews might be a place she would use."

John put down his empty mug. "I would prefer to be there when you talk to my dad," he said to Ramsay. "Mac has some memory issues."

Although John had addressed Ramsay, Faraday was the one who replied. "I've instructed Detective Ramsay to include both of you in the Cobble Cove interviews."

"Let's get going then," Ramsay urged. "Rush hour traffic is a bitch this time of day."

Faraday raised his eyebrows, but didn't reprimand his partner for his use of language. "Good luck," he said, standing. "Keep me informed. I'm still checking out more leads up here."

Ramsay nodded and rushed out the door.

"Excuse my partner's behavior," Faraday said when he heard the engine of Ramsay's police cruiser gun up with an abrupt start. "He can be brusque at times, but I've already told you he's an excellent cop. He'll catch Ryan if anyone can and get to the bottom of all this."

Alicia was glad they weren't driving with Ramsay, who probably felt he had the privilege to exceed the speed limit because of his badge.

"Take these." Faraday closed the donut box and pushed it toward John. "My waistline can't take any more of this stuff. You can take the rest with you on your drive."

Alicia wondered why Faraday remained so slim, and Ramsay, who hadn't touched a bite, was obese. *The quirks of metabolism*, she thought. John accepted the donuts.

"Thanks."

"Be careful," Faraday said as they went to the door. "This Ryan woman sounds dangerous."

"I've dealt with her," John told him. "I never imagined she was so screwed up, but now I've heard her background, I can see the affect that type of upbringing must've had on her. She hid it well."

"They usually do." Faraday's phone buzzed. He

answered it, waving them away.

Alicia was quiet on the ride back to Cobble Cove. Her mind was on the drive in her purse. What message had Maura recorded on it the day Peter died? She almost told John, but she knew she had to listen to it herself first. She could do that in the computer at the library as long as she had a few minutes alone.

"What are you thinking?" John asked when he caught her staring out the window. The weather had taken a cold turn. As they made their way north, a few flurries began to hit the windshield.

She decided the weather was a safe topic. "It's starting to snow. When we left, it was so warm."

"Snow can come early in Cobble Cove," John said. "Even though we've been lucky with unseasonable weather lately, that can change in a second. It's end of November already."

Alicia remembered Dora asking John to plant her bulbs while the weather still permitted. "I guess Dora's bulb planting will have to wait until next year."

"Not necessarily. I'll see how hard the earth is at the inn on Sunday. It might still be possible."

The small talk was making her edgy. "John, isn't Ramsay supposed to meet us at the library?"

"Yes. He wants to check some things there before we speak with Betty. I'm going home first to drop off my stuff and prepare Dad before Ramsay talks to him."

"That's a good idea." Alicia wondered if John would notice the recording missing when he unpacked, but it was likely he wouldn't do that until later. "Do you mind dropping me at the library before you go to your dad's? I'd like to check on Sneaky and drop my things off too."

John smiled. "That cat will be fine. I'm sure Dad spoiled him while we were away. I don't mind dropping you first, but are you sure you'll be okay alone with Ramsay? It's possible he might beat us there, especially since he had an early start and probably blew a few lights on his way."

Alicia could well imagine Ramsay running through red lights, even those with cameras. If he was at the library, she wouldn't have time to listen to the drive. "I'll be fine," she said, "but isn't Mac opening the library today?"

"I think he mentioned he might, but maybe he decided to keep it closed for the Thanksgiving weekend. I'm still sure he came by early this morning to feed Sneaky, if that's what worries you."

"No," Alicia said. "I was hoping for a little bit of time alone." That wasn't a lie.

"Well, if you're lucky, Ramsay will stop for food. He didn't eat any of the donuts Faraday offered us. Casey serves breakfast on the weekends. Ramsay might even decide to question him."

"Did Casey know Tina? I mean Maura."

"We ate there once. I don't think he knew her, but who knows? There are a lot of things about Maura we're starting to discover."

"How did it end," Alicia asked, "between you and her?" It was a question she'd wanted to ask for a long time.

John sighed. They had reached the toll. He

slowed down so the machine could read his EZ-Pass. When the gate opened and they drove through, he answered. "She broke it off. It was sudden. I'd been away at a library conference. Dad sent me because he wasn't up to it. I was only gone a few days at the end of April. When I returned, she was like a different person. She said we could remain friends, but she didn't feel we were a good match."

"Were you hurt?" Alicia didn't want to probe, but he seemed amenable to answering her questions.

"Not at all." He laughed. "I was actually relieved. I was beginning to see things about her that weren't so nice. I wouldn't say she was capable of murder at that point, but I did notice a few things that worried me."

This was news to Alicia. "Why didn't you tell this to the detectives?"

John's eyes were on the road ahead. They were approaching a bottleneck. "I didn't have anything concrete to tell them. It was just my gut feeling. Turns out I should've listened to that instinct."

By the time they arrived in Cobble Cove, snow covered the streets. Alicia had to admit it cast a pretty glow on the town. She would love to head up to Cove Point and look down at the frosted mountains or walk through the green and see the gazebo and shop fronts adorned in winter finery. The library even looked festive with its ice-tipped bushes. She noticed someone, probably Mac, had hung a wreath on the library door. She remembered the Christmas Fair Committee meeting she'd missed and somehow felt disappointed she hadn't been able to attend.

"Looks like we beat Ramsay," John said. "Let me walk you in." He turned off the car but left it pulled up in front of the library. Alicia got out as he was taking her case out of the back. "I can handle that, John." He ignored her, insisting on carrying the bag as he walked her to the door. He took out his key and opened the library. Alicia switched on the lights.

After checking around, John gave the place an all clear.

Out of nowhere, Sneaky came running to Alicia, purring against her leg. "Hey, boy," she said, bending down to scratch his head, "Looks like you missed me."

"Hmmm. He probably wants to be fed again."

Alicia worried Mac may have forgotten. "I'll go up, feed him, and unpack. Does Ramsay have a key to the library?"

John shook his head. "I doubt it. If he shows up, you can let him in. I shouldn't be long." He paused and gave her a quick kiss on the cheek. "See you in a bit, Ali. Everything's going to be okay."

CHAPTER 19

As soon as John locked the door behind him—not providing much consolation because whoever got in last time had a key—Alicia went upstairs and fed Sneaky. She noticed his bowls were empty. She found that unusual because she put out so much dry food when she left and Mac was known to overfeed the cat. As soon as she refilled the bowls, Sneaky gobbled down the food so quickly he barfed some up. "Oh, Sneaky, just what I need when I'm in a rush." Alicia really wanted to listen to the contents of the drive before Ramsay arrived. She cleaned up the mess, thinking it was possible Mac had indeed forgotten to feed the cat. She also wondered if the litter box had been scooped but didn't want to check it yet.

She left her overnight bag in the bedroom and closed the door. That could also wait until tonight. There was no time to spare. She opened her purse and took out the drive that had been covered over with all the small scraps of paper, wads of tissues, gum wrappers and other miscellanea that always kept her from finding anything at the bottom of her bag. This time, she was glad her purse was so untidy because the drive had been well hidden.

She went downstairs and booted up the computer. When the desktop appeared, she inserted the drive into the USB port. A folder appeared containing a file dated the same as the one on the label. Media Player opened, and the file began to play. She adjusted the volume and heard an unfamiliar female voice speaking low, almost in a whisper. She hoped the highest volume setting would enable her to hear the monologue.

"My name is Maura Ryan. Some people may know me as Tina Deerborn. If you're listening to this recording, I may not be alive, so please bring it to the police."

Alicia held her breath. Reading Maura's diary hadn't given her a clear indication of the woman's character. Without seeing or hearing her, Alicia couldn't form a true picture of Maura's personality. After seeing her photo and now hearing her voice, Alicia began to compose an image of the person who'd pretended to be Tina Deerborn.

Maura continued after a breath.

"I worked for East Coast Publishing as a sales rep in their White Plains division from May 2000 to November 2013. In May of 2013, I attended their annual conference where employees from all divisions gathered. The conference took place at a hotel in Westchester."

Maura paused for a longer time and then picked up the story.

"The first night of the conference, some of the East Coast employees mingled in the hotel bar. I saw a man sitting alone, so I asked if I could join him. We began talking, and he introduced himself as Peter Fairmont from the Long Island division. I noticed he wasn't wearing a wedding ring, so I assumed he was single. He didn't mention a wife during our conversation. We seemed to talk easily together. At the end of the evening, he invited me to his room."

Another pause. Alicia strained to hear the words because they had grown lower. She was also keeping an ear out for Ramsay's approach.

"I knew I should've been more careful, but Peter treated me well. He wasn't exactly a stranger. He worked for the same company I did except in another division. We spent the entire week's conference together, either in his room or mine. When the conference ended, we exchanged cell numbers."

Alicia winced. Even though the evidence had pointed to Peter having an affair, the verbal confirmation of his cheating punched her in the stomach.

"I didn't hear from him again for a while and thought it had only been a week's fling, but he

called me a month later saying he was going to be in my area. We met at my place in White Plains. This went on for a few weeks, hearing from him off and on, but always meeting at my place. I should've seen the signs earlier, but I guess I didn't want to."

She swallowed. Alicia wondered if Maura was drinking anything while making the recording, but she didn't sound drunk. She sounded quite sober.

"I finally confronted him and asked why we couldn't meet at his place. I started to think he was concealing something." Maura paused again. "He admitted he was married, but he told me he wasn't happy anymore. He said he realized that when he met me. I know men say things like that. I shouldn't have believed him, but I'd fallen in love. I didn't come from a happy home, and he was the first man I'd met who seemed to care for me. Maybe I was too innocent back then, but I still couldn't condone having an affair with a married man. I told him we had to stop seeing one another."

Her voice quickened.

"He got upset. He said he'd ask his wife for a divorce. He'd do anything to keep me. He started to beg. I hated that. I told him I didn't want to be a homewrecker. It hurt to let him go, but I knew I had no other choice."

The recording was silent for a few seconds and then Maura continued in a slightly higher voice.

"I thought it was over. I was sad for a while, but then there was a training workshop. I thought it was just for my division, but Peter attended. It was unsettling for both of us. This was around October a year and a half ago. During the lunch break, he asked if I'd take a walk with him. The grounds of the White Plains office are lovely in the fall, like a college campus. We walked among the red and gold leaves. It was a sunny, crisp day. I felt invigorated but also cautious. I probably never should've accepted, but I'd been so lonely without him."

Alicia was amazed at how descriptive Maura related her tale compared to her diary entries. She could almost see them—Maura with her long black hair and gypsy features hand in hand with tall, fair Peter. She nearly ejected the drive, but she had to hear the rest.

"We started seeing each other again, but I knew things had to be different. I didn't like being deceptive. Then I saw the ad for a library position upstate in Cobble Cove, New York. Peter hadn't told me much about his past, so I had no idea that town was his birthplace. I applied for the job, thinking it was best I quit East Coast. It was too risky for us to be in the same company. Maybe, in the back of my mind, I hoped the change would help me forget him. I didn't have a library degree, but I had knowledge of libraries from selling library products. I decided to use an alias for the position. I wanted to make a fresh start."

Another pause.

"I was surprised the library director in Cobble Cove, Mrs. Sheila Whitehead, hired me on the spot. I packed up my stuff that night and called Peter on his cell. He wanted to see me before I left, but I told him I didn't think that would be wise. I didn't tell him where I was going."

Alicia was becoming anxious Ramsay would arrive before the recording finished. Although the drive seemed to have been playing forever, the WAV file only registered a quarter of the way through.

"When I started working at the Cobble Cove Library, I met a man. He was older than I was, like Peter, but nothing like Peter. His name was John McKinney. His father was the head librarian there. I found out from Sheila—Mrs. Whitehead insisted I use her first name—that John's wife died a long time ago, but he'd never gotten over her death. I think she was trying to match make us, but I was hesitant after my experience with Peter. However, as friendship grew between us, I became more and more attracted to John."

Alicia's heart took another leap. Was Maura reading from a script or actually relating this all from memory?

"When John invited me to the cottage where he was staying, one thing led to another. We ended up

in his bed. Our affair lasted a little over a year. I knew he enjoyed our encounters, but I felt there was a part of him still hung up on his wife. I also enjoyed our lovemaking, but I was still grieving for what I'd had with Peter. The strange part was, because I was using a different name, I almost felt as though Tina was having the affair with John, not Maura. I wanted to tell him my true identity, but I didn't want to spoil his opinion of me. I didn't want to be seen as a liar."

Maura's voice rose.

"Last week, John went to a library conference because his dad wasn't feeling well. While he was away, Peter found me. I don't know how. He told me it didn't matter. He was supposed to be at another sales conference. Instead of attending the conference, he'd booked a hotel near Cobble Cove. I joined him there, and it was as if we picked up where we left off. He told me about Cobble Cove and how he had lived there until he was ten. Like me, he found it a coincidence that was the place where I'd chosen to move. He didn't think anyone would recognize him after all these years. Just in case, he wanted us to keep a low profile. I met him at the hotel after work most nights that week, but I did invite him to John's cottage once while John was away. I know I shouldn't have risked that, but there was only a senile old woman living next door. I still had the key John had given me to make it easier to meet him. Before Peter left Cobble Cove, he said he was going to tell his wife about us, and I

finally agreed that would be the best plan. I also told John when he returned from the library conference that things weren't working between us. I thought he took it well, but I later learned he hadn't. How I wish I'd seen the signs of his obsessiveness earlier."

Alicia was transfixed by this strange tale. In some ways, it followed the information she already knew, but many of the blanks were now being filled in.

Maura's voice quickened once more.

"I found out, to my dismay, Peter was planning to kill his wife. He said a divorce would be messy. He said he could make it look like an accident. I should've gone to the police then, but I feared I'd be seen as an accomplice."

Alicia couldn't believe what she was hearing. So it was Peter who'd rigged the basement stairs. She stared at the sound waves counting down on the computer. There was still about a third of the recording left.

Maura continued, breathless.

"I became frightened of Peter. I wanted to confide in John, but we'd broken up."

She paused again.

"I knew I had to do something before he killed his wife. I finally spoke to John. I asked him to join

me at the cottage the day before yesterday. He thought we were getting back together again, and it was possible we would have. But when I told him about Peter, he reacted much differently than I expected. He wanted me to leave Cobble Cove. He said I wouldn't be safe there. He asked me to tell Sheila I was going home to take care of my mother. I had never told anyone about my family or lack of, so he figured she would believe me. He promised to find me a place, maybe in New Paltz, somewhere not too far where we could still meet and be together. He said he'd take care of Peter. I wasn't sure what he meant. I thought he was going to speak with him. I told him that probably wouldn't do any good. He said he had a better idea and asked me if he could use my car because he had to have his pickup serviced soon for a problem that started on his conference trip. I still wasn't sure what he was planning. He asked me a lot of questions about Peter. He wanted to know what his morning routine was and where he lived and worked. I couldn't answer everything, but I did my best. Peter had started telling me more about his life, and I shared all I knew with John. I put my trust in someone who was no better than the one I feared."

She almost spat out the words, and Alicia could only wonder what would be revealed next.

"It wasn't until John returned and met me late that night at the cottage that I discovered what John had done to take care of Peter. He told me he

followed Peter as he was jogging to work that morning and had run him down. I was horrified. He had used my car to kill Peter. I knew I had no choice but to go to the police. I pretended I was thankful he'd gotten Peter out of my life. I promised him we'd be together after he found a place for us. We could eventually return to Cobble Cove if he wanted, or we could start anew somewhere else. I could go back to my real name, maybe we would marry. I knew this is what he wanted. But after what he'd done, I realized his wife's death had driven him insane. I had to protect myself, so I told Sheila yesterday that I had an emergency call from my mother at home and had to leave. Before I left the library, I made this recording. I'm planning to take it to the police. I know they're looking for my car, and I'm a suspect in Peter's murder. If they knew the whole truth, I would be cleared and could go on with my life. They would see I was just an innocent woman who trusted two dangerous men."

Alicia thought the recording was over until Maura whispered the last words.

"I only hope I'm alive when the police hear this."

The recording ended. Alicia sat there stunned. How much of this was true? If it was false, where was Maura, and why had the recording been in John's bag? Ramsay would arrive any minute. She ejected the drive and held it in her hand. Should she hand it over to the police? It might incriminate

John, but could she still trust him after hearing Maura's account? As she was trying to make up her mind what to do, she heard a car pull up outside and saw it was John. She hurriedly put the drive back in her purse and went to the library door.

As soon as she saw John get out of his car, she knew something was wrong. His face was pale, his dark hair mussed as if he'd been running his fingers through it. Her heart leaped at the thought he might've realized the drive was missing. When he called to her, she discovered the real cause of his disheveled appearance. "Ali, Dad's missing. He didn't answer the door. I thought he was hurt or worse, but he's not in the house at all. I've made a few calls. Dora hasn't seen him, and he hasn't been at Casey's. I'm not sure if he left voluntarily. The door was open, but he usually didn't lock it. You haven't seen him, have you?"

Alicia hoped her doubts and fears didn't show when she replied. "No. He hasn't been here, but neither has Ramsay."

As if she conjured him, the police car appeared, and Ramsay pulled up behind John's car. Getting out, the gruff officer exclaimed, "I've been around town checking on some things. I found that homebound's house and the cottage next to it. I'm ready to conduct the interview. You both can ride in my car if you'd like."

John shook his head. "There's been another development, Detective Ramsay. My father is missing."

Ramsay seemed more annoyed than interested. "How long has he been gone, McKinney? We don't usually consider people missing unless it's been forty-eight hours. I imagine you saw him before you left yesterday."

John's face went from white to red. "You don't understand, Ramsay. My dad has dementia. He might've walked out the door and lost his way or even injured himself."

"People know your father," Ramsay said. "He didn't have a car, so he couldn't have gotten far. As for him hurting himself, you didn't see any traces of blood at his house, did you?"

John ignored the question. Instead he turned to Alicia. "You can go on Betty's interview with Detective Ramsay. I need to find my father." With that, he got back in his car and sped away. Alicia didn't like being left alone with Ramsay, but she reminded herself he was an officer. If John was guilty of what Maura alleged on the drive in her purse, she was far safer with Ramsay.

"Okay then," Ramsay said, shifting gears. "Let's talk to this homebound lady. If McKinney's father turns up, I have lots of questions for him. It's also possible he's hiding out from us. We haven't removed him from our suspect list."

Alicia didn't enjoy riding next to Ramsay. There were McDonald's wrappers on the floor by her feet, and some remains of a Big Mac and fries. She figured Ramsay had recovered from his donut denial by pigging out on fast food. She also noted a smell of sweat coming off him despite the cold temperature and, in the confined space of the squad car, it was suffocating. She thought she would gag if she couldn't open the window. Luckily, their drive was brief. They could've walked it, but Alicia realized Ramsay did as little of that as possible, which was part of the reason for his girth.

Betty's house was dark, as usual. It was still snowing, and her walk was covered. Their two sets of footprints were the first to christen the virgin snow. Ramsay stomped to the door and pressed the bell. "Is the lady deaf?" he asked Alicia after he'd rung the bell several times.

She shrugged. "I don't think so."

Ramsay huffed, and his sour breath came out like smoke on the cold air. He opened the outside door and rapped on the inside one. He rapped so hard Alicia worried he might break a knuckle even through the gloves he wore. A few minutes later, without a reply, he knocked again. Finally, she saw Betty's shadow peering through the kitchen curtain. Ramsay saw it too. "Open up," he demanded, taking out his badge. "Police here."

The door opened slowly, but the woman stood back. "What do you want?" she asked in her screechy voice.

"Open that door or I'll shoot it open," Ramsay said, taking out his gun. Alicia forgot about being safe with him. She felt like running back to the library, but her unbooted feet were frozen to the spot.

The threat of violence got through to Betty, and she opened the door. "All right. Come in already then." Ramsay automatically replaced his gun in his side holster.

The room into which they walked was as dark as the exterior of the house. Alicia imagined Betty saved tons on electricity. The kitchen was small with dark cabinets and drawers fronted by dull bronze knobs. The table was uncovered, a deep walnut with two matching wooden chairs positioned opposite one another. A tall candleholder with half melted wax stood in the middle of the table. Alicia assumed that's all Betty used to light the house after dark.

"Why are you here?" she asked Ramsay and then, turning to Alicia, "You came before. You're the new librarian."

Alicia was surprised Betty remembered her, but the woman seemed to have intervals of recollection. "Yes. I'm Alicia Fairmont." She didn't know why she felt compelled to introduce herself again.

Dragging her cane, Betty walked over to her. Alicia noted how hunched the woman was. She probably suffered from osteoporosis. Either that or her body had become accustomed to bending in the stooped position she used to look out her window at everyone.

She pointed a bony finger at Alicia. "You. I told you to go away."

Alicia expected Ramsay to fend the woman off her. Instead, he took out a pad and pen. "I have some questions for you, ma'am. Did you leave some notes in a library book brought to you recently by Mrs. Fairmont and Mrs. Whitehead?"

Betty's reaction was quick. She turned her finger toward Ramsay. It still hung in midair. "What if I did? Haven't you heard of freedom of speech, Officer?"

"The name is Ramsay, Detective Ramsay. Take

that finger away from me, or I'll charge you with assault."

"If I wanted to assault you, Ramsay, I'd throw some boiling water at you." She laughed. It sounded like a witch's cackle.

Ramsay wasn't amused. Alicia still smelled his sweat. It was worsening along with his anger. "Okay, lady. I'm going to give you one last chance. Tell me why you wrote those notes and what you saw in the house next door this past May."

"I saw nothing," Betty said, allowing her finger and whole hand to drop. She braced her cane. "Even if I did, I'm not going to tell you."

"I can subpoena you and bring you down to the station unless you comply with this questioning."

Betty hesitated. It was obvious she didn't want to leave her house.

"Let me make this easier on you." Ramsay brought two photos from his pocket. Alicia recognized the photo of Maura, but she had no idea how Ramsay had gotten one of Peter. "Do either of these people look familiar?"

Betty grabbed the photos from Ramsay's hands and studied them, her small eyes squinting as she brought the pictures closer. Alicia wondered if the woman needed glasses.

"Yes. I've seen these two." She put the photos down on the table.

"Where did you see them?" Ramsay asked. "Were they in the house next door?" Alicia felt that, in court, that might've been considered a leading question, but she waited for Betty's reply.

"They were there together once. She was usually

292

with the other one."

"Is this the other one?" Ramsay withdrew another photo. This one was of John.

Betty nodded. "That's him, all right. The killer."

Alicia's heart sank even as she wondered why Betty hadn't had that reaction when John had come there with her recently.

"Pardon, ma'am?" Ramsay said, "Please explain that statement."

"Nothing to explain. He killed that other guy. They were in it together for the money." She smiled weirdly, baring a few yellowed teeth. She turned to Alicia. "Better mystery than the rotten ones you brought me."

Ramsay frantically wrote in his book. "What money are you talking about, and how do you know this, ma'am? How was the murder committed?"

Betty took a few minutes to answer and then said, "His sister's money, of course. My eyes may be getting weak, but I still have my hearing."

"Let me get this straight, ma'am." Ramsay's eyes glinted as if he were coming close to a great discovery, "You heard Tina Deerborn discuss the murder of Peter Fairmont with John McKinney, and their motive was Mr. Fairmont's sister's money?" Alicia understood why Ramsay had used Maura's alias when asking Betty, but the woman's reply was vague. "Not sure you got that right, police officer. I heard them fight about Peter, and I know his sister lives up in that North Shore with tons of money. I just couldn't figure how they planned to get it from her, but my mind gets mixed up sometimes."

Ramsay looked disappointed by Betty's

293

admission. He tried another tactic. "Do you know where Tina Deerborn is now? Have you seen her recently?"

Betty shook her head. "I think she skipped with the money. That's what those girls do." On that note, she turned toward her living room. "I'm tired now, Police Officer. Please leave my home."

Alicia expected Ramsay to keep battering Betty with questions but, surprisingly, he honored her request. "Very well. We may be back, though." He didn't thank her for her time or her answers but turned and walked out the door. Alicia almost felt as if he'd forgotten she was with him, but when she followed him out, he said to her, "That lady is mostly senile, but some of what she told us might be worth investigating. I'm sending a report of the interview to Faraday." He opened the door to the police car. "I'll take you back to the library. If McKinney has shown up, I'd like to speak with him."

As Alicia sat in the foul-smelling car, she gazed out the window at the cottage next door to Betty. It was completely dark, as if no one had occupied it in years. She thought of John with Maura, and she felt sick. The account Betty gave contradicted some of the information on the drive she'd found in John's bag, but she wondered if either version were true or if the true version was yet to be known. Riding through the snow next to Ramsay, she remained quiet. The dark was setting in, although it was just after four p.m. The snow was still piling up, and it appeared Cobble Cove was going to get a significant amount through the night, according to the weather station Ramsay had on. "Looks like I'm going to be staying at that dingy inn tonight," the officer muttered next to her. "If this case doesn't break, I may be there a few more days."

Alicia didn't know if he was expecting a reply, but she remained lost in her thoughts.

When they arrived at the library, she saw John's pickup and Sheila's car in the front parking spots. So Sheila had returned. Alicia was surprised because she thought she was staying longer at her daughter's house. Faraday's call may have prompted her to cut her visit short.

Ramsay opened his door, and without a look back at her, strode into the library. She followed, astounded by the detective's rudeness. He didn't even hold the door open for her.

The scene they met when they got inside was disconcerting. John and Sheila were seated on the couch in the reading room. John had his head in his hands. Sheila was trying to console him. Alicia wanted to join her, put her arms around John and hug him, but so many questions were in her mind. If she trusted Peter for over twenty years and he had betrayed her, how could she trust a literal stranger she'd known less than a month?

"No luck on your father, I presume," Ramsay said, walking over to them. John looked up, his eyes red. "There's no sign of him anywhere. He must be lost in this storm. I don't know how far he could've gotten with his cane. Maybe he fell. Can't you do something?"

"Like I said," Ramsay repeated, "We have to wait forty-eight hours. Maybe he's out with a lady friend or something,"

John's sadness shifted to anger. "What kind of cop are you? My father has mourned the loss of my mother for years. He's eighty years old." John got up and went over to Ramsay. He towered over the short, stocky officer. "I want to speak to Faraday. Call him for me."

Ramsay took out his cell phone. "I need to talk to my partner, anyway."

While they waited for Faraday to answer, Sheila walked over to Alicia and said in a low voice, "I came back after I had that call from the police asking about Tina. John has filled me in on some of it. Now I hear the awful news Mac is missing."

"I'm glad you're back."

Sheila smiled. "I'm staying here in John's place tonight. He needs to be at Mac's house to see if he returns. The snow may get pretty bad, and I'm sure you could use the company."

Alicia nodded. She felt relieved.

They heard Faraday over the cell phone Ramsay had put on speaker. "Faraday here."

"Ramsay calling from Cobble Cove. I'll be emailing you the report on my interview with the homebound tonight. Not sure what she told me is reliable, but there's a new development you should also be informed of. The elder McKinney is missing. At least he's been gone since yesterday morning."

"Protocol is to wait forty-eight hours before a search," Faraday said. Alicia couldn't help but notice a weird smile touch the corner of Ramsay's mouth.

"Let me have that phone," John said, reaching for it.

Ramsay passed it to him.

"Faraday, John McKinney here. Your partner informed me you can't start looking for my father yet, but he has dementia. There's a winter storm passing through here, and he could be in danger. Can't you make an exception and bring a search party up here?"

"Sorry, Mr. McKinney, but we're very short staffed at the moment. There was a shooting earlier today. I have men on that case. We're also getting snow down here, so it doesn't make things any easier."

"I don't believe this." John passed the phone back to Ramsay and headed for the door. "I'm going home and hoping Mac shows up there tonight. If he doesn't, I swear someone's going to pay." Alicia shivered at the tone in John's voice and the sound of the door slamming behind him.

Ramsay spoke into his phone again, ignoring the outburst. "I'll get that report out to you ASAP. I'll be staying at the Cobble Cove Inn tonight. I'll contact you from there later. Over and out." He clicked the off button and put the phone back in his pocket. "I'll be in touch tomorrow morning," he said to Alicia and Sheila as he left the library.

When both men were gone, Sheila told Alicia, "I can sleep down here tonight if you want to stay upstairs. I picked up a casserole for us for dinner."

Alicia wasn't in the mood to eat. "I'm not hungry right now, but thank you."

CHAPTER 20

Alicia stood before the long library windows watching the snow gather on the ground. Sheila had gone upstairs to start dinner. She told Alicia she could heat it up later when she got hungry. Alicia doubted her appetite would return that night. Her mind was in a whirlwind like the swirling snow. After contemplating the situation, she decided she had to share the contents of the drive with someone before bringing it to the police, and it couldn't be John. Besides not being sure he could be trusted, there was the matter of Mac's disappearance that preoccupied him. It would make more sense to show it to Sheila. They were spending the night together in the storm, so there would be plenty of time.

Alicia climbed the stairs to see Sheila feeding Sneaky. "I fed him earlier."

Sheila was pouring some dry food into the cat's bowl. She had already replaced his canned food. "I know you have a lot on your mind, Alicia. I figured I could do cat duty for once, but I would appreciate you handling the litter box. It's in a terrible state."

So Mac hadn't scooped Sneaky's box. "Of course. I'll take care of that later."

"Thank you. Are you hungry yet? I'm just heating the casserole I picked up at the market. They were pretty busy with people scrambling to buy provisions for the storm. Bread would've been nice with it too, but not one loaf was left on the shelves."

Alicia was surprised. "I thought they only panicked down by us. Aren't they used to snowstorms here?"

"Not really. Further north they're more relaxed about it." Sheila cleaned her hands at the sink. "I hope Mac is okay. John is really distraught."

"Can I talk to you about something?"

"Sure." Sheila checked the oven. "It'll be a few more minutes. Come sit with me. I can put on some tea if you'd like or we can share a bottle of the red wine I brought over." She indicated the bottle on the table.

"The wine sounds good," Alicia said, sitting at the table. It would help her gain the courage to show Sheila the drive.

Sheila took some glasses out of the cupboard over the sink and poured them both some wine. "There you go." She sat across from Alicia. "What did you want to tell me?"

Alicia noticed how relaxed Sheila had become around her recently. Although she was still technically her boss, she seemed warmer, more approachable.

"I came across something the other day by

accident. It's a USB drive. It has a recording on it."

Sheila looked slightly puzzled. "Was it left in our computer by a patron?"

Alicia took a large gulp of wine and swallowed. It burned her throat. "No. You'll understand when you hear it."

They brought their wine downstairs, although Alicia knew Sheila had a taboo about drinking or eating in the library. She figured this was a special circumstance.

Gathering her pocketbook from the chair in the reading room where she'd left it, Alicia removed the drive. Her hands shook as she booted up the computer and inserted it. Sheila pulled up a chair next to her. Alicia clicked on the folder that appeared and opened the WAV file. She took a breath as the recording began.

As soon as Sheila recognized the voice, she gasped. "Oh, my God! Where did you find this, Alicia?"

"I'll tell you later. Please, just listen for now."

Alicia watched Sheila's face as the file played. She couldn't bear to listen to it again herself, so she blocked it out, concentrating instead on Sheila's expression, which went from surprise to shock to anger.

When the recording stopped, Sheila had composed herself. "All of that is a lie," she said calmly. "I've known John McKinney since I was a young girl. I'm older than he is. I actually babysat him for a time." She smiled at the memory. "Then, when he returned to Cobble Cove after I lost my husband, I knew him as a man who had suffered a great loss but was able to pick up his life. His strength gave me the inspiration to cope with raising my daughter alone. When I began working as director at the library ten years ago after Mac went part-time, I came to know John even better. He's not capable of murder. That woman, Maura she says her real name is, I had no idea about her. I made a mistake hiring her without checking her background. That recording's purpose is clearly blackmail. I don't know where it came from, but you must get rid of it."

"I found it in John's suitcase when I was helping him pack. It was under some of his clothes."

"John had it?" Sheila looked puzzled. "I don't know how he could've gotten that. Did you ask him?"

"I was afraid to." Alicia ejected the drive and placed it next to the computer.

"Afraid? Why? Alicia, certainly you don't think there's any truth in that? I mean, I know she sounds convincing, but that's part of an act."

"I hope you're right, Sheila, but I don't think the drive should be destroyed. Do you have another idea of what I can do with it?"

"Now is not the right time to show it to John, and we can't let the police have it yet, either. I really dislike Detective Ramsay. He's got something stuck up his ass, excuse the expression."

Alicia laughed, and it felt good. "I know what you mean. Can you take the drive? It's been burning a hole in my purse."

Sheila picked it up. "I know a good place for it. Actually, the library has a safe. I had it installed when I became director. I don't believe I ever showed it to you." She walked to the far side of the reading room. Alicia followed. She watched Sheila take out a key and insert it into the lock of a small gray door built into the wall. It opened silently.

"What do you keep in there?"

"Usually the receipts for the day or items found around the library no one retrieves from our lost and found. There was a set of false teeth in here once."

"Oh, gosh," Alicia said. "Did the owner ever claim them?"

"Yes. He finally realized he'd left them in the library bathroom while returning some books."

"Who else has a key to the safe?"

"I gave the only other copy to John. I couldn't trust Mac with one once he started having memory issues, and I never gave one to Tina. I'm glad now I didn't."

"What if John opens the safe?"

"He never uses the safe. I don't intend on keeping it in there long, anyway. I'll probably find a place for it at my house as soon as the storm lets up and I can go back there. Don't worry. It'll be well hidden." As Sheila placed the drive at the bottom of the safe and started to close the door, Alicia caught sight of something familiar. "What's that?" she asked. "That book in the safe?"

"Book? I thought the safe was empty. I instructed Mac to put his receipts in the drawer with the ledgers until I got back." She reached in and pulled out the book lying face down in the safe. It was Tina's diary. "How did this get in here?"

"You said you're the only one who uses the

safe," Alicia pointed out. "That diary was taken from my room on Thanksgiving." Alicia didn't want to consider that John also had a key and had been in her room before it disappeared, but he had helped her search for it and seemed so sincere in his surprise at her discovering it. Was that only an act and this further proof of his guilt?

"I have no idea how it got in the safe. I was in California on Thanksgiving," Sheila said, looking genuinely startled. "I'm going to take both of these to my house. Someone is playing games, and it's not funny."

Before she could comment, Alicia's cell phone buzzed, making her jump. "Hello," she said, her voice quivering.

"Ali, it's me. Dad's not back yet. I'm checking to see if you're okay. It's getting pretty bad outside."

"John." She had to admit it was good to hear his voice. "I'm okay. Sheila's with me."

"Good. I've got Fido here. Looks like Dad's been gone awhile. Fido's food was pretty bare. I restocked it, and he was appreciative."

"Same thing with Sneaky." She watched Sheila remove the drive and diary from the safe and close it. She then put them in a library tote bag she took from behind the desk. The bag was large enough to contain them both.

"I'm thinking that once the storm stops, I may take Fido around town to look for Dad. He's not trained as a police dog or anything, but who knows? He and Dad are pretty close. If the snow doesn't cover Mac's scent, Fido might be able to track him down."

Alicia nodded, although she knew he couldn't see through the phone.

"Can I talk with John?" Sheila asked. She strapped the library bag to the back of a chair.

"Sheila wants to talk to you."

"Put her on. I'll let you go. Have a good night, and be careful, honey. I miss you."

"Miss you too," she felt compelled to add, although it was actually true. She handed Sheila the phone.

"Hi, John. I heard there's no luck on Mac. Alicia and I are hanging in here for now. Ramsay said he was going to stay at the inn tonight. I think you share the same feeling we all have about him. I'm hoping the other detective can make it through the storm tomorrow and lend us a hand."

"I don't put much stock in either of them. They're like doctors. They keep looking for a problem but, by the time they uncover it, the patient could be dead. My dad is out there somewhere in this blizzard, and they insist on waiting to do a search."

"I'm sure they'll start tomorrow when the weather clears. Sit tight, John. I know that's easier said than done, but there are some strange things going on here." She looked over at Alicia. "We may need all the help we can get to figure out what's happening."

After John's call, Sheila suggested they go upstairs to eat. "I know neither of us is probably hungry now, but dinner should be ready.

Alicia had some questions she thought Sheila

could answer, so she followed her upstairs and helped her set the table. The aroma of the casserole, a mixture of cinnamon and other spices, assaulted her as she entered the kitchen. Her stomach growled. She couldn't remember when she ate last.

"Sounds like you're hungry," Sheila said. "It sure smells good." Placing oven mitts over her hands, Sheila removed the hot metal tray. She cut two equal squares of the casserole and placed one on each plate. "The grocer's wife makes these herself. I wish I cooked as well as she does."

The food turned out to be immensely satisfying, and Alicia felt much better by the time she'd finished her serving.

"I'm going to put on the fire downstairs," Sheila told her as they cleaned up their plates. "As I said, I'll be sleeping down there tonight unless you want to switch?"

"No, I'm fine up here."

"Okay. I usually read before bed, but it's too early right now. Care to join me in the reading room, and we can chat a little? I'll put on some tea."

It sounded like a good idea to Alicia. She had so many questions and some of them she was certain Sheila could answer.

***

When they were settled by the fire with their tea mugs, the snow still falling softly outside the reading room's windows, Alicia posed her question. "Sheila, can you tell me about the day Tina—I mean, Maura—left?" she asked, taking a sip of the herbal chamomile tea Sheila insisted would calm their nerves.

Sheila considered a moment, resting her elbow on the tapestry-covered chair's armrest and balancing her tea cup in the other. She looked into the fire. "To really answer your question, Alicia, we need to go back a bit further. The two weeks before she left were strange."

"Strange in what way?"

Sheila remained staring into the fire, her green eyes alight with the flames. "John attended a library conference for Mac at the end of April. You already know he and Tina—sorry, but let me refer to her by that name for now—were involved. They didn't flaunt their attraction, and I was actually happy for him. He'd been lonely for a long time." She turned and looked at Alicia. "That's not to say I thought he was in love. I know what love looks like, and I didn't see it between them."

Alicia was wondering if Sheila was saying this for her benefit or because it was true. John had described his affair with Tina as a physical attraction. Perhaps it was.

"While John was gone," Sheila continued, "I came back to the library one night because I forgot something. Tina wasn't here. At first, I thought she'd just stepped out. Looking back, I think she was staying in the cottage with someone. I knew John had given her the key. They used to meet there occasionally. John would never use the library for their, uh, I guess 'trysts' is the proper word." She looked back into the fire and took a sip of tea. "I saw a stranger leave from the cottage one night when I was driving home. I only saw him from the back. He was fair and tall. Had I seen his face, I may not have recognized him after all these years. It must've been your husband."

"What happened when John returned?"

"They had an argument. Tina was working at the reference desk that day. Mac was there too. I got in late because I overslept. I'm not a morning person, but I usually get up on time. Somehow, I slept through my alarm. When I got to the library, they were yelling at each other right there in public. Luckily, no patrons were around, but I was so surprised because it wasn't like John at all." She finished her tea in a gulp and continued. "Actually, it was Tina doing all the yelling. John was just standing there taking it all."

"What was the argument about?" Alicia wanted to know. "What was Tina saying to John?"

"I could only hear a few words because, as I entered the library, she calmed down. I think I heard John tell her they would talk about it later. The only words I could make out from Tina were 'How dare you accuse me of seeing him to get you jealous. At least he's not pining over his dead wife.' That hit John below the belt, but mind you, this isn't verbatim. Although my memory is better than Mac's, it's not that great."

Verbatim or not, Alicia thought it odd. "What other strange things happened?"

"I can't remember the exact date. It was probably mid-May. Tina told me she needed some time off the next morning to see her dentist in White Plains. She said her tooth had been bothering her for a while, and she was sure she needed a root canal. It would take a few hours between travel and the procedure. I told her it was fine, but I also recommended our local dentist, Mr. Klein, who's been my dentist for years. She said she preferred her own dentist, and I understood. If you find a dentist you're comfortable with, it's probably a good idea to stick with him or her if you can."

Alicia nodded, wondering if she was due for her six-month dental checkup. Since Peter died, she'd stopped keeping track of appointments. "What happened then?"

"Tina came back around lunch time. Mac was still at the desk. It was almost his time to leave, so I was glad to see her. The strange part was, when she spoke, she didn't sound numb, so I wondered if she'd had the root canal. I couldn't imagine not having Novocain for that type of work. I even asked her how it went, and she said it wasn't too bad. Then she broke the news to us. She said she'd heard from her mother in Florida who had taken ill suddenly. She was sorry, but she had to leave right away to go down there and take care of her."

"So you and Mac were there when she said this, John wasn't?"

"That's correct, and I don't think he would've protested at that point. He probably was hoping to be rid of her."

That sounded similar to John's response when Alicia asked him about the breakup before she realized he had a recording Maura made in his overnight bag.

Sheila continued without further prompting. "I

thought what Tina said was odd because I couldn't see how she'd heard from her mother right after being at the dentist. She'd rushed into the library, as if she'd just come from there, but maybe I was wrong. She went upstairs without a further word and started packing. She definitely seemed in a hurry, and I worried her mother was so ill she feared she would die before she got to her."

"What did Mac say?"

"He was surprised too. He was concerned we would be short staffed and even offered to start up full-time again until we found someone else. I told him that wasn't necessary. I suggested maybe Tina would be back after her mother either died or recovered. I didn't say those words exactly, but that's what I thought."

"And Tina left the following morning?"

"Yes. Her bags were packed, and I helped her put them in the car. She only had one full case and a travel bag. She said she wanted to say goodbye to John and asked where she could find him. I thought he would be at the newspaper office, or maybe at home with Mac, who had called in sick that day. I never saw her again."

"Did John say he saw her that day?"

"I didn't ask. I figured it was between them."

Now it was Alicia's turn to stare into the fire. "Where do you think she is now?"

Sheila sighed. "I have no idea. She never contacted me afterwards." She stood up and walked to the window. "Let's hope the snow stops soon and John finds Mac. I'm sorry you got involved in all this, Alicia. It seems I made a bad decision that affected everyone. If I had any idea Tina wasn't who she said she was, none of this would've happened."

Alicia didn't think Sheila should blame herself, but was her guilt only related to hiring Tina or was there more to it than that? She couldn't help but think Sheila may have been the last person to see Tina. She was also the only one who normally used the safe where Tina's diary turned up, although it was highly unlikely she could've taken it while she was onboard a plane. But here Alicia was, alone on a stormy night, with this woman who might know more than she was telling.

CHAPTER 21

Alicia didn't sleep well that night. When she finally managed to fall asleep, she fell into a deep slumber. She had another dream, like the one with the beach and the wedding rings.

There was snow in this one. She and John were trudging through knee deep snow. As they walked, their footprints were disappearing in the swirling snow. Alicia kept falling, and John kept helping her up, his arm guiding her as they made their way slowly up a hill. She finally realized they were headed for the top of Cove Point and then, as they grew closer to their destination, the snow whipping into her hair and face, stinging with its coldness, she saw the cottage. It was at the top of the hill where she and John had their picnic not long ago.

As they approached, she noticed someone standing outside the cottage beckoning them. It was a woman completely dressed in white, so it was hard to distinguish her against the white landscape. The woman's dark hair stood out, stark black against all the white. Alicia realized who the woman was and what she was wearing. It was Maura in a wedding gown. Just as she and John crested the last rise of the hill, Alicia heard a noise that started as a low hum and then grew louder. John began running toward the cottage and Maura, but Alicia suddenly couldn't move. She was stuck in a snowdrift. She called to John, but he didn't look back. As John reached the cottage, Maura disappeared into the whiteness. John fell into a snowbank, the snow completely covering him. Alicia couldn't make it any further. She screamed John's name, but there was no answer except the roaring of the wind.

Alicia sat up shivering, even though the room was warm. She still heard the noise from the dream and Sheila calling her from downstairs. "Are you up, Alicia? John is here."

Alicia grabbed her robe and slipped into it. Still sleepy and remembering the dream, she joined Sheila downstairs. John wasn't with her, but she saw him through the library windows. He was on a snow blower, clearing the walk. Fido ran next to him, snow hitting his furry face. Alicia realized the noise of the blower was what she'd heard in her dream.

"What time is it?" she asked Sheila, who was also in her robe.

Although the sun wasn't fully up, the snow made the sky appear lighter by its reflection.

"Six a.m. I have a feeling John didn't sleep well. I'm glad he's clearing our walk. I'm putting on some coffee for us. I'm sure he'll appreciate a cup after he finishes."

It wasn't long before John rapped on the door. Sheila opened it, and John and Fido bounded in, both shedding snow over the library entryway.

"Look at you two," Sheila exclaimed. "You'd better mop up this floor later, John. You know animals aren't allowed in the library." She was half smiling as she admonished him.

"What about Sneaky?" John asked.

"That's different. He's a library cat."

"Well, maybe you should get a library dog too. Fido would make a good watch dog. You should consider it."

Hearing his name and sensing an animal intruder, Sneaky appeared out of nowhere, arching his spine and hissing at the dog. Fido backed away in mock terror.

"Some watchdog, afraid of a cat." Sheila laughed.

John turned to Fido. "It's okay, boy, that's only a kitty." Sneaky scooted away, and Fido relaxed at John's side.

"You're in time for coffee. We aren't even dressed yet."

John smiled. "I've been up for hours. I've already cleared the snow at the inn. Ramsay tells me Faraday is going to be delayed because of the storm. The roads are still pretty bad. Dora gave me some fresh muffins for snow blowing the walk, and I brought them here for you ladies to share with me. I'll get them from the truck and be right back. Fido can stay outside. It's not that cold right now, and he loves the snow."

When John returned with a brown bag of muffins, he hung up his coat. Sheila had brought a towel down from the bathroom so he could wipe his boots. "Are you sure Fido is safe outside? He's welcome to come in. It's Sunday, and I was just kidding about the no animal rule."

"Fido is fine outside, and I don't plan to be here long. I need to continue searching for Dad." John turned to Alicia. "Would you mind coming with me, Ali?"

Before Alicia could reply, Sheila said, "We'll both go. Come upstairs and warm up, John. Let's have Dora's delicious muffins before we brave the cold. I'm glad I took my winter boots out early." She looked down at Alicia's feet. "I have another pair that may fit you at my house, Alicia. You can try them on when we get there. I think we're about the same size."

"Thanks," Alicia said, following Sheila and John upstairs.

When they were eating at the table, Sheila pulled over the desk chair from the storage room so John could join them. Alicia asked if Ramsay was finally looking for Mac.

"He is, but he's pursuing some other avenues as well," John said. He bit into a muffin, swallowed some coffee, and then wiped his mouth with one of the napkins Dora also supplied in the breakfast bag. "He said he was heading to the green after breakfast to talk to some people. Most of the stores are closed on Sunday or they open pretty late, so I don't know how much luck he'll have. Unlike Faraday, I'm not too convinced of his competency and that's why I want to do more searching on my own and bring Fido along."

"We have to be careful, John," Sheila warned. She had eaten half a muffin and taken a few sips of coffee. "We can't take this into our own hands. When the roads clear, Faraday will be here and maybe some officers from New Paltz or somewhere else."

Alicia wondered if Sheila would mention the drive or the diary to John, but she was glad when she didn't. She noticed Sheila had filled the tote bag with some library books to keep them hidden until she brought the bag to her house to find a place for them.

"So where do you intend to start searching for Mac?" Alicia asked.

"I'm going to let Fido guide us. I hope he can smell Dad's scent through all this snow."

***

Before they left, Sheila reminded John they had to stop at her house to pick up the extra pair of snow boots for Alicia. John pulled the pickup close to the library's front door, and Alicia, wearing sneakers, got into the front seat. Sheila sat in back with Fido, who had been waiting patiently for John outside. "Great, so I get to sit with the dog," she exclaimed.

John laughed. "I hope it isn't too cold back there. I opened the windows so Fido could enjoy the ride, and you wouldn't get so choked up by his fur."

Alicia hadn't yet been to Sheila's house and

didn't realize it was so close to the library. It was the opposite direction from Betty's house and the cottage, a few blocks before the green. It was a nice looking home with a white fence around the front. Unlike some of the houses she'd seen so far, this one was more of a country-style modern ranch. Instead of brick or stone, the exterior was of lemon yellow aluminum siding with white-trimmed windows. There was a wraparound porch where some flower pots hung now covered in snow. The walk hadn't been cleared, but John had loaded the snow blower into the rear of the pickup behind Sheila and Fido, along with a few shovels. Since the path to the door was short, he got out and started to shovel while Fido frolicked again in the snowy wonderland.

"For Pete's sake, John," Sheila said, grabbing the second shovel from the back of the pickup. "Let me give you a hand with that before you have a heart attack."

Alicia watched as Sheila worked alongside John. It wasn't something she'd expected from the library director. Nor was the easy friendship she felt the two shared that included the joking way they regarded one another. It wasn't jealousy she felt, at least not in the romantic sense. She only wished she could feel that type of trust with someone. She thought she'd felt it with Peter, but she learned it was invested in the wrong place. When she started to feel it with John, occurrences began happening that raised too many doubts in her mind.

Alicia was surprised at how easily Sheila and John dug through the snow piles. She felt slightly guilty sitting in the car while they were working so hard, but she definitely didn't have the footwear to help. She made a note to visit a Cobble Cove shoe store soon to outfit herself for the upcoming winter season.

When Sheila and John were done, Sheila opened her door and waved Alicia to come inside. She switched on a light, and Alicia's senses were bathed in warmth and mellowness. Another surprise. She should've expected a handsomely decorated home from someone who dressed as smart as Sheila. The living area was a yellow similar to the exterior with cream accents. The room featured a few watercolor paintings; a beige couch with ivory-tasseled pillows; an audio system and large screen TV set into the wall opposite a cream-fronted fireplace with a trio of photos upon its mantel; and a bookcase full of books.

"I know you want to get started looking as soon as possible, John," Sheila said, "but I can put on some coffee or tea to warm us up first if you'd like." They were standing in the kitchen where pine cabinets and white appliances lined the wall-papered room. The wall paper featured a pattern of white chef hats and kitchen utensils against a sunny yellow background. It was bordered in a soft white shade that matched the ceiling.

"That's okay. Maybe later, Sheila. Thanks."

"I'll get the boots then," she said. "Both of you, please have a seat while you wait."

John sat on the couch. "Come sit with me, Ali," he said, patting a space beside him. She sank down into the soft contours of the cushions. It felt like sitting on a layer of padded cotton. She was reminded of the dreamy divan in Pamela Morgan's bedroom.

"Was that Sheila's husband and her family?" Alicia asked, looking across at the three photos on the fireplace mantel. The first was a wedding shot of a younger Sheila in a white gown. She held a bouquet of pink roses and stood next to a dark-haired man in a tuxedo. The middle photo featured Sheila holding a curly-haired baby in a pink dress on her lap. The dark-haired man sat next to them. The last, a more current picture, featured Sheila with a dark-haired young woman and two red-haired young girls.

"Yes," John said. "Doug died young. Sheila doesn't speak of him much. He had a brain aneurysm. It was quite sudden. Sheila's daughter was only five years old when it happened. That was over twenty years ago. I was still in New York."

"That's terrible." Alicia could barely imagine the strength Sheila must've had to raise her young daughter on her own after such a sudden tragedy.

John moved closer to her. "Ali, I've noticed something different between us. Is something bothering you?" His blue eyes looked into hers. Up close, she could see dark circles under them. She looked away.

"Sorry, John. It's nothing. I'm just upset about all of this.

"I know." He sighed. "I didn't sleep much at all last night worrying over Dad and everything else. I wish this would all come to an end. If Maura's around, I hope she shows herself." His hands balled into fists.

Alicia wondered what was taking Sheila so long down the hall and figured she was hiding the drive and diary because she'd brought the tote bag with her. She glanced at the books on the bookshelves. It was a modern collection consisting of mostly mysteries and thrillers. Authors such as Harlan Coben, James Patterson, and Tess Gerritsen lined the shelves. She even saw *Gone Girl*, the recent blockbuster turned movie. Why did Sheila buy books if she could borrow them from the library? Alicia knew she was guilty of the same money waster, but the thought brought her back to her lost home and furnishings, including some of the favorite books in her own library. Even though the arsonist was caught, it would be several months if not longer before she received a settlement. She was glad she would at least get some compensation eventually.

Sheila returned carrying a purse and a pair of white calf-length snow boots. "Here you go, Alicia. I hope they fit." She placed them on the floor before Alicia and watched as she slipped off her sneakers and tried on the boots. Her feet glided into them easily. There was a bit of room in the toes but not so much to consider them loose. She zipped up the sides and stood.

"They feel good," Alicia said, walking around the room.

"Look good too," Sheila commented, appearing satisfied she'd done a good deed.

John got up. "Okay. We're all set. Let's get going. I'm sure Fido is as eager as we are."

As they left, Sheila grabbed her purse. "I have an extra pair of gloves in here in case you need them too," she told Alicia.

The three of them took the same seats they'd occupied last time. Fido was waiting for them with his head halfway out an open window, his tongue lolling, cold air forming a cloud of smoke as he breathed. John walked by and petted his head. "We're ready, Fido. Let's go find Dad."

***

They drove back to the library. John suggested that might be a good starting point for their search because that was the last place Mac was supposed to be.

"It's strange because he hung up a Christmas wreath," Sheila said, "but according to Alicia, Sneaky hadn't been fed. I saw the litter box, and it was a mess. I doubt it's been scooped since we left."

"The Christmas Fair Committee meeting was supposed to be on Friday," John told her. "Maybe Edith or Rose came by and convinced Dad to put up some decorations. It's possible he closed the library early. He said he might do that if it wasn't busy. Maybe he just forgot to feed Sneaky before he left."

"That's possible," Sheila mused. They had all gotten out of the pickup and stood knee deep in snow. Alicia was thankful for the borrowed boots. She watched as John released Fido, who came bounding out the back door, eager to play in the snow again.

"No, boy," he said. "No play time now. I'll toss you some snowballs later." He smiled and then, changing his voice to one of authority, he commanded the dog, "Sit, Fido, sit." At once, the golden retriever obeyed.

"Nice trick," Sheila said.

"Dad trained him. Let me try this." He pulled a red handkerchief from his pocket and held it up to the dog's nose as he changed his voice again and issued another order. "Find Mac, Fido, find Mac."

"Fingers crossed Mac's scent is strong enough on that handkerchief that Fido can detect it through all this snow," Sheila said.

The dog didn't move. John waited a few more minutes before he repeated the handkerchief command ritual.

"Looks like it's not working," Sheila said after the dog remained frozen by John's side.

"Sorry, John," Alicia added.

Then, as if being dared, Fido sniffed the handkerchief John held in front of his nose. He turned his head first left and then right. His tail grew erect. He began walking in the opposite direction of the library from Sheila's house. John brightened as he took after the dog. "Good boy, Fido. Keep going."

Alicia and Sheila walked a few paces behind John, trying to keep up with him through the snow. They lost sight of him once making a turn, but then he called out to them, "Sheila, Ali, come here."

Following his voice, the women found him standing by Fido in front of the cottage next to Betty's house.

"I should've known," John said when they'd joined him by the door. To Alicia, the place still looked unoccupied with the curtains drawn and lights off. John tried the door knob. It turned but didn't open. "Locked," he said, looking back at the ladies.

He began rapping on the door. "Dad, are you in there?" There was no response, but Fido's ears perked up as if he heard someone on the other side of the door.

John fished a key out of his pocket. "I still have the key from when I stayed here. Why don't you two stay outside while I go in?"

Alicia knew he was suggesting this in case there was something inside that wouldn't be suitable for them to see. She felt a prick of fear touch her spine in the icy air.

Sheila put her arm out and guided Alicia back. "Do as John says. He'll call us if he needs us."

At that moment, Detective Ramsay pulled up in his police car. He got out as swiftly as he could given his girth and the weight of the gun he extended. "Hold up, folks," he exclaimed. "Are you harboring Mr. McKinney in there?"

"Harboring?" Sheila put her no-nonsense face on. "Who do you think you are, Detective Ramsay? This is my employee's cottage. His son has a key. We were trying to find him because you were dragging your hide in the matter. I personally would like to speak to your partner when he arrives to let him know how incompetent you've been here."

Alicia felt like clapping, but Ramsay's face turned scarlet. "Okay, lady, move aside so I can get in that cottage."

Sheila blocked the door, and Alicia thought nonsensically of the childhood tale of the *Three Little Pigs and the Big Bad Wolf.* Ramsay certainly looked as though he was ready to huff and puff. But as Ramsay and Sheila stared each other down, Fido began barking. Alicia thought he might attack the detective. Instead, he darted past Sheila into the cottage.

"It's okay," John called out. You can all come in."

Sheila turned and walked in before Ramsay could get through the door. Alicia was last to enter the cottage. The lights were still out, although enough daylight peeked through the curtains for her to see the scene before her.

The cottage consisted of a large room and a smaller one to the side that must've been a bathroom. The large room contained a simple double bed with a nightstand, unplugged lamp, and a bureau. There was a chair and table by the window. John sat at the table, which was covered in open food wrappers and several half full water bottles. The scent of spoiled food wafted in the air and almost made Alicia's stomach turn.

On the bed, sitting quite calmly, was Mac, petting Fido. When he saw them all, he said, "Greetings. I've been waiting for someone to find me."

"Dad, can you please tell us what's going on here?" John asked. "I saw you have more food stocked in the closet. Why were you hiding out here?"

Although his tone sounded reprimanding, Alicia could tell he was glad he'd found his father and Mac wasn't hurt.

Before Mac could answer his son's questions, Ramsay stepped forward. "Excuse me, Mr. McKinney, but I'm the officer here, and I'm the one who asks the questions."

Sheila gave Ramsay such a look Alicia almost laughed, but Mac had a better response. "Well, Officer, I'm the one who answers the questions, and I think it's rather rude of you to interrupt my son."

Alicia could tell Ramsay sought a fitting response, but before he could think of one, his cell phone buzzed. "Just a minute," he said, tapping the screen and putting the receiver to his ear. "Ramsay here. Is that you, Faraday? What? You're in town? Where? At the library? Okay, you might want to come down here. I found the old man." While Ramsay gave the directions to the cottage, Alicia couldn't help marveling at his taking all the credit for finding Mac. She secretly wished Fido would take a piece out of Ramsay's ample derrière.

As he switched off his phone, Ramsay said, "Faraday's on his way. When he gets here, we can all have a nice little chat."

CHAPTER 22

It didn't take Faraday long to arrive. When he walked in, his pant legs covered in snow, he scanned the room, observing them all standing around Mac, who seemed to enjoy being the center of attention. "Heck of a storm that was, and half the roads aren't plowed yet. I had to take several detours." He turned to Ramsay. "So, fill me in, Ron. What's going on here, and why are you holding that gun?"

Ramsay nervously put the gun back in his holster." I was having some trouble gaining entry to this cottage." In place of the gun, he pointed his finger at Sheila. "She blocked my way."

Faraday ignored the comment. "I see Mr. McKinney has been located and is safe, so let's get on with our jobs. We still have to find Ms. Ryan. Any sign of her?"

Ramsay shook his head.

"Excuse me, Detective Faraday," Mac said, standing with the assistance of his cane at the side of the bed. "My son asked me some questions your partner rudely interrupted. I would like to answer those questions now, and please put my replies on record."

Faraday looked puzzled, but he took out his cell phone and opened what Alicia assumed was Evernote or another note-taking app. He must've decided it would be faster using technology than a pen and pad. "What did your son ask you, Mr. McKinney?"

"He wanted to know why I was hiding. The thing is, I wasn't hiding. I was meditating."

A slight smile touched the corners of Faraday's mouth, but Ramsay, who had also taken out his cell phone, retained his grim expression. Alicia saw him press a voice memo icon, so she assumed he was trying to record Mac's account.

Mac turned to John. "Remember, John, when we used to go camping on Bear Mountain? We'd pitch a tent and bring an oil lamp, a few sandwiches, and jerky strips?"

"Yes, Dad. I enjoyed that time with you, but is that what you were doing here alone with the lights out in a snowstorm, pretending to camp?"

"I needed time and space to think. When you're surrounded by all the modern contraptions— computers, cell phones, gadgets, and such, you can't really think. There's no way to concentrate." Mac walked toward the detectives, who stood side by side. He turned his face toward Ramsay. "I would recommend you try it, Detective Ramsay. You seem too wound up. Too stressed. Meditation will relax you and clear your mind."

"Get to the point, McKinney," Ramsay said.

"Why were you holing out here away from everyone? You're wasting our time here."

Mac smiled. "It's true, time is very precious. While I was here meditating on some issues, I came to a decision. Please take this down, Detectives." He glanced at John. Fido had left the bedside and gone to stand by his younger master. "I apologize, son, for not being the kind of dad you imagined I was." As he spoke, Alicia noticed a framed picture on the nightstand near a flashlight. It was a photo of a blonde woman, a much younger Carol Parsons.

Before John could say anything, Mac continued, addressing everyone this time. "I'm eighty years old, and I'm not proud of all the things I've done in this life, but there are choices we all face sometimes that are difficult to make. You do the best you can." He sat back down on the bed and covered his head with his hands, similar to the way John had the afternoon before when Alicia saw him with Sheila at the library.

Ramsay was about to comment when Faraday whispered something to him. Alicia thought he said, "Let him continue."

"You won't find Tina or whatever her name is because I killed her," Mac said. There was a collective gasp around the room, but Alicia saw the biggest reaction from Sheila, who turned completely white. "No, Mac," she said. "Please don't."

But the story spilled from him once he'd loosened it from his memory. It seemed as if it were an effort for him to hold it back. "She was going to blackmail my son. I had to stop her."

"Mr. McKinney," Faraday said. "We can't take this down without reading you your Miranda rights." He nudged Ramsay to turn off the voice app.

"I don't care about my rights," Mac said. "I'm an old man. I've kept this secret for too long."

John went to his father. "Dad, we can get a lawyer. Don't say anything more."

Mac ignored him. "Sorry, son, but it has to be said. The truth must be told. I've deceived too many people. First it was Carol. I loved her too much to let her go. But she left me anyway, and yet I destroyed her family. I never had the chance to tell her the truth, to admit what I'd done. Then Tina came, and, even though she was young, I thought she would make a nice match with you. I had no idea she was so evil. When she called the house the day she was leaving and I told her you weren't home, she asked me to meet her here at the cottage. I had called in sick at work that morning because my allergies were bothering me. They hit pretty hard in the spring. When I showed up, she showed me a computer drive she said contained evidence you murdered Peter Fairmont. If I didn't give her a million dollars, she would release it to the police. I didn't have the money, but she thought I could get it from my daughter, Pamela Morgan." He looked over at Alicia. "When you came to town, Alicia, I was concerned you might find out some things that were better left alone. I typed a note to try to persuade you to leave. I came in the library and left it. Then I went out again and returned. You asked me if I saw anyone on my way in, so I knew you didn't suspect me. As time passed, I regretted that foolish action because I realized you might be the right one for my son. Tina had hurt you, as well. I also put the diary in the library safe on Thanksgiving morning. Before we left for the inn, I went back upstairs for my jacket while you and John were waiting for me in the car. I heard some scratching coming from the bedroom. It seems Sneaky was locked inside. When I opened the door and released him, I noticed the diary by the bed. I didn't have much time to decide what to do with it. I brought it downstairs and tried the safe because I'd found it unlocked in the past. I was in luck, and Sheila had left it open again. I figured I could leave it in there and deal with it later. After Thanksgiving, I completely forgot about it when I made my plan to disappear." He took a breath.

"Please, Mac," Sheila said, joining John by the old man's side. "You don't have to do this."

Faraday signaled to Ramsay, who began reading Mac his Miranda rights.

"No," Sheila screamed, and suddenly everyone was quiet. Ramsay stopped in mid-sentence. She withdrew the drive and diary from her purse and threw them toward the detectives. They landed on the ground near Ramsay's foot, and both he and Faraday dived toward them like single women at a wedding trying to catch the bridal bouquet. Faraday retrieved the drive while Ramsay grabbed the diary.

"I was going to destroy these or hide them somewhere in my house where they wouldn't be found, but now I'm glad I didn't. I was here that day too. I followed Tina to the cottage. I heard her and Mac arguing. I heard the terrible things she was saying. When he ignored her demands, she attacked him. He almost fell. Then he picked up his cane." She paused, her voice breaking. "I was at the door. I saw him hit her, but it was self-defense. He only meant to stop her, but he hit her with his cane, and she fell and hit her head against the bedside table. I tried to revive her, but she was already dead."

Mac picked up the story. "I didn't know what to do. I wanted to go to the police, but Sheila had another idea. We got the keys to Tina's car, and Sheila put the body in it. She tossed the suitcases in the cove, and I thought she would throw Tina in along with them, but Sheila wanted to bury her. The inn was closed that day because Dora was out celebrating her birthday. Sheila had given her a plant as a gift the day before that she planted in her garden. I helped Sheila dig a grave near that plant in the soil that was still soft. She wrapped the body in some blankets she got from her house and said a prayer as we covered the dirt over. Then she drove Tina's car while I followed in the pickup. She abandoned it, and I drove her back to Cobble Cove. She wanted me to get rid of the drive too, although I'd never heard what was on it. I told her I would, but I brought it home and hid it in my house instead. I put it in a drawer under some clothes and forgot about it. I was so nervous that day I hardly knew what I was doing."

Everyone was silent, only the sound of Faraday and Ramsay tapping the keys on their phones could be heard. Even Fido stood quietly by John's side. Alicia now realized how the drive ended up in

John's overnight bag. Mac must've hidden the drive in one of John's drawers and when John packed hurriedly to leave for Long Island, he must've thrown it in his case along with the clothes on top of it. Alicia also realized Betty, the homebound, had written her note for Sheila, not Tina. When she wrote, *'I know what you did. I saw you with him,'* she was referring to seeing Sheila with Mac disposing of Maura's body and luggage. How Maura knew Pamela was Mac's daughter still needed to be explained, but after having gone to Brookville under the pretense of selling books to Pamela for her home library and seeing how wealthy Peter's sister was, Alicia knew it wouldn't have been hard for Maura to hatch up a blackmail scheme.

After a few minutes, Faraday spoke. "It appears to me we need to recover the body and make an arrest. Because of the storm, it may take some time because the ground is frozen and difficult to dig. We don't have jurisdiction here, but I plan to contact the officers at the nearest police precinct."

"Can I cuff them?" Ramsay eagerly asked.

"No need. They're not resisting arrest. Mr. McKinney has willingly admitted his guilt, and Mrs. Whitehead will be considered an accomplice in the matter."

John looked from his father to the library director. "What can I do?" he asked. "Surely, if Dad was protecting himself and Maura was threatening to blackmail him, he should be released."

"No, son," Mac said. "I should be tried for my crimes. If anyone should be released, it should be

Sheila. She was only protecting me."

"That's for the law to decide," Faraday said. "I need both of you to come with me to the New Paltz station and make a statement." He turned to John and Alicia. "You two need to come, also. You can drive with Ramsay."

Faraday's partner seemed disappointed he wasn't transporting the alleged criminals, but Alicia thought she and John were getting the raw end of the deal.

"What am I supposed to do with that animal?" Ramsay asked as Fido followed John.

"He can sit in the back with us."

"Just keep him quiet and don't let him block my view."

"He likes to look out the window," John said as he opened the door for Alicia. Faraday had pulled his car up in front of his partner's, and Sheila and Mac were already inside. Faraday started the engine and was waiting for Ramsay to follow.

Alicia was relieved when Ramsay used the automatic release to roll down the back windows. Fido stuck his head out of the one behind the passenger seat. John slid in next to him. "Good boy. Sit, Fido."

Alicia sat by the window behind Ramsay. She breathed in the fresh, cold air, a relief from the stale, sweat-filled interior of the police car. As she filled her lungs with clean oxygen, she also attempted to clear her mind. Did Mac really kill Maura, or was it an accident as Sheila claimed? What about John? Was Maura actually trying to blackmail Mac about John's involvement in Peter's hit and run? Were her accusations false, or was the recording accurate? She glanced over at John petting Fido and hoped the truth would prove both him and his father innocent.

CHAPTER 23

The New Paltz police station was a stone building located on Clearwater Road. Alicia noticed the parking lot was cleared and only a large mound of melting snow remained piled on the side of the curb. Ramsay took the parking spot next to Faraday. His partner had already gotten out along with Sheila and Mac.

Ramsay rolled up the windows, and John tugged at Fido's leash just in time to save his head from being caught.

"That dog won't be allowed in the station," Ramsay growled.

Faraday approached their car. "If John keeps him on the leash, he'll be fine. I radioed ahead that we were on our way and filled them in as much as I could."

Ramsay joined Faraday while John and Alicia exited the police car. John held tight to Fido's leash. The dog walked obediently by his side.

The two officers led the way into the building. Sheila walked next to Mac, who was hurrying on his cane to keep up with the policemen's brisk pace. Alicia was surprised at Ramsay's quick strides, but she heard him puffing and imagined it wasn't too easy for him to match his partner's steps. Ramsay flashed his badge at the man at the desk.

Faraday said, "Good afternoon. I'm Michael Faraday, and this is Ronald Ramsay. We're from Precinct 2 on Long Island. I called a few minutes ago and spoke with Detective Carter about the McKinney case."

The young man, whose badge read Craig Wilson, nodded. "Yes. He's in his office. He already told me to let you in when you arrived. I'll show you the way." He got up, and they followed him down the fluorescent lit corridor that smelled of Lysol.

Fido remained quiet by John's side. Ramsay stared at the dog from time to time but knew he had nothing to complain about.

When they were escorted to Carter's office, John asked Wilson if it was okay to bring Fido in with them.

"It shouldn't be a problem. We get lots of seeing eye dogs here."

"The Cobble Cove people have arrived," Wilson announced in the doorway. He moved aside to allow all of them to enter. "Should I bring some extra chairs?"

"That won't be necessary. We'll move to the conference room," a balding man in his fifties said from behind a desk. "I'm Detective Carter." He stood and extended his hand to shake Faraday's and then Ramsay's. He smiled over their heads at

Alicia, John, Sheila, and Mac. Walking around the desk, he indicated they should follow. "The conference room will be a more comfortable place for us all to talk. There's coffee and donuts in there too." Alicia noticed Ramsay's eyes widen at the mention of food and drink. She couldn't consider eating or drinking while Mac's, John's, and Sheila's fates were about to be determined.

They gathered around the long conference table. A side table contained a coffeemaker, a tower of white Styrofoam cups, a few half and half containers, some napkins, and a box of Dunkin Donuts and Munchkins. A Windows PC sat in the corner.

"Before we begin, please help yourselves to refreshments," Carter said, heading to the table for a cup of coffee.

No one else moved from their seat except Ramsay, who grabbed a Boston Cream donut and a bunch of munchkins that he scooped up in a napkin and brought back to his seat along with coffee.

John, who sat between Mac and Alicia, glanced over at his father. "Dad, would you like me to get you something?"

"No thanks, John. I'm fine."

Fido sniffed the air and opened his mouth for the first time since he left Cobble Cove. He let out a low whimper.

"Looks like your dog's hungry," Carter said. "I have a Golden at home too." He brought a plain munchkin over to Fido, who ate it from his hand. Ramsay looked on in disgust from across the room.

"Thanks," John said. "Dad likes to give him

sweets once in a while. I'm afraid he's a bit spoiled."

Carter laughed. "I do the same with Clyde."

"Aren't you going to question them already?" Ramsay cut in. He was clearly annoyed with all the attention the dog was receiving.

Carter walked back to his seat. Fido's big brown eyes followed him, but he stayed at John's side. "Yes. I won't keep you waiting, Detective Ramsay. I know how busy you are." Alicia wondered if the comment was sarcastic. Carter continued, "Please, folks, take your coats off. You can leave them on the backs of your chairs."

Everyone complied except Sheila and Mac. Sheila kept on her short fur stole, and Mac retained his quilted plaid vest.

A slim woman in a brown tailored suit stepped silently into the room carrying a small machine. She took the single chair next to the computer and placed her device on the desk. "This is Miss Marek," Carter introduced her. "She's our stenographer. She'll be taking some notes as we talk." He turned to Faraday on his right. "Can you please repeat some of the information you told me on the phone, Detective Faraday?"

Ramsay looked disappointed he hadn't been permitted to speak first, and Alicia imagined him controlling the impulse to raise his hand.

Faraday gave a brief background to the events in Cobble Cove and Long Island. He ended with Mac's confession and how they hadn't been allowed to read him his Miranda rights.

The room was quiet except for Miss Marek's

keyboarding as Carter considered the presented facts. "May I have the recording and the diary," he said finally.

Faraday reached into the pocket of the coat behind him and retrieved the drive. He handed it to Carter.

"And the diary?" Carter turned to Ramsay.

"I haven't had time to review it," Ramsay said. He was chewing a munchkin, and his words were a bit garbled.

"We'll take care of that."

Ramsay got up, dusted some of the powder from the donut off his pants, and searched through his coat. Locating the diary, he reluctantly gave it to Carter.

"Were either of these items checked for prints?" the New Paltz detective asked.

"No," Faraday admitted. "We should've done that, but we didn't have a kit with us. We know both of them have been handled by Ms. Fairmont, Ms. Whitehead, and most likely Ms. Ryan."

Carter glanced behind him at Miss Marek. "Amanda, please take these down to fingerprinting after the recording is played." He looked back at the people around the table. "I don't know if you've all heard this, but we need to play it. This is not an interrogation. No one is on trial here. We just need to examine the evidence and decide how to proceed."

"That's fine, detective," Sheila said. "Alicia and I have heard it. I don't think the others have. Just keep in mind the background of the woman who recorded it. I believe that report will be shared with you."

"I've already requested it be emailed," Faraday said. "The file on Maura Ryan should be in your inbox, Detective Carter."

Carter took his cell phone out of his shirt pocket, turned it on, and tapped the screen. "Yes, it's here. Perfect. I also see you included the report on Mr. Fairmont's hit and run. Thank you. I'll read these over later." He got up and brought the drive to the computer. "Excuse me, Miss Marek." He bent over her and inserted the drive into the machine.

Alicia watched the others for their reactions as the audio began to play. Carter, who had returned to his seat at the head of the table, had his eyes closed as if to shut out any visual disturbances that would interfere with his hearing the recording. Faraday, next to him on the right, had his head down, eyes on the table, as if concentrating on some imperfections in the wood. Ramsay, on the other side, was still munching donuts, his face smeared with sugar. He seemed more interested in eating than listening. Sheila, next to Faraday, was staring ahead in the distance at a spot on the gray wall across from them. She seemed lost in her thoughts. Mac, between John and Sheila, was fiddling his thumbs, fidgety in his seat. John, by her side, was watching Fido, but she could tell he was listening intently to Maura's words.

When the recording ended, Carter opened his eyes and stood up. He went to the computer, ejected the drive, and handed it along with the diary to Miss Marek. "You can bring these to fingerprinting now. Please also email me a copy of the notes you took of Detective Faraday's case summary. Thank you."

"Yes, sir." She smiled at all of them and exited the room.

Carter remained standing at the front of the table. He faced the group. "After hearing that audio, I believe we have two crimes here to investigate. We need to determine who drove the car that hit and killed Mr. Fairmont, and we need to decide if Ms. Ryan's death was accidental as Mrs. Whitehead contends or if Mr. McKinney murdered her." He paused. "We are not going to determine that today. First, we have to exhume Ms. Ryan's body from the inn's grounds and conduct an autopsy. We also need to examine the cottage where Ms. Ryan met her death." He walked over to John. "Since one of the suspects in Mr. Fairmont's murder is already dead, it's going to be difficult for us to figure out exactly what transpired that morning in May." Fido watched as Carter approached his master. "If you have an alibi for that morning, it would be of great help to us, Mr. McKinney."

"I would have to think about that, Detective. It was six months ago."

"Okay, you do that. In the meantime, all of you may leave. We'll be in touch with a trial date unless the case is dismissed."

"Wait," Ramsay said from across the table. "Aren't you locking them up? Those two could be murderers." He glanced from John to his father,

Carter shook his head. "We have no concrete evidence right now, Detective Ramsay, and they've both been cooperative. I see no need to put them behind bars."

Leaving crumbs and his dirty napkin behind, Ramsay stood and walked from the room.

"Excuse my partner," Faraday said. "He takes his job a bit too seriously. Thank you for your time this afternoon, Detective. I'll drive these folks back to Cobble Cove."

Alicia wondered if there was room enough in Faraday's cruiser for all of them including Fido, but Ramsay was waiting outside in the parking lot for them when they came out of the building. She, John, and Fido got into the police cruiser, taking the same seats as before. Sheila and Mac went with Faraday.

Before Faraday got behind the wheel, he stopped by Ramsay's open car window. "After I drop off Whitehead and McKinney, I'll meet you in town at the diner. We can have a bite for lunch and wrap things up. I think the roads will be safe enough for us to leave and now that the case is handed over, we really won't be needed except for any further information we'll be asked to supply electronically."

Ramsay grunted. "Fine by me." Alicia could tell he wasn't happy with matters being taken out of his hands.

The ride back to Cobble Cove was quiet. John sat next to her petting Fido. It seemed like he was miles away.

"Where do you two want me to let you off?" Ramsay asked when they entered town.

Alicia hadn't considered where she should go. The library was closed, but she had the key. Sheila would most likely return to her house.

"Please drop me at my father's house on Stone Throw Road," John replied. "I'll direct you." So John was going to stay with Mac. That made sense.

"What about you?"

"Leave me at the library," she said. A piece of her heart felt like it was being torn out, but what had she expected John to do? He and his father were suspects in two murder cases.

They arrived at the library first. Ramsay must've had it programmed into the police car's GPS. When they pulled up, John said, "May I take Ms. Fairmont inside, please?"

"Go ahead, but make it quick, and if you leave that mutt in the back, he better behave himself. When you bring him home, I'm checking for dog poop. If I find any, you'll be cleaning it up."

"I take full responsibility," John agreed. Alicia found it ironic the detective was worried about Fido making a mess in his car when the entire front seat was covered in Ramsay's garbage.

"You wait here, boy," John told Fido. "I won't be long, and then we're going right to Dad's."

Alicia opened the library, and John walked in behind her. She switched on the lights. The space looked different to her suddenly, bare even though it was crammed with books. How suddenly life could change. One moment she was happily married to Peter; the next, the man she now loved might be guilty of his murder.

"Alicia," John said from beside her.

She snapped back to the present. "Yes, John."

"I couldn't talk in the car with Ramsay. I need to ask you something." He tilted up her chin with his finger and looked into her eyes. "Do you believe I'm innocent?"

She met his gaze. They were standing in the alcove to the reading room where so much had happened, where she'd found the threatening note Mac admitted to writing, where she'd discovered Betty's messages in her book returns, where Sheila had attempted to hide the drive in a wall safe and uncovered Maura's diary that Mac later explained he'd placed there.

"I want to, John."

He let his finger drop and stepped away.

"That's what I thought. Okay, Alicia. I have to get back to Dad. Dora should be notified about the police search, so she can prepare the inn. You might consider going back there. Dora likes cats, so she won't mind you bringing Sneaky. I'm sure Sheila will close the library until after this is all settled. This news will spread like wildfire." He smiled ruefully. "It's something that would've made a great story for the *Cobble Cove Courier*."

"Oh, John." Alicia wanted to open her arms and embrace him, but she knew it wasn't the right place or time.

"At least it's beginning to warm up," John added. "I think that storm was just an anomaly. There'll be worse ones to come, but if the temps rise again for even a short time, they'll be able to dig up Maura's grave. The sooner that's done, the better." He turned toward the door. "I should get going. Dad might be home already, and I need to rescue Fido from Ramsay, although it would give me some pleasure to sic him on that idiot."

Alicia smiled. Same old John. "Wait."

He looked back at her. She went to him and placed a soft kiss on his lips. "Good luck."

"Thank you." His eyes warmed a moment. "That means a lot to me, Ali."

***

The investigation took place over the next few weeks. The police scoured the cottage, took fingerprints, and found some traces of blood that matched Maura's on the nightstand. New Paltz detectives visited Long Island where they conferred with Faraday and Ramsay and spoke with Pamela Morgan and Mrs. Clemens, the only witness to Peter Fairmont's accident. With the permission of the White Plains police department, they also located Maura Ryan's dentist and learned that she hadn't had an appointment on the morning of Peter's death. The police took advantage of the change in the weather during the first week of December to expedite the exhumation of Maura's body. Alicia was back at the inn staying with Dora and Charlie when the job was done. Charlie was out picking up some groceries that morning. Alicia and Dora avoided watching the work outside. They stayed in the kitchen mindlessly chatting about everyday things and eating muffins without tasting them. When Carter rapped at the door, both of them jumped. Dora went to answer it with Alicia behind her.

"Excuse me, ladies. My men will clean up the garden after we remove the corpse. Thank you for your cooperation."

Dora nodded. "I appreciate that, Detective." Since learning what had transpired at the cottage next to Betty's house, Dora had closed the inn but welcomed Alicia and Sneaky to stay there with her and Charlie. She hadn't spoken much about the allegations made against John, Mac, and Sheila, and Alicia felt that was best. The rest of the town residents whispered about the events as the library remained closed. The annual Christmas Fair was cancelled, the first time since the tradition began twenty years ago. The homes still featured some festive decorations, but the mood in Cobble Cove was somber.

Alicia hadn't seen or heard from John since he'd left her back at the library after their return trip from the New Paltz police station in Ramsay's car. She missed him so much but resisted the urge to reach out to him. Had she done the right thing? Would her support make any difference?

Alicia finally heard from John on a cold, sunny day a week before Christmas. He arrived at the inn after she'd finished breakfast with Dora and Charlie. When the bell rang and she answered it, she took a deep breath when she saw him standing on the porch.

"Hi, Alicia. How are you?"

"John. Is there news?" Her voice quivered.

"Yes, but I'd like to discuss it somewhere else. Can you come with me?"

Alicia agreed. She went back for her coat and told Dora that she was going out with John.

Dora saw her to the door and invited John to

come in first and have some of the leftover breakfast muffins.

"Thanks, Dora, but I ate already. I'm sorry I interrupted your breakfast."

"Not at all, John. We've missed you around here." She glanced at Alicia, and there was a twinkle in her eye. "I'll let you two go and catch up."

They waved to Dora as they got in John's pickup. Alicia was trying to read John's expression to see if the news he was about to share was good or bad, but his face remained neutral.

A few snowflakes began to fall. Alicia watched as John's wipers caught the small flakes. It was too warm for much of an accumulation.

As they entered town, Alicia realized where they were headed—Cove Point. John parked at the foot of the hill. "Are you up for a little walk?"

Alicia had recently bought the comfortable pair of boots she was wearing. "I'm all set."

John took her hand and they climbed to the top. Light snow covered the tiny rooftops of the houses below. The cold sunshine gave everything a golden glow. It was an enchanting scene.

"Have a seat," John offered, indicating a large rock. Alicia sat upon it, bracing herself for the news.

John sat next to her. "There's no sense beating around the bush when I know you're eager to know what's happened, Ali. I just didn't want to announce it publicly yet, although the news will spread fast." He wasn't looking directly at her, so she feared his next words. Her heart thumping, she began to feel woozy. She thought she might be hyperventilating.

"They dismissed the cases."

Alicia couldn't believe it. "Oh, John. Thank God!"

"After Pamela was questioned, she contacted me and asked to help. I didn't want her involved, but she insisted. I think she spoke with some people, greased some palms. I don't know if it mattered much. As far as I'm concerned, Dad acted in self-defense when he hit Maura, and it was just bad luck that her fall against the nightstand killed her. Sheila may have faced charges for disposal of evidence or obstruction of justice by burying Maura, but I know she made that decision to protect my father."

"What about you?" Alicia was more concerned with how John was cleared from Peter's murder.

He turned to face her, the beginnings of a smile forming on his lips. "Seems I had an alibi. I was able to provide a statement that I'd met with a psychiatrist, Dr. Sherman Gross, from eight to nine on the morning of May 13 at his office in Carlsville."

John had never mentioned to her that he'd been seeing a psychiatrist. Alicia imagined his providing this detail must've been difficult, but it was the alibi that proved his innocence.

"I'd been seeing Dr. Gross for years. No one knew. He always saw me early. I went once a month on a Wednesday. It helped to talk about the feelings I still had after Jenny. I didn't realize I'd gone there that day until I called his office to check. It actually was my last visit. I thought about going back since this all happened, but I think I can deal with things on my own now." John moved closer to her on the rock.

"I'm glad this is all over, Ali. I was hoping things would turn out the way they did. I planned to bring you here if they did."

Alicia turned to him. "Why?"

"Because we've been apart. It had to be that way. Now it can be different." He looked out across the mountain.

"I'm glad you brought me here to tell me the news. I'm sorry if you ever thought I didn't believe you."

"Shhh!" John put his finger to her lips. "That's all over. I want us to start again. I didn't only bring you here to give you the good news. I also wanted to give you this." He withdrew a wrapped box from his coat pocket. "It's an early Christmas present, but maybe it'll be more than that one day. I guess it would be more appropriate for me to give it to you on my knees."

Alicia's heart began to pound again as he kneeled before her and handed her the small box.

"I know it's way too early for you to give me an answer, so I won't ask. Consider it just a gift for now. You don't even have to wear it."

Alicia took the present. A few stray flakes fell on the red, green, and white holly-patterned paper.

"Open it. Please."

She unwrapped it with trembling fingers. The ring inside the box was a diamond set in a silver band. It sparkled in the clear light.

"It was Jenny's. If you want something else, I'll understand. If you don't accept it, that's okay too."

"John."

He stood up. "I'd better get back to Dad."

"Wait. I can't."

"I know. It wasn't a smart idea."

Alicia got off the rock. She placed the ring around her finger. "No. It's lovely. It's a special gift. Thank you."

John turned, but she stood in front of him. "Look at me, John. You can't just give me something like this and walk away."

He lifted his head, and his blue eyes met hers. "I love you, Alicia. I think I did since the day I walked into Dora's kitchen and saw you. I know so many things have happened since then. If you decide to leave Cobble Cove, I won't blame you, but the ring is yours. You're the one I want to have it."

Alicia hugged him, and his arms tightened around her. "I love you too, John, and I'm not going anywhere. I don't know why I ever doubted you. I made a big mistake with Peter. I was afraid of making that mistake again."

"Mistakes are good. We learn from them."

Alicia looked up at him and smiled. She knew he was right.

EPILOGUE

Seventeen months later, in the spring of 2017, a very pregnant Alicia McKinney sat behind the reference desk, her new leather desk chair pushed back to allow room for her stomach. It was a Sunday at the end of May. The library was now open all weekend. John came through the library door, whistling and carrying a picnic basket. "Hello, there, Mrs. McKinney. Are you ready to join me for lunch?"

***

Many things had happened in Cobble Cove since that snowy morning Mac and Sheila made their confessions in the cottage. Plans were underway for the building of the Fairmont Library Wing, an addition to the current library that would feature computer stations and Wi-Fi availability. Already, renovations had started on the main library including a completely automated computer catalog and a children's room. The top floor was no longer a living space. It was now an area for offices and public programs including author talks. The storage room still remained behind the staff lounge with a cat door for Sneaky to come and go as he pleased. Mac removed the letters and replaced the clawed box with a scratching post he made himself.

The groundbreaking for the McKinney Elementary School next door was scheduled the following Sunday. The school would provide education to students through Middle School. One day, a high school might be added, as well. Construction in the rest of Cobble Cove was booming, and the McKinney and Son's real estate firm was doing great business.

Mac still worked part time at the library, and you could find him often in the expanded reading room working on a newspaper puzzle eating a peanut butter and jelly sandwich with Sneaky at his feet begging for scraps. Although food wasn't allowed in the library, they made an exception for Mac as long as he cleaned up afterwards.

Sheila postponed her move out West for a few more years until they hired a suitable library director. She was quite strict about the qualifications and background checks of each applicant. They also now employed a full-time and part-time clerk to help check books in and out and shelve them. Applications were being considered for a children's librarian and a custodian, and the town was planning to schedule elections for a few people to run on the newly created Board of Directors.

Dora had married Charlie in a double ceremony

with John and Alicia at the Cobble Cove Church the previous year on her seventy-first birthday. It was a year since Maura and Peter's deaths. Both couples celebrated their reception at the inn. Gilly came up to attend with her boys and had given John and Alicia a crockpot with a collection of her own recipes as a wedding gift. Pamela was there too, in a designer gown, wishing the couple her best and stuffing a $10,000 check into John's tux.

Dora expanded the inn to keep up with the increased visitors. She hired Edith and Rose to work with her there. Since she'd agreed to babysit John and Alicia's twins after they were born so Alicia could still work part-time at the library if that's what she chose to do, it made sense to have extra help. Rose was a wonderful cook, and Edith excelled at crocheting beautiful accents for the inn's rooms.

Jim Casey, in anticipation of competition, enlarged his restaurant and modernized it. The new design added more tables as well as booth seating. He hired a chef from the Culinary Institute to revamp his kitchen and menus.

Another development was John selling his mystery series, co-authored by his wife, to a New York publisher. The first in the Groucho Marks mysteries was due to come out that fall. Although the characters were all fictional, Detective Marks was loosely based on Ron Ramsay, who had since retired early from the force. John still edited the *Cobble Cove Courier*, now published on a weekly basis. It was additionally staffed by recent journalism graduates from a nearby college.

John and Alicia spent a brief honeymoon at the Mohonk Mountain House in New Paltz, and Alicia commented on the stone structure that reminded her of some of the stone houses in Cobble Cove.

Pamela Morgan, who endowed the library and town with the money for all these changes and also paid the right people to prevent the case from being brought to trial, visited her father the spring after the case was dismissed. When Pamela visited, she brought her two grown daughters with her to meet their grandfather, and the reunited family spent a week catching up on their dissimilar lives.

Faraday stopped in once at the library after it was all over to chat with John, Alicia, Sheila, and Mac. He told them the authorities in Florida were unable to locate any of Maura's relatives, so the body had been turned over to the county to be disposed of. Sheila organized a memorial on Cove Point where the minister said a few words for the troubled woman the town knew as Tina Deerborn. People gathered in the inn's garden afterwards to pay homage to the lost soul. The following fall, John planted the bulbs Dora wanted in the area where they'd dug up Maura's body, and lovely spring plants bloomed in profusion that April.

There were still a lot of unanswered questions from the happenings two years ago, but John surmised Maura's original goal was to persuade Peter to leave Alicia and marry her. She quit the job at East Coast, left town, and took up with John to try to make Peter jealous. Even though she claimed on the audio recording that Peter found her in Cobble Cove when John was away, it was more likely she contacted Peter sooner than that and met with him while she was seeing John. In fact, John admitted later that he thought Maura was seeing someone while they were together, but he had no idea who. While John was at the conference, Maura must've given Peter an ultimatum. When he turned her down and refused to seek a divorce, Maura planned to kill Alicia and make it appear an accident. She found a way to get into Peter's home and rigged the stairs, causing Alicia's fall in the basement. Having failed in that attempt to get rid of Alicia and finally realizing that Peter would never marry her, she decided to screw both men by killing Peter and hatching up her blackmail scheme to frame John. When Maura called Mac's house the day she was leaving and was told John wasn't there, she asked Mac to the cottage instead. When he arrived, she threatened to turn the recording implicating his son in Peter's death over to the police if he didn't get the money from his daughter that she requested. It was also probable Maura found the letters Mac had in the storage room and pieced together his long ago affair with Carol that resulted in Pamela's birth.

Alicia and John were both surprised and delighted when, the summer after their wedding, Alicia became pregnant. They later learned, despite her advanced maternal age, the babies were healthy—a boy and a girl. They planned to name the boy John Mac III, Little Mac for short, and the girl, Carol Abigail McKinney. They had moved into Mac's house, adding a room for a nursery/playroom with two bedrooms for each child as they grew.

Mac relocated to the cottage that had been rebuilt and expanded.

***

Alicia smiled. "Yes, the babies and I are hungry." She patted her stomach. "We were hoping Daddy would get here soon."

John grinned, exhibiting his dimple.

As Alicia wobbled out from behind the desk, Mac came into the library. He was working the afternoon shift that day because Sheila had called in sick.

"Just in time, Dad. I'm here to take Ali on a picnic." The way John said 'picnic' and the look he exchanged with his father, made her wonder if they were hiding something from her.

"Have fun. I'll hold the fort." The old man's eyes twinkled almost as bright as when they'd announced he would be a grandfather. Although he already had granddaughters by Pamela, he would be able to see John's children as babies and, if he stayed healthy and his dementia didn't progress too quickly, he might see them grow into older children with minds and personalities of their own.

"So what are we feasting on?" Alicia inquired, stealing a peek in the basket, but John pulled the cover back tight. "Not yet, dear. Have a little patience."

The pickup was parked outside the door. John assisted Alicia into the passenger seat and adjusted the seatbelt under her bulging stomach. Then he got into the driver's seat. When he turned right instead of left toward Cove Point, Alicia asked, "I thought we were picnicking where we usually do."

A secretive smile spread across his face. "Not today. I thought it would be nicer to spend this beautiful spring afternoon on a picnic bench in the inn's garden."

When they arrived at the inn, Alicia marveled at the changes since she'd stayed there, first with John when she arrived in town and then alone with Sneaky before the cases were dismissed. The white trim around the windows on the main floor and the added dormer upstairs shone pristine in the sunlight. Although the exterior was now a pale blue vinyl siding, it still retained the flavor of a country inn. The front walk's cobblestones had been replaced with more even ones. Colorful pansies, impatiens, and other spring flowers bordered the entryway. Real geraniums burst from the hanging baskets. Dora stood out front. She hurried down the porch steps to greet them as John helped Alicia from the truck. The innkeeper's face too, held a hint of mischief, and Alicia again wondered what was being hidden from her.

"Hey, there, mama," Dora said. "Come out back. I have the picnic table all set. I thought I'd join you both, if you don't mind."

John smiled. "Of course not, Dora. You were kind enough to allow us to use the inn." The three of them walked to the gate that opened into the newly built patio deck.

"Watch your step," Dora warned Alicia as she unlatched the gate and beckoned her to follow. John was guiding his wife from behind.

There was one step down onto the deck. Alicia was watching her footing, so it wasn't until she looked up that she saw the deck and garden full of people with Sheila, looking quite well, up in front. A long white banner was strung across the yard from fence to fence proclaiming in pink and blue letters: *'Happy Baby Shower, Alicia'*. As she read the words, the crowd screamed, "Surprise." Dora's and John's faces broke into wide smiles.

"No picnic today, Ali," John said beside her, "but don't worry, there's plenty of food."

"You tricked me." She laughed, delighted. There were several tables in addition to the long picnic table full of food she later learned had been supplied by Casey, who couldn't attend because only women and the father were allowed as guests at baby showers. A huge number of gifts were displayed on another table, most wrapped in pastel colors—pink, blue, and yellow. John directed her to a beautiful hand-carved wooden rocker among the guests. "Sit down, honey, on our present from Dad. He built it himself."

"This is amazing," Alicia said, awestruck. She looked around at everyone. "All of this. How did you...?"

Sheila stepped forward and kissed her on the cheek. "Dora and I put it together and, of course, your darling husband. Charlie helped move all the tables. He went out to join Casey at the restaurant while we girls have our party." She paused. "Stay there one second." She dashed in the back door and came out wheeling a yellow-cushioned double stroller adorned with a huge pink and blue bow.

Alicia could imagine walking her twins in it through the pretty streets of Cobble Cove. "Oh, Sheila. Thank you so much. It's wonderful."

Dora turned to Alicia and handed her an envelope from her pocket. "There's a gift certificate in here for the new baby store in town. I'm sure you'll find something perfect for your twins." Alicia took the envelope and smiled. She was overwhelmed. "Thank you, Dora. I know I will."

As Dora and Sheila stepped away, other women approached Alicia, one by one, to greet her, kiss her, and hug her. She recognized townspeople and library patrons. Edith and Rose proudly showed her the baby shower cake Rose baked and decorated and the lovely pink and blue baby booties and hats Edith crocheted. Wilma from the beauty salon, who had finally had a chance to do Alicia's hair for the wedding a year ago and who she now went to regularly to have it trimmed and styled, gave her two sets of combs and brushes for the twins.

Alicia was even happier when she saw Gilly and Pamela, who had both traveled to attend the shower. Gilly said her boys were at Casey's and were probably depleting his stock of hamburgers and hot dogs while driving Casey and Charlie crazy with Boy Scout tales and magic tricks. She told Alicia she'd brought her famous chocolate chip cookies up with her for dessert to eat along with Rose's cake. She kissed Alicia warmly and had her swear to send photos of the babies as soon as she could. Gilly hoped Alicia would like the gift she'd brought and, like the Gilly she remembered, gave it away by saying there was a great sale at BJ's and she knew, from her experience with the boys, a new mom never had enough diapers.

Then Pamela was there smiling with her blonde twin daughters by her side. "I guess twins run in our family, brother," she said to John. When she bent down to kiss Alicia's cheek, Alicia caught a whiff of her exotic perfume. "Thank you so much, Pamela. Have you seen the town? What your generosity has done?"

Pamela waved off the comment. "I'm glad the money could do some good finally." She turned to her daughters. "Cynthia, Caroline, why don't you show your aunt what we've given her as a baby shower gift?"

Cynthia and Caroline were beautiful young women in their mid-twenties. Both had the same shade of blonde hair as their mother, layered at their shoulders. Their eyes were the color of John's, and their smiles displayed perfect white teeth, most likely the result of orthodontic treatments. They both had lovely tanned skin, a sun-kissed color from their recent trip to the Greek Isles to study ancient art. They exchanged glances, and Caroline stepped forward. "Aunt Alicia, Mom checked with Uncle John before she chose this gift." She turned to her mother. "Shall we get her now?"

Pamela nodded, and the two sisters rushed as fast as they could in their three-inch heels to the back of the garden where a tarp-like white blanket covered something moving. Alicia couldn't believe it when Cynthia and Caroline took opposite sides of the blanket and pulled it down. A beautiful chestnut horse stood staring at them. It was a wonder it had stayed quiet. The general noise of the crowd may have concealed its low neighing. Alicia's nieces led the young horse by its lead rope to her side.

"All children need a horse," Pamela said. "Starburst is only six months old and recently separated from her dam, who is my best horse. Cobble Cove stables is not far from here. I've already made arrangements with the owner. John has all the details."

Alicia was overwhelmed. She felt tears gather at the sides of her eyes. "Thank you so much, Pamela, for everything. And you too, Cynthia and Caroline."

Alicia then caught sight of a small, stooped woman with a cane ambling slowly toward her. As she grew closer, Alicia realized it was Betty, the homebound. She held a pink rattle in one hand and a blue one in the other. Alicia couldn't believe her eyes.

"Hello, Mrs. McKinney," Betty said. "I've come to bring you presents for the babies and to thank you. Sheila put an invitation to this shower in my last book delivery, and I knew I had to come. After your father-in-law made his confession, I began to realize some things," she said quietly, gently, as if to a child.

"Fifty years ago, I had a family too, a husband and two young children. We lived in the city. My youngest was only a baby, his sister a toddler. We went for a walk one early evening as we usually did—me, Sam, and the kids. I was wheeling little Sam in a carriage. It was after dinner in the summer, just turning dusk. Two masked men came up behind us."

Her voice choked. "One had a gun, the other a knife. They wanted our money. Sam gave them all he had in his wallet. It wasn't much. We weren't rich, but we dressed nicely, wore clean clothes and decent walking shoes." She sniffed, and Alicia could see a tear run down her wrinkled cheek. "It wasn't enough. The gunman shot Sam and Jessica. His partner stuck a knife in little Sam and then in my stomach."

Her voice grew loud with sobs. "I spent a month in the hospital. When I was released, my family gone, I took all my stuff and left the city. I moved here to Cobble Cove in that small house and became a hermit. I didn't want to face the world. I wanted to die there, but the townspeople here wouldn't allow that. They brought me food. The library brought me books. But I feared everyone. I couldn't leave that house." She tapped her cane. "Mac was right. If you think long and hard enough, you'll find the truth and what you must do for it to set you free." She handed Alicia the rattles as the tears fell more profusely down her cheeks. "I hope your little ones enjoy these."

Alicia was crying now too. She got up from the rocker and embraced Betty, her stomach keeping them apart. "Thank you for coming, Betty. It means so much to me." She thought to herself she would speak with John and Mac afterwards about finding Betty a nicer home here in Cobble Cove, one that would be filled with light and sunshine to wipe out the shadows of her dark past.

***

After the shower wound down, and everyone had eaten, chatted, and given Alicia their best wishes, John loaded the pickup with all their gifts while Alicia thanked everyone, especially Dora and Sheila. She had Gilly and Pamela vow to visit often, and she promised them lots of photos of the babies.

Back at their house, Alicia sat on the porch swing resting as John unpacked the truck and brought all the gifts inside. When he was done, he joined her on the swing.

"We don't have to open everything now. You look tired, and I don't blame you after all the excitement of the day."

Alicia smiled and reached out a hand to touch his face. "You look tired too, and I guess I'll forgive you your treachery about the picnic."

"You know," John said, "I can't help thinking how all the pain we went through has brought us to such a better place. This town…" He waved his arms to encompass the whole of Cobble Cove. "It's blossomed, and, even with the newcomers, the renovations, the changes, it still has the same small town feel, a great place to raise kids."

Alicia felt the same. "I guess your dad was right all along, John. Everything happens for a reason." He kissed her, and she knew, like Betty, their shadows were gone too.

ACKNOWLEDGEMENTS

Writing a book starts with an idea, but it also begins with encouragement. I want to thank library patron, Eleanor Di Primo, for all her gentle nudges to motivate me to keep writing.

Writing a book also involves patience on the part of the author as well as the author's family, so I would like to thank my husband, Anthony, and daughter, Holly, for putting up with me while I worked on this book.

It's important for an author to receive support from fellow writers and other professionals as they journey toward publication. I would like to thank Amy Shojai, author of the September Day mystery series and founder of the Cat Writer's Association, for all her helpful answers to my publishing questions. I would also like to thank my nephew, Justin William Smiloff, Esq. for reviewing my contract and explaining some of the legal terms.

Of course, there can't be a book without a publisher, so I would like to thank the wonderful staff at Limitless Publishing, LLC, for their faith in me and "A Stone's Throw," especially Lori Whitwam, Managing Editor of Limitless Publishing, who favorited my pitch on Twitter and reviewed my submission; Jessica Gunhammer, Vice President of Limitless Publishing, for her help with the contract and inviting me to join this wonderful team; Toni Rakestraw, my insightful editor, Dixie Matthews who formatted my manuscript into a book; and, of course, Jennifer O'Neill, the President. I also want to extend a special thank you to my beta readers and fellow authors, Kiarra Taylor and Sara Schoen for their helpful suggestions on fine-tuning my manuscript. I wish I could also individually thank all the talented and welcoming Limitless fellow writers who have reached out to me and made me a part of their group, but there are way too many of them. I wish them all the best in their endeavors and hope I can support them as much as they've supported me.

Another important part of producing a book is the research to make it as realistic as possible. I would like to thank Elizabeth Roderick, a fellow Limitless Publishing author who is also a paralegal, for her feedback on some of my questions and also Scott M. Schmidt, CFSP-President NYS Association of Coroners and Medical Examiners for his help with information regarding autopsy after exhumation.

Since in today's publishing world, social networking has become so important, I would additionally like to thank my followers on Twitter and Facebook as well as the members of the writing groups in which I participate. I especially need to thank Kristen D. Van Risseghem, who sponsored the Twitter Pitch2Pub event that provided the opportunity for me to be contacted by Limitless Publishing, and Holly Miller, PhD, a long-time online friend and fellow library professional who assisted me in setting up my WordPress author's blog: https://debbiedelouise.wordpress.com/.

Last but not least, I want to thank my readers. A book is not just a collection of words. It's thoughts, feelings, and ideas that each reader processes in their own way. Readers make books come alive in their minds. Thanks for giving my characters a stage on which to act. I hope you enjoy the performance.

ABOUT THE AUTHOR

Debbie De Louise is a reference librarian at a public library on Long Island. She was awarded the Lawrence C. Lobaugh Memorial Award in Journalism from Long Island University/C.W. Post where she earned a B.A. in English and a M.L.S. in Library Science. Her romantic suspense novel, *Cloudy Rainbow*, received an honorable mention in the *Writer's Digest* self-published awards. A member of the Cat Writer's Association, she has published articles in *Cats Magazine*, *Catnip* (Tufts University Veterinary Newsletter), and *Catster*. Her short mystery, *Stitches in Time*, was published in the *Cat Crimes Through Time* Anthology. She lives on Long Island with her husband, daughter, and two cats.

Facebook:
https://www.facebook.com/debbie.delouise.author?f
ref=ts

Twitter:
https://twitter.com/Deblibrarian

Website:
https://debbiedelouise.wordpress.com/

Goodreads Author:
http://www.goodreads.com/author/show/2750133.D
ebbie_De_Louise

31442480R10235

Made in the USA
Middletown, DE
30 April 2016